BROKEN
BOUNDARIES

Helen Aitchison

Published by Write on the Tyne

Printed and bound in Great Britain by Clays Ltd, Elcograf S.p.A

ISBN: 978-1-7394882-8-4 (Paperback)

Cover image & design: Jarmila Takac (Instagram: @jarmila.covers)

Published by Write on the Tyne
www.writeonthetyne.com

For Alison and Caroline —

your support goes beyond friendship.

Prologue

The sound of screaming reverberated in the otherwise quiet night on Lawson Lane, East Hertfordshire. Ceasing, the air turned eerily silent for a few minutes — as if the world had paused — before the frantic sirens of the approaching emergency services rang, shrieking as they travelled closer to their destination.

An unfamiliar car had been parked at the top of the lane for a couple of hours earlier that evening. Yet to rouse any level of suspicion, a resident had spotted the vehicle whilst walking her dog. A new neighbour had moved in a few months back, so maybe it was associated with him. Or perhaps it belonged to someone visiting a house in the next lane.

The handful of houses in the rural street, thirty miles from London, provided torch rays of light, illuminating the dark winter night in the normally peaceful village of Much Hadham. Front doors open, residents huddled in their gardens, eyes darting up and down the street, trying to discover what the frenzied commotion was about.

What had happened? Were they safe?

The blaring of the advancing emergency service vehicles indicated something had most definitely happened. Something involving Nate Lundie, and by the sound of it, it could be deadly.

Nine Months Earlier

Chapter 1: Nate

Nate sighed and stretched back into his Eames-style lounge chair, as he placed his feet on the matching black leather footstool, encased in rosewood veneer. Shutting his eyes momentarily, he tried to close the diary of appointments in his mind. It was the end of a long day at work. Nathaniel Lundie, Nate as he liked to be called, was a therapist based in King's Cross, London.

His office, just a few minutes' walk from King's Cross St Pancras Station, proved as convenient as hectic. Although its visibility definitely worked as a marketing technique, he frequently craved the tranquil surroundings of the countryside, as opposed to the constant tooting of horns, foul-mouth road-ragers, whizzing cyclists, and barging commuters that the city provided as background audio to his private therapy sessions.

Having qualified in counselling and a range of specialist therapies five years earlier, Nate had set up his own business just under four years ago. Despite the recession and the world changing, he had a successful, satisfying, sometimes stressful business in Lundie Therapy. A lone ranger in the fight to help people recover from trauma and mental health issues, he loved his job. However, it was far from easy. Operating a business resulted in extra work and stress at times, and limited ears to listen to his own problems. Nevertheless, his job was an emancipation from the crippling corporate circle he had been in most of his life.

Nate had spent fifteen years as a teacher before retraining in mental health, counselling, and therapies. Being his own boss was different class to being controlled and criticised by incompetent managers and colleagues, and although practising as a therapist certainly wasn't Monday-Friday, 9-5 — especially in the never-quiet city — he had more autonomy as a sole trader. At the age of forty-five, he now knew what he wanted to be as an adult. And he was right there, feet up on his significantly cheaper, designer-style office chair, thinking about what he would eat for dinner. Life was good, work was good, and despite a few things missing, he couldn't be happier.

Taking a deep breath, he interlocked his hands, placed them behind his neck, and stretched his arms out, letting his breath pour out for ten seconds. Standing, he grabbed his laptop and bag, and left his small office, locking the door.

'Night,' he said to the building's receptionist, with a bounce in his step, before pushing the main door open, revealing the late summer evening.

The sky was blue, a covering of white with pink and gold ribbons dancing through it. Walking the few minutes to his car, parked in the extortionately priced but convenient car park, the end of the work day meant the start of the city centre evening buzz. Colleagues going for after-work beers, or a bite to eat. Weary shoppers and London tourists coming towards the end of their day of purchasing and sightseeing. Theatre and concert-goers arriving in the capital for pre-event drinks. The scent of the final days of summer, mixed with sprays of aftershave and perfume, and a nasal tantalising spectrum of food fragrances from the nearby array of world cuisine restaurants and takeaways.

Walking to his car from work could be a colourful affair, and tonight was no exception. Strolling to the pedestrian lights, Nate glanced at the pub on the corner of the street. People were sitting outside, chatting and joking as they swigged beer or sipped cocktails. Others stood smoking, away from the entrance, laughing and playfully shoving one another. Two women were swaying from side to side, their arms around each other's shoulders, pink cowboy hats on, singing Madonna as their free hand grasped glasses of alcohol. Nate smiled to himself as a dart of envy clipped his ear.

Despite being in control of his diary, he didn't have a great work-life balance. It wasn't because he was overworked, more that he was underplayed. At the age where most of his friends were married, settled, and some becoming grandparents, it meant nights out in town, or anywhere else, were limited. Added to this was that Nate was single and childless, having split from his wife, Sarah, five years ago. He had tried to save the marriage, the blame for its demise being projected onto him, and rightly so, but it wasn't to be. And really, Nate couldn't decide to that day whether Sarah had just become a habit.

When the divorce eventually came through, he was relieved and already onto a new chapter in his life of dating, being promiscuous, and partying with anyone he could. Then he realised he was closer to fifty than forty and choices for longer-term partners were like Greggs bakery at the end of the day: limited and not as appealing as one may think. Still, Nate had experienced a few dates, a few flings, and found there was life after divorce. He just hadn't met the right woman for relationship material yet.

Chapter 2: Melody

'Hi, Dad,' Melody called with forced enthusiasm as she shut the door behind her and unzipped her black ankle boots. Grimacing, she pulled her feet out of the leather shoes, before sighing in satisfaction as she vowed not to wear new boots with a heel for the first time at work again.

'Hi, love, you're early,' came a voice as her father, Matthew, hurried down the stairs. He walked towards his daughter and embraced her lightly before they went into the lounge.

'You okay?' His voice was gentle, concerned, as his head pushed slightly forward from his neck.

Placing her handbag onto the wooden floor, leaning it against the sage green sofa, she nodded. 'Yeah, fine. Just took an hour toil.' Her tone was tinged with abruptness.

Matthew looked at her, waiting for something else. It didn't come. After a few seconds, he cleared his throat. 'Cuppa?'

She nodded and feigned a weak smile. Matthew walked through to the kitchen of their family home, followed by Melody. So much had changed over the last two years, yet at the same time, the house remained unchanged, a continuous reminder of the missing person — missing people. The empty room, the cold seats at the dining table. Melody swallowed and closed her eyes for a second, as her father had his back to her. She didn't know how he could still live here, yet she understood entirely.

Placing her long, wavy brown hair up in a bobble, her head

thumped from her day working for Crawford's Insurance in King's Cross, with customers speaking to her like she had man-handled their child. Melody had been employed at the call centre for just over two years. She disliked her job, but it paid okay; enough for her to have moved out of the family home and into a rented flat. Plus, Crawford's had been where she met Brandon, who worked for their contracted IT company. Pressing her lips together at the thought, she plonked herself on one of the breakfast bar stools.

'Good day? You look pale. Are you looking after yourself?' Matthew was trying to make conversation and not start with his usual panic act, but it seeped out like fat from a roasting meat joint.

Melody felt lost, deaf from the screaming voices all day and her own frustrated, devastated voice that played in stereo in her mind. She shrugged, watching her dad take two cups from the cupboard as the kettle boiled, before his eyes focused on her again.

'Are you managing?' There was a slightly heightened tone in his voice.

Gritting her teeth, she couldn't be bothered with another checklist of personal health and safety. Matthew had already texted her that day asking her to check her car tyre pressure, and her mum had asked twice if she needed anything from the shops.

Rolling her eyes, she spoke. 'Same shit, different day. Isn't that what they say?' She let out a sarcastic laugh.

Matthew turned from the kitchen bench to the fridge, re-trieving the milk. He sighed, placing the milk down, then leant across the breakfast bar. Tapping her hand gently, he spoke. 'It will get easier, Melly. I promise. But you know you can always move back in if things are hard. It can be lonely here all alone.' He released a sad chuckle.

Melody bit back the emotion and guilt that threatened to escape her mouth. Then a rush of anger lashed against her ankles that her mum, Zoe, had just left it all; leaving Matthew for her to support and reassure. How could she tell her dad what had happened two nights earlier? His paranoia and protection of her would rush right back up the thermometer like the raging Las Vegas summer sun. Instead, she nodded in silence as the feelings that haunted her and goaded her to crack into a million pieces, began bubbling. And this time, she wasn't sure the medication could stop them.

Melody put her head back against the door of her flat and made an urgh sound. Trying to hold things together in front of her parents could be borderline impossible and she often lied to them. Especially to her dad, so he didn't have the claws of anxiety disembowelling him. It was exhausting, even more so since her parents had separated. Whilst Matthew was panicky, like an introvert expected to perform at a comedy club, Zoe, babified her, focusing on the practical rather than the emotional but still flapping around — voice bouncy, body language animated, each time she saw her. When all she wanted was for them to acknowledge life would never be the same and no amount of cups of tea would make it better.

Grace, Melody's flatmate, was out at work. She was a bartender at South of Here, a popular venue near King's Cross, alongside studying business at university. Grace and Melody were both twenty-four years old and had met at the Italian restaurant they had worked at three years ago, becoming close friends. The shared bills, alongside their friendship, were

6

definitely a bonus — although Zoe, in particular, helped financially. She adored Grace and living together with different working patterns meant contact and company, balanced with privacy and space. Their flat in Walthamstow was less than ten miles from her employment office. Enough to be handy, and just over half the monthly rent of the average £3,500 per calendar month price tag that the city centre demanded for a flat with two box bedrooms.

Unzipping her uncomfortable shoes yet again, she slid her now pudding-like feet out of the boots and kicked them to the side of the tiny hallway, before dropping her handbag and heading straight to the bathroom. Feeling the hot water soothing her aching shoulders, Melody closed her eyes in the shower and let the water bounce off her skin as she absorbed the silence. Listening to people rant all day on the phone inevitably resulted in her own mind being distracted — a good thing. However, it meant that by the end of the day, she needed to process a saturated sponge of intrusive, often unmanageable thoughts that frequently kept her awake, or at the least, polluted her evening. And the last two days had been almost unbearable.

After a long shower, Melody put on her pyjamas and a cream fleece jumper. Sliding her feet into her fur-lined slippers, she sighed. The peace and quiet of the flat were welcome, but her thoughts began ricocheting around her head. Walking through to the kitchen, she opened the fridge to look for something for dinner. Scanning the almost empty shelves, she curled her lip, shook her head, and shut the fridge door. Opening a kitchen cupboard, she pulled out a cup of dried noodles. That would do. Melody mechanically filled the kettle and switched it to boil, before leaning against the grey kitchen bench. Running her tongue over her top teeth, she stared into space for thirty seconds and swallowed the lump in her throat.

Don't go there, she thought to herself, closing her eyes and clenching her fists quickly. She immediately softened, knowing it was normal, expected, yet still disappointed that she couldn't control herself. He wouldn't want her to be like this. Not after everything. Not over him, and certainly not over some stupid man. Yet, by the time she had poured water over her cup of noodles and they lay, marinating and expanding in the steaming liquid as she stirred absentmindedly, fat tears were plopping down her cheeks.

She sat at the tiny kitchen table, her head in her hands, her knees bouncing. Feeling as much anger as sadness, Melody looked down at the grey lino and thought about Felix. All the things she would say to her big brother if she were to look up and see him sat opposite her on the cold, plastic seat. The answers that she needed as much as the water she drank. Only the water was poisonous as she would never get them now. Instead, she had the constant taste of sickness in her throat and a stabbing of guilt for the moments she enjoyed life. The moments she forgot, along with the flashing reprieve of anger for the tremor in their world that he caused — that led to irreparable destruction.

The nights when she slept okay and didn't wake up thinking of him as her first, uncontrollable thought of the day. Those fleeting, free, forgotten thoughts that Felix was dead. And that he had taken his own life; deleted himself from their family, without warning, without their ability to intervene, and with a book full of questions they needed answers to, that was thicker than the Bible.

And alongside the grief she had been trying to process for the last two years, since her older brother took his own life, she watched her parents carry a darkness in their eyes that the brightest of lights could no longer reach. Their hearts in the pitch black, like the anglerfish's existence. Searching, getting by, surviving — just. Because they had to. Because even if each other wasn't enough, they had Melody. Their family, cracked all those years ago, then broken by Felix's death, and destroyed by Matthew and Zoe's separation as grief, blame, and pain shattered their family like one hundred lightbulbs dropped from a balcony.

Zoe had left the family home, moving to a flat closer to the law firm where she worked as a solicitor. The pain of their family home was too crippling, knowing her firstborn died there. Yet unable to let go completely, Matthew remained in the house, never to be sold, but never to be their family home again. Zoe became the best actress going, masking her own pain in front of her daughter in a desperate attempt to ensure her only living child wouldn't deteriorate. Whereas Matthew became terrified he would lose another child. His son was gone. His wife, gone. Only Melody left.

Struggling with mental health wasn't new to Matthew and Zoe's children and what happened to Felix could happen to her. Both shouldered an uncontrollable fear of losing their daughter that manifested in different ways, and their separation twelve months after Felix's death made Melody grow closer to Matthew.

Although she loved her parents, Melody had felt smothered at home, unable to grieve and with the constant reminder of her brother being gone. His bedroom left; a shrine to his life and death. The family photos on the wall, haunting her. His belongings, mementos of his life everywhere she looked, and the broken souls of her parents trying to glue their family back together like ornaments smashed in an argument.

She moved into her flat eight months after Felix died, and four months later, Zoe left. Melody felt resentment towards her parents that they lived with a hangover of worry that her past would resurface. Matthew and Zoe wanted to wrap their daughter up and keep her away from the world and any danger; desperate to protect her from harm. She knew that, but it was claustrophobic — from her father, in particular.

After moving into her flat, she visited her dad and the ghost of her brother a few times a week and her mother less often, around Zoe's work schedule. Only then, once she had moved out, could Melody start to process her emotions and past trauma, away from their obsession with protecting her. She wasn't a child anymore.

It was Brandon who had given her the confidence to look for a flat, helping her to realise it wasn't healthy for her or her parents to remain in the mousetrap of grief and paranoia.

'You need some distance, some space,' he had said within a few weeks of meeting her before they dated. Confiding in him about some of her struggles, Melody shared her difficulties in managing her overbearing father and burying-her-head mother. He had held her hand tenderly, his green-brown eyes reassuring her, and she knew then that they would become more than friends.

As her relationship with Brandon developed, her parents were pleased. Matthew knew Brandon was a good guy. Well, his definition of one. He'd studied hard, came from a good home, and had a good work ethic. And Zoe was just delighted to see her daughter happy.

'And he doesn't do drugs,' she had said to Matthew, knowing that her parents would ask. It was an issue that would forever be the beast of burden Melody carried, even if its skeleton had disintegrated over time.

Tutting to herself at the thought, she wrapped her fork in some of the curry-flavoured noodles, sitting on the kitchen chair, one foot tucked under her leg. Of course, as an overprotective father, Brandon Steel was never quite good enough for Matthew Dartford's daughter. No one would be. The truth was, both Matthew and Zoe couldn't bear the thought of losing their daughter. They'd already lost Felix, without warning, like a shark attack on their family. They wouldn't, couldn't, lose their daughter. Instead, Matthew in particular kept her on reins that made Melody's loss more painful and made telling her father the truth impossible.

Chapter 3: Melody

Grace arrived home at just past midnight. She struggled through the door; hands full and her laptop case hanging off her wrist. Placing her bags on the hallway floor, she walked a few steps into the flat and raised a hand to her chest.

'Shit!' she exclaimed to Melody, who lay in near darkness on the sofa. 'You gave me a shock!'

Only the light escaping the ajar bathroom door illuminated the lounge. 'What are you doing up still?'

Melody pulled herself up from a lying position on the grey sofa, watching as Grace kicked her trainers off before turning back to her flatmate's silhouette.

'Couldn't sleep.' She sniffed, placing her feet on the floor, making space for her friend to sit down.

Taking a seat, Grace switched on the small salt lamp that rested on the IKEA side table. She looked at Melody, who turned her red, puffy eyes away.

'Has he not been in touch?'

Melody rubbed her hands together and shook her head.

'Screw him, hun. It's his loss.' Grace clasped her hand over her friend's hands.

'It's my fault. I shouldn't have done it.' Melody sighed and glanced down at her lap, her shoulders pulled in.

'Probably not, but there was no need for him to react like that.' Grace's voice was calm, gentle, soothing.

Melody nodded and picked at the mustard cushion on the

sofa next to her. She hadn't told Grace the full details of the messages and conversations that had been exchanged between her and Brandon's ex-girlfriend.

'I'll get my pjs on and make us a cuppa, eh? I think I've still got some of that chocolate left.' Grace smiled at her friend and tapped her shoulder as she got up, leaving Melody remaining on the sofa, clutching a fleece blanket.

The act of comfort and care did little to steady the choppy sea Melody felt she was swimming in. She raised a hand to her head — chipped nail-varnished fingernails pressing lightly into her scalp. The scene with Brandon had played over in her head those past few days. She had never seen him so angry. The whites of his eyes were almost bloodshot with venom as he shouted at her, before he had told her to get out of his car. His usual perfect teeth smile nowhere to be seen. She had cried, tried to explain, apologise, and beg, but none of it worked.

'It's one thing too many with you. You're not right in the head.' He had banged his finger against his temple as he spoke. Snarling, disgust was plastered across his face as his brown hair, which usually fell in the exact right position, had ruffled up.

She had tried explaining through the tears. It was because she loved him. Didn't it show that she loved him?

He'd laughed, saying he wanted, 'Fuck all to do with a love like that.' It wasn't what he had signed up for and she was lucky his ex, Hannah, wasn't going to the police.

Melody had felt tiny as he'd continued the lecture. Eyes colder than January in London, he'd said that he had stopped Hannah from taking it further, and she should be grateful. But all Melody could think about was that Brandon had been talking to his ex. Meeting up with her, calming her down from the 'attack' she claimed Melody had perpetrated.

'She's lying,' she had stated, chin tilted up.

He'd put his hands in the air. 'Stop with this shit. I've got screenshots and you're on her Ring doorbell.' Brandon had clenched his chiselled jaw, shaking his head as his eyes stabbed her heart. 'Social media was bad enough. You said you'd not message her again. But she showed me. For Christ's sake, you set up fake accounts to warn her to keep away from me. She's blocked you six times, Melody. Six fucking times!' He had placed his hands on his head and laughed. 'Hannah isn't even interested in me. She's seeing someone else. We're just friends.'

She had cried and touched Brandon's leg but he'd snatched it away, revolted, as if she were coming towards him with a handful of dog crap.

'She thinks you're a psycho. And so do I. Who the hell do you think you are threatening to hurt her?' He'd pushed his face forward, scowling.

'I, I...'

'You what?' he'd screamed.

'I just love you so much. I was scared that you were going off me and would go back to her. I just...' she'd spat out quickly. He had glared at her for a moment as Melody licked her dry lips and swallowed, wiping her hand under her nose.

Releasing a sarcastic laugh, he had shifted in the driver's seat. 'So, you thought telling my ex, my *friend*, that if she contacted me again, you'd follow her in your car when she's running and knock her over was fucking reasonable?' He'd puffed out air and slammed his hands on either side of the steering wheel.

'I was joking,' she had pleaded.

Brandon had shaken his head frantically. 'You weren't. Nor were you joking when you said you'd poison her dog in a Facebook message. Or that you'd tell her work she sent naked photos to me, which she never did! She showed me all the messages. So, stop lying!' He had sneered.

'I didn't mean any of it. I'm sorry, Brandon. I love you so much,' Melody had grabbed the sleeve of his green sweatshirt.

He'd yanked his arm away. 'You need help. It's sick.' He had looked straight ahead, out into the car park as workers began returning to their vehicles to battle rush hour traffic home. Gaze remaining fixed, he'd continued, with no tone in his voice. 'It's over. Get out and don't contact me again. You're lucky Hannah isn't going to the police. But she will if you message her again.'

'But…' Melody's voice had cracked as her watery eyes focused on him.

'Out!' he had screamed into her face, eyes bulging.

As she sobbed, Brandon's face had remained unchanged. And as she got out of his car, teary-eyed and with weak, wobbly legs, Melody had felt a flicker of regret — before she'd wiped it away and thought to herself that Hannah deserved every one of those messages.

Chapter 4: Nate

Sitting in his office with a coffee on the side table, Nate tapped a pen against his mouth, scanning his diary for the week. He had several regular clients, many who received a weekly session, which became fortnightly, then monthly — before they no longer required therapy, having developed their own toolkit to manage life's pressures and unexpected events. It was the end result; he had done his job correctly once someone was discharged from his practice. However, the door was always open.

People often came back for the odd session in a time of distress or if a trigger had resulted in their lives being flooded and they couldn't quite stay on their life raft. Nate was a competent, skilled therapist. Testimonials on his website, the smiles, confidence, and ultimate mental health management that people left Lundie Therapy with, were his accolade of success.

Of course, it wasn't always easy. Some people were simply more complex, more challenging, and less likeable than others. It was life. It happened to him as a teacher, and being a therapist was no different. It didn't make Nate any less professional. Some people weren't ready to address their issues; perhaps coming to therapy with misconceptions. Thinking they would leave after one session, covered in a protective glitter that held the answers to everything and kept shit away. Some attended by coercion through a partner, spouse, or parent. Others expected him to 'fix' them, with little input and responsibility from themselves.

Nate was always clear. He wasn't there to dictate or find the answers for the client. He was there to find the answers *with* the client. After years of training, he had his preferred methods. Person-centred therapy and dialectical behaviour therapy, with an understanding of the impact of trauma. Continuous professional development had allowed him to learn specialisms such as the complexities of domestic abuse or eating distress, alongside addiction and PTSD. And Nate used his own adversity, not to share with clients, but to know that sometimes, a textbook can't teach you the basics of human empathy and experience.

His childhood involved being raised by a single parent after his mother left his abusive father. Her resilience and care for Nate and his older sister, alongside his mother's work ethic, helped support him through university, then later manage his marital problems. He understood people, and a common reason for individuals accessing Lundie Therapy was marriage and relationship issues. He used to hate the thought of people giving up on a relationship that wasn't abusive. Until his own marriage presented itself with a problem that wouldn't go away, continuously growing in their home like a persistent weed in the garden. And Nate admitted defeat, knowing it would never be the same again. So, he felt personally and professionally experienced in helping clients and sometimes, their problems made him feel a lot better about his own failings and shortcomings.

Perusing his diary, he had a few days of regular clients. It was important to not see too many people in one day. His mind-cup would overflow, saturated with the problems of clients. Friday was free, meaning a day of admin from home and perhaps a spinning class in the morning. Plus, he had a first date on Friday night from a dating app with a promising woman who looked stunning in her profile picture and seemed to have the intelligence to match. Leaning back in his armchair, a grin spread across his chiselled face as he thought about their message exchanges.

Many of the dates didn't go far. Dating was like fast fashion: disposable, addictive, and sometimes not as nice on. However, it gave him a social life, and sex now and then. He wanted to love again, but he enjoyed the dating and flirting after a long marriage. He let out a light chuckle. And why not? He was a good-looking man. Over six feet, 185 lbs of lean muscle, and a head of blond-grey hair that put him straight into the silver fox category. With Pacific Ocean blue eyes and straight, white teeth, he looked the part. And the women loved it, even the younger ones.

Nate bit his lip as he had a quick scroll on the site, looking at his Friday night date before being interrupted by his five-minute warning alarm, alerting him a client would be arriving. Snapping out of his fantasy daydream, he stood and walked to the small kitchenette in his office, filling a jug of water for his next appointment.

After a break in between sessions, it was soon 6 pm and Nate was getting ready to finish for the day. Clicking his neck and stretching his back, he washed the dishes, before ensuring all of his notes were locked away and the room looked fresh for the next day. Grabbing his bag, he was about to leave when a call came through his work mobile phone. It was the receptionist of his building.

'Hello.'

'Hi, Nate. There's a lady here wanting to make enquiries and I have none of your business cards left.'

He glanced over to his desk where a stock of new business cards lay. He had been meaning to replenish reception with a pile for over a week. 'Thanks. I'm actually locking up now so I'll come and speak to her. Be two minutes.'

Ending the call, Nate walked to his desk, retrieving a pile of the new business cards, before locking up. After taking the two flights of stairs, he entered the reception area. Thanking the receptionist, he introduced himself to the young blonde woman standing in the foyer.

'Hi, I'm Nate Lundie.' He smiled at the woman, stretching out a hand.

She shook it, a slight tilt of her head and her thick, blonde ponytail fell to the side. 'Hi, I'm Grace. I just wanted to get a business card, please? I pass here most days for work and knew there was a therapy service somewhere on this street.' She let out a light laugh, the apples in her cheeks rounding.

He smiled again. 'Yeah, these buildings can all look the same, but I am pleased we stood out a little.' Nate handed her a business card and her eyes glanced at it before back to him.

Moving slightly on the spot, Grace continued. 'It's not for me.' She tapped her collarbone with her free hand. 'Although, if I needed a therapist, I'm sure you would be great.' She blushed slightly and puffed out air. 'It's for my flatmate. She's had a lot happen in her life and well, the doctors...'

Nate nodded. 'Waiting lists?'

'I think so. I just want to be a friend and try to help. Give her options.' She shrugged.

'Good friend,' he replied, holding her eye contact.

She pressed her lips together.

'All the information is on the website, but your friend can email or call if she wants. No pressure.' He held his palms up.

'Thanks. That's great. Anyway, I better get off to work.' Grace put the card in her bag and turned to leave. 'Bye.'

Nate said goodbye and watched her walk out of the double doors onto the busy street. Part of him wanted to know where she worked. He shook his head to himself and turned to the receptionist, who raised her eyebrows at him. Saying goodnight, he left, feeling a little like one of the schoolchildren he used to tell off.

Chapter 5: Melody

'I don't need to see a therapist!' Melody said firmly to Grace, brow furrowed as she held the business card.

Grace tilted her head. 'It could help. You've been through a lot,' she said softly.

Melody sighed and slumped back into their sofa. 'I'm on the counselling waiting list with the doctor.'

Grace tapped her friend's arm. 'I know, but it's been over a year and you still haven't been offered the help. You'll be waiting forever.'

She cupped her face in her hand. 'But the meds, they help.'

'Just even enquiring could be useful. In case you need it. I hate seeing you like this,' said Grace, as she watched her friend bite the skin around her fingernail.

Melody could feel herself getting upset. The reality was that Brandon had made it eternally clear that they were over and there was no way of going back. After the crescendo in the car park and a few days of no communication, she had emailed him. She was blocked on WhatsApp, his phone, and social media. But the email she sent showed a read receipt, meaning he hadn't blocked her there.

An hour after the read receipt alerted her, Melody had checked her phone at least fifty times whilst at work, much to the dirty looks from colleagues. She wanted to scream at them and the customers. Instead, she had to be the one screamed at and called useless by tens of callers a day. They had no respect, no appreciation that it wasn't her personally who had upped their insurance quote, or who added the clause, meaning they couldn't claim for X, Y, and Z.

In that hour, after Brandon read the email, Melody felt she was being pushed along a gangplank. She had mentioned Felix in her email — desperate for him to understand she was grieving, struggling, not herself.

Melody, DO NOT contact me. And don't blame Felix's death for your behaviour, that's low. I DO NOT want to hear from you or see you again. You brought all this on yourself and I WON'T forgive you. So, LEAVE ME ALONE and please get some help!

After finishing her call with 'Arsehole number seventeen of the day' she rushed to the toilets. Locking herself in the cubicle, she read the email from Brandon over and over whilst crying. How could he be so heartless? Then she wanted to repeatedly punch the mirror above the sink until her hand turned red with blood.

Grace broke Melody's suffocating thoughts by rising from their sofa to make cups of tea. Tilting her head back, she took a deep breath. In a way, Grace was right. And Melody knew her friend was being exactly that — a friend. It was what she needed. Friends weren't forthcoming and she certainly couldn't speak to her parents about it. Not unless she wanted to have her every moment monitored as if she were a newborn baby.

Returning to the lounge as the kettle boiled, Grace placed their Christmas-themed biscuit tin on the coffee table.

'This therapy. It's not going to help me get over it all. Felix, my parents' separation, Brandon... It's not going to change what I've lost.' Melody gulped in air, feeling tears forming.

'I know, hun, I know. But it may help to talk to someone. Someone trained and that,' Grace soothed, squeezing her hand

and looking at her with kind eyes.

Later that night, as she sat in bed, her eyes flitted to the card for Lundie Therapy that lay on her dressing table. Maybe Grace had a point and she didn't know the half of it; the extent of Melody's past and how she felt. The emotions of loss were pretty universal. Grace understood that. However, this time with Brandon, the jealousy that she wore tight around her, like a crippling corset, was what turned the milk of their relationship sour. She couldn't tell Grace the extent of the messages she had sent to Hannah. Grace wouldn't understand and would judge.

She couldn't explain her feelings about Brandon and the risk of losing him, which had now become her reality. Melody knew she could be jealous, but she was loyal, loving, passionate. She only became jealous if someone she cared about gave her reason to. She was 'fiery' as her mum would say and went 'all in' with her emotions.

Sniffling, she closed her eyes as Grace clattered around in the kitchen, and her thoughts returned to her past. When she was eleven, a new girl, Courtney, had started at school. Courtney had made a beeline for Lily, Melody's best friend. As the first week of Courtney's arrival at Greenside School progressed, she became closer to Lily, and Melody felt left out. Two weeks later, having gone through the emotions of being upset and feeling excluded, she was full of anger, wanting to take control.

One day after class, as they were tidying up from an art session, Melody had taken a pair of scissors and cut an enormous chunk from Courtney's hair. She had received a five-day suspension from school, despite claiming Courtney had asked for a haircut, and Courtney agreeing out of fear.

Courtney quickly moved on to new friends. Melody struggled with Lily not realising, not understanding and appreciating that she did it because she loved Lily so much. She couldn't stand for anyone to come between them, dilute their friendship, weaken their bond. It was as simple as that.

Then there was Laura at the Italian restaurant she and Grace used to work at in Soho. At the time, Melody was learning to drive and wanted to save up for a car. Laura was dominant and pretty. The customers loved her, and so did the married couple who ran the restaurant. She would get extra shifts because she was a great server and a marketing tool for the business. Grace wasn't bothered about shifts; she was studying and it was a part-time job, topped up by her student loan and parents' support. Other members of the team were at university or had a second job. For Melody, this was her income, and her way of saving for a car.

It began with her putting laxatives in Laura's water bottle in the staff fridge or sliding some into her coffee. Laura would rush to the toilet within the hour, sometimes looking peaky on the restaurant floor and touching her stomach. Melody would snigger in secret, thinking the greedy bitch deserved it. Laura would leave her shift early and, eventually left the job before she got sacked — after commenting the place needed a hygiene rating review.

No, she couldn't tell Grace all of that. Grace would think she was unhinged, irrational, mad. And if she wanted help and to skip the ever-growing NHS list for therapy by going private, she would need money. Something Melody didn't have going spare. But her parents did and that would mean having to tell them she was struggling once again.

Chapter 6: Nate

The date arranged through the dating app was a success, and Nate felt confident there would be a second. He was his usual naturally charming self and they had plenty to talk about. His date was intelligent, attractive, and their night passed quickly and pleasantly. A peck on the cheek as they said goodbye, with a promise to keep in touch satisfied him. Did he want a long-term relationship in the future? Absolutely. But he was also happy to not rush and never settle. The world was full of beautiful, interesting women, and London had its fair share.

He had worked from home that Friday and after a spinning class, a haircut, and preparing for the date, Nate hadn't done the amount of admin he needed to. It meant a few hours on Saturday morning to catch up with his website, enquiries, and client notes. After making some toast with marmalade and a strong coffee, he moved to his upstairs office of his three-bedroom Victorian terraced house in Stratford, East London, and powered up his laptop. Taking a seat in his olive-green wingback armchair, he took a bite of toast. His teeth sunk into the sweet golden spread, the tang of the orange peel tickled his tongue and he let out a 'mmmm.' There was something about toast that always felt satisfying, almost as much as a cold beer in the summer.

Putting his empty plate on his oak side table, he leant over and rubbed his hands over it, making sure any crumbs were collected, then picked up his laptop. Nate checked his website before going to his emails. Two SEO sales pitches sat in his inbox, asking him if he wanted a quote to attract more traffic to his website and boost its visibility. He rolled his eyes, directing them to spam. There was a further email which, on first impression, could have also been spam. An email from mel-ody.darty. Sighing, Nate clicked on the email. It was a genuine enquiry from a Melody Dartford.

Hello Mr Lundie, my name is Melody Dartford and my friend passed on your business card. She popped by last week. I'm not sure if I am ready to access any therapy and I looked at your website, which was useful. If I do decide it's right for me, what is your waiting list? Thank you.

Melody

He thought for a second as he gulped some of his coffee. Running a hand through his thick blond-grey hair, it clicked. The pretty, young girl who worked in the city centre somewhere. 'What was her name?' he said aloud. He couldn't remember but recalled her saying it was for her friend. Sometimes, people really meant for themselves when they made comments like that. A protection, a denial, a sussing something or someone out. Either way, it was a possible new referral and within two weeks, he was dropping one client down to monthly and another would be signed off, meaning he had capacity.

Hi Melody, I hope you are well. Many thanks for your enquiry. At the moment, I have a two-week waiting list. Usually, the first session is a thirty-minute, free consultation. This can be face-to-face at my office in King's Cross, or via telephone, or via Zoom (whichever you prefer). After that, if you wish to progress with therapy, I would be able to offer appointments that fit around your schedule. I hope this answers your query and if

you do wish to proceed, please do let me know.
Kind regards, Nate Lundie

After a further ninety minutes on his laptop, Nate felt suitably caught up. It would be an afternoon of housework before going to his sister, Julie's house for dinner that evening. Music on, he began cleaning, starting with his laundry. He found housework therapeutic and felt it linked to the need to feel organised, have clarity, and the satisfaction of a job well done. Granted, he got more of a buzz from the gym, but it was still soothing and, for Nate, a tidy house meant a tidy mind. His lips curled into a sad smile as he set the washing machine away — his cleanliness was something Sarah always loved about him.

It was soon 7 pm and he was pulling up at Julie's house. Cutting the car engine, he picked up the bottle of Merlot from the passenger seat and exited his vehicle, before rushing up her driveway. His brother-in-law, Brian, opened the door with a warm welcome and ushered him inside, where Julie hugged him and took the wine. Nate inhaled the smell of garlic and creamy, earthy mushrooms.

'Risotto,' Julie beamed as they walked into the kitchen diner.

'Mmmm. Can I not just move in?' he said in a whiny voice to his older sister.

'Yes, if you clean for your supper!' she replied, elbowing him and winking.

'Done!' Nate laughed as Brian appeared with two bottles of Peroni.

Forty-five minutes later, they had all finished their meals and Julie placed a cheesecake on the maple wood dining table.

'Is that…?' Nate looked at the sweet delight that almost glistened from the ceiling light, then back at his sister and licked his lips.

'Yup, it's white chocolate and Biscoff.'

'She wants us all fat for the winter. Like geese!' said Brian, tapping his stomach.

Julie laughed and leant over to cut the cheesecake that looked like a work of art on the table. Nate almost didn't want the knife to penetrate it, but he was salivating for a slice. They tucked in and he closed his eyes as his tongue danced with the mascarpone topping, sprinkled with heavenly white chocolate and cinnamon-infused caramel notes of Biscoff.

'Mmmm. This is so my Death Row meal,' he said as he opened his eyes and shovelled more onto his spoon.

Brian nodded, and Julie smiled before speaking, her mouth straightening and her eyes focusing on him.

'I saw Ian Graham the other day.'

The mood across the table changed immediately — a much more unpleasant cut of the knife than through that work-of-art cheesecake. Brian looked at his wife, then to Nate, who had put his spoon down. Julie swallowed and continued to talk.

'He was in the new deli at the shopping centre. I think he wanted to avoid me at first, to be honest.' Julie's eyes darted to Brian, who shook his head slightly. 'But he couldn't as the shop was so small.' Her gaze flitted nervously to Nate, then Brian, then back to Nate, as he put his hand to the back of his neck and moved in his seat, remaining silent.

'It wasn't as bad as it could have been. He was okay.' Julie shrugged, and he noticed her cheeks were flushed. 'He didn't make a scene like last time. But I suppose... time and all that.'

Brian coughed and picked up his beer. Nate glanced at him and he raised his eyebrows. He was the easy-going type and Nate could almost read his thoughts of, *'Let sleeping dogs lie.'*

She continued. 'He said Annabelle was working in Shoreditch at Amazon now and had a boyfriend the family love.' Focused on her brother, she knew his eyes always gave away his mood. They had since he was a child, just like their father's used to. Icy cold blue when he was angry, sparkling warm ocean blue when he was happy. 'That she was okay, now since, you know.'

The room went quiet and Julie's gaze remained on Nate. His face unmoving. His piercing icy cold blue eyes unblinking.

Chapter 7: Melody

Melody had re-read the email before pressing send. There was no harm in enquiring about the therapy service, and after a shitty week at work, it was something positive on a Friday evening. It wasn't as if she was committing to anything, simply finding a little more out. Self-care, her parents would say. She rolled her eyes as she watched the sent message alert flick up on her screen. Letting out a deep breath, she rested her head back on the sofa. It had been a long week and her tolerance and energy were depleted. She knew that if she were to seek private therapy, she couldn't afford it herself and would have to ask her parents.

Grace was right, the waiting list through her GP wasn't getting shorter any time soon. They were dealing with people who were in crisis, not those who were still managing, holding down a job, functioning. She was medicated and stable, according to her last review. Melody shook her head as she bit her bottom lip. Of course, she couldn't tell her family doctor about the recent communication with Brandon's ex, Hannah. Perhaps he would deem her as a little less stable if he knew about that. Even if she explained, she knew what it sounded like and for that reason, she hadn't even told Grace.

After looking at Lundie Therapy website, Melody felt perhaps it would be an option and it wasn't like she had to commit to so many sessions. After all, it wasn't free. She realised she would have to tell her parents about the break-up and perhaps the promise of attending therapy may reduce their anxiety about her well-being. They could afford to pay for therapy sessions and would do anything to help their daughter, especially Matthew, in his frequent fog of panic. She ran a hand through her dark brown hair and pulled the grey fleece blanket on her knee further up.

Her dad had been in touch multiple times a day that week after she lied, saying she had some sort of bug and couldn't come around for their usual catch-up. Zoe had also been concerned, offering to visit. Matthew had rung and texted, wanting updates, trying to make her laugh with memes and checking if she needed anything.

Feeling like she told a child Santa didn't exist, she had felt awful for hours after initially lying to her parents but needed some space and time. Dreading telling her folks that she and Brandon had split up, Melody had to be sure that they would not get back together before explaining to them. She put her hands to her face, rubbing her palms over her eyebrows, knowing now that there was no chance of Brandon forgiving her.

She just had to be sure of the next steps, as Matthew's reaction, especially, would be of spiralling concern for her well-being. Likely to intensify the welfare checks, calls, concerns about tyre pressure, carbon monoxide levels, eating raw fish, and other endless irrational fears that her dad liked to plague her with. The truth, well her version of it would only encourage the mother-hen routine from Zoe. As if her mind wasn't already a tennis game of emotions, her parents unwittingly added more anxiety and stress.

Melody looked out the lounge window at the marshmallow-white clouds in the grey-blue sky and felt bad. She loved her parents, she really did, but her dad was overbearing, paranoid, and drained her to almost empty at times. She needed to slacken the crushing belt of overprotection around her that Matthew had enforced. Sometimes, after an evening with him, she felt her energy was like a bath full of water with the plug pulled. Shutting the front door of her family home and getting ready to drive home, she would feel as if the last of her energy was trickling away, down the plughole.

Matthew and Zoe would never get over losing Felix, but Matthew couldn't seem to manage to live without being inside a vacuum of intensity that sucked her in, whether she liked it or not. Melody tried to rationalise it. Her parents didn't want her to be poorly. They didn't want her to go backwards when she had come so far. They didn't want their daughter to struggle like she had to such catastrophic levels in the past. They had all worked so hard to keep her safe, well, happy — perhaps to the point of not seeing Felix was struggling. But Felix's untimely death threatened all of that, and now Matthew felt like his daughter was walking on an eroding cliff. And although she would never admit it, so did Melody.

It was Saturday morning. She had cried sickness to her parents all week. Now it was time to Facetime her mum then visit her dad to share the news about her break-up with Brandon — omitting the full truth. Checking her emails, the therapist had replied, explaining the referral process. Melody shrugged as she read it, eating her yoghurt, granola, and fruit. It sounded okay; she would chat with her parents about it. It would be a softener for her dad and she would speak to him about paying in an attempt to make him feel he was helping.

Sighing, she rose from the kitchen table, placed her dishes in the dishwasher, and walked to her bedroom. Pulling on her jeans and T-shirt, she felt the September coolness, and taking a baby-blue sweatshirt out of her cupboard, put it on, then placed her brown hair in a messy bun. Grace was asleep after working late the night before. Quietly, Melody went to the bathroom, brushed her teeth and put some mascara on the lashes of her big brown eyes, hoping that as she pulled the wand through, it wouldn't look like she had been crying and sleep deprived for most of the past week. Although, her parents always seemed to know.

She rubbed her forefinger over her mouth. In a way, it was kind of nice. After the troubles in her teens, and now not having her older brother, it made her feel protected. But Matthew took it too far after Felix's death and his separation from Zoe. Fatherly protection accelerated to a level that felt almost institutional. She washed her hands and glanced again at herself in the mirror, her full lips with cracks in, her eyebrows overgrown — she vowed to get back to her self-care and pampering next week.

After Facetiming her mum and the conversation going easier than she imagined, they arranged to meet for Sunday lunch the next day to talk in more detail. Zoe offered to pay for the therapy, but they both agreed that Matthew would likely want to finance it. Plus, Zoe already gave Melody money towards her monthly rent. Ending the call with her mum, she felt positive and grabbed a banana before heading out of the flat to drive to her father's.

Fifteen minutes later, Melody arrived at her family home. Cutting the engine, she took a deep breath, closed her eyes, and rehearsed what she would say in her head one last time. Her thought process was terminated as Matthew opened the front door and began walking up the drive. She sighed, knowing that he would be eager to see her, giving her fake illness that week. Getting out of the car, she said a chirpy hello to her dad as they met halfway up the driveway.

'How are you, love?' Matthew asked, head tilted and eyes wide.

'Much better, thanks, Dad. You okay?'

He nodded without speaking and they walked back down the drive. She glanced at the apple tree in the corner of the garden. It was a fixture from her childhood — but not this tree. This tree was a replica, planted in the new home that the family had moved into eight years ago. Where the family of four had tried to duplicate positive parts of their home, before it was destroyed. She smiled to herself, thinking about the old house and the aged apple tree that stood proud in the garden; part of their family.

The original tree had remained strong as Felix climbed it almost daily. Its branch arms carrying him, holding him as he grew. The apples she and Lily used to pick when her friend visited on weekends. Then they would pester Zoe to help them make something from the fruit. Usually, it would be apple tarts or crumble, and they would wait impatiently, looking into the oven every three minutes, despite Zoe telling them it would take even longer if they persisted on checking.

The two friends would be giddy with excitement to devour their creation, and it always seemed to taste better than the week before. She closed her eyes. The memory of their past now left a bad taste in her mouth. Melody walked into her family home, which still felt like Felix and Zoe should be there. Everything else unchanged, just their presence gone.

'Cuppa?' she said to her dad.

'I've just put the kettle on. Got some of that fruit cake from your auntie Glynis as well.'

She smiled. 'Great. I'll make them.'

Melody knew that her dad struggled, he had done since losing Felix, and then when Zoe moved out, he struggled further. Zoe didn't visit their family home; swapping grieving collectively for case after case at the law firm where she worked. And as the days passed, the distance between her and Matthew widened. She got further away as Matthew remained stuck on the spot — trying to learn to walk again.

Melody knew that he needed looking after too. He was the protector, or in Matthew's case, the overprotector. And as a parent, he would almost always be the one who looked after her. *But who looked after him? Not many people*, she thought. Auntie Glynis, his work colleagues, friends. Matthew had people around him but he didn't have Zoe.

The three of them were trying to heal. Like an ornament, smashed and glued back together. The lines still showed. The cracks, the weakness. Always there. Physically, he had changed. At five foot ten, he seemed to have shrunk with grief, his shoulders narrower and his brown eyes more sunken.

She swallowed down the lump of guilt that was growing in her throat. Melody would do better. She would tell her dad about Brandon, get help, and help him more. After all, her mother didn't seem to want to help her ex-husband. She flared her nostrils as she poured water into their cups. His overprotective care of her wasn't just about Felix dying. It was about her past, and she had to take some responsibility for that.

Matthew cut slices of cake as she made the cups of tea. Felix's favourite cup sat unmoved in the cupboard. Reminders of his shadow everywhere. Melody hadn't even begun to process her grief. She hid it inside a mini safe in her mind, which had a combination lock even she couldn't open. Not yet, anyway.

'Here you go,' she said a few minutes later, placing two cups on the breakfast bar that Matthew sat at. Pulling out a wooden stool, she sat opposite him and took a slice of cake. Auntie Glynis made the best fruit cake that felt healthy yet such a treat. No doubt it was laced in sugar, but the succulent sultanas and tang of lemon peel made it feel luxurious and most definitely moreish. Melody bit into the cake, making a mmmm sound and nodding to Matthew, who took an even thicker slice.

'You must be feeling okay now, then?' he mocked as his daughter chomped on the sweet treat.

She swallowed. 'Yeah, much better. Must have been some bug I caught at work. I think I was feeling a little run down, actually.'

Matthew raised his eyebrows.

'Nothing to worry about, Dad. I just had a bad few days before I was feeling unwell.' She looked down at her plate and pressed her finger on the crumbs that had accumulated before putting them in her mouth. 'Brandon and me split up.'

Matthew's jaw dropped before he placed his hand to his chin. 'Oh, darling. I'm so sorry to hear that.' He reached over the cream breakfast bar and squeezed her hand. 'What happened?'

Melody pushed her shoulders back. 'We just weren't getting on.' She put her hand to the bun on the top of her head and twisted a bit of loose hair back into the messy nest. Matthew was leaning forward slightly, wanting to know more.

'I think… we just want different things. At different points, you know?' She shrugged.

Matthew nodded. 'That happens. You're only twenty-four, Melly.'

Knowing he meant well, despite feeling patronised, Melody smiled weakly at her father. 'Better to know now, I guess.'

'Maybe some time apart and you may get back together in the future?'

'I don't know, Dad.' She paused and puffed out air. 'I feel that it's maybe time to see someone. You know, someone professional.'

Matthew's back straightened. 'You haven't done…'

She held her palm up. 'No, Dad, nothing…'

He pursed his lips and breathed out.

'The waiting list for a counsellor is massive and I feel ready now. To talk about Felix, you and Mum, the past, Brandon, everything.'

Melody tried to sound casual, and inside she felt panic rising. She knew, deep down, that there was an issue in the way she contacted Brandon's ex. If it wasn't a problem, why hadn't she told Grace? But it wasn't just Brandon, it was everything; an emotional volcano inside her that always felt on the periphery of erupting.

Matthew nodded. 'So, a private therapist?'

She took a sip of tea. 'Yeah, just to even try it. I think it will help.'

A smile grew on Matthew's face. 'Well, anything to help, Melly.'

She moved slightly on the stool. 'And Dad, it will hopefully stop you worrying so much. It's not good for you, either, or for Mum.'

Matthew glanced to the side, then back to his daughter. He feigned a jokey, upbeat tone in his voice. 'It's my job to worry, Melly. I'm your dad.'

She let out a strained laugh. 'I know. But this could make

you worry *less*. The problem is, it's not cheap.'

'That's not a problem, love. Just tell me how much and I will transfer it. You're priceless.' He squeezed her hand, smiling. She felt relief. Seeing a therapist would help her and her dad, and even her mum, who hid her anxiety better than Matthew — she felt confident about that.

Leaving her father's, Melody had a calmness she hadn't experienced in a long time. A relief, a positivity, a hope that things would get better. She dreamt of the time she would be off her medication, discharged from therapy. And that life wasn't the turbulent journey of pockets of happiness and stability that sky-dived rapidly out of nowhere until she hit the ground and couldn't get up. She was trying to take control, help herself, and Melody felt sure she was moving in the right direction.

On her return to the flat, Grace was pottering around in her loungewear. Dancing to Taylor Swift, she turned and grabbed her hand to dance alongside her. Melody laughed, slightly embarrassed, but happily danced along for a minute before Grace hugged her and they both giggled.

There was a playfulness, a carefree lightness that she should also carry as a twenty-four-year-old. That Grace wore like a second skin. Melody wanted that. She wanted to dance in the kitchen and smile. She craved to stay up all night and watch movies with Grace, eat popcorn, and experiment with the latest make-up trends. Melody wanted to date men without becoming too emotionally dependent on them. And she desired to be honest about her past and her problems, as well as manage the pain that lived in her. She wanted to recover and thrive and hoped Lundie Therapy might help her do just that.

Chapter 8: Nate

Leaving Julie's, Nate couldn't wait to get home and drink alcohol. He understood why Julie brought up Annabelle Graham, but it was jarring, and he felt a cocktail of emotions that needed to be dissected alone. For all Nate Lundie was a qualified therapist who was apt at helping other people to process and manage their problems, he had a habit of burying his own. However, Annabelle Graham had exhumed all elements of his life for far too long. He knew Julie was trying to reassure him; tell him that everyone and everything was okay now and all had moved on. Nate had moved on. But it still stung, like nettles against his mind.

Arriving home, he failed to get a parking space outside of his house and instead, grumpily parked six houses away from his Victorian terrace. Walking to his home, Nate knew it was too big for one person. But after the divorce, Sarah hadn't wanted to live there and it made sense for him to buy her out at the time, meaning she could purchase an apartment. It was the least he could have done, given the circumstances.

After seeing what his neighbour's property two doors down sold for, Nate was now considering selling. His house was stunning, but he dreamt of moving somewhere quiet. Work in the city centre was bustling and his residential area was much more desirable than when they purchased it — with small bistros, micro-pubs, and an influx of young professionals and families.

The garden gate squeaked as he pushed it open and walked

to his front door, the hanging basket he purchased almost three months ago, still in bloom, cascading like a colourful waterfall. Entering his home, he took off his trainers and stretched his toes out on the geometric tiles in the hallway. Puffing out air, he ran a hand over his thick hair, before throwing his keys onto the stairs and going through to the kitchen.

Opening the cupboard that hid his built-in fridge freezer, Nate pulled out a bottle of Captain Morgan's rum and two cans of Coca-Cola. Tucking the bottle in his arm, he reached for a glass from the kitchen sink draining board. Carrying them through to the lounge, he sat on his black leather L-shaped sofa, and poured himself a drink. Releasing a sigh, the only noise he could hear was the ticking of the Karlson clock on his wall as the scenes with Annabelle Graham played on repeat in his mind.

Nate jerked on the sofa. A shooting pain darted through his neck and he licked his dry lips. Looking at the clock, it was after 2 am. He had fallen asleep after drinking a good few shots of rum. He picked up his mobile phone from the seat beside him and saw a text message from a gym mate, asking if he was up for the charity spin-a-thon at their gym in November. Pulling himself up from the sofa, he yawned. Leaving the glass, empty pop cans, and bottle with a slither of rum left on the side table, he headed upstairs, hoping in the morning, the punchbag of his mind would feel less assaulted.

Seven hours later, Nate was up, ready, and heading to the gym. After a litre of water with a hydration tablet in, some porridge, and a cold shower, he felt human enough to do a workout. Exercise was his medication and as well as keeping his endorphins going and providing mental clarity, it helped him keep in shape and look his best. It was also nice to catch up with people he knew there, including those who had become friends and a few attractive females that he often said hello to.

Following an intense cardio workout, he headed back home and showered, then sat down with his laptop. He checked his emails and schedule for the next week. There was a reply from the enquiry he received the day before.

Hi Nate, thanks for the reply. That sounds great. I'm happy to come to your office. I work early shift on a Thursday and finish at 3 pm. Do you have any availability on a Thursday from 3:30 pm onwards, please?

Thanks.

Melody

He was pleased with the prospect of a new client. Few people came for a free assessment and then never engaged in the therapy appointments. People came to therapy when they were ready, well, ninety per cent of them. His approach of making people feel at ease and his supportive, empathetic demeanour, meant that rapport was built and clients felt empowered to begin their therapy journey. Pulling up his online calendar, Nate looked at the following Thursday commitments. He had a regular client at 2 pm, the last appointment of that day so far. Perfect. He would offer 3:30 pm next Thursday to Melody. Returning to the emails, he replied:

Hello Melody,

I am pleased you wish to proceed. I actually have next Thursday from 3:30 pm free, if that is convenient? If so, the address is on the footer of this email, and our building is opposite the Mexican takeaway, El Cortez. If next

Thursday doesn't work, let me know and I will look towards the end of the month and for October.

Kind regards, Nate

After dealing with some work admin, Nate logged onto his online dating profile. There were a few messages, including one from his date from Friday. He exchanged several messages with her and alluded to another date next week, but he still messaged some other women he had been chatting with. Nate would not close his account after one date, no matter how enjoyable it was. He knew better than that, and the online dating scene was ruthless.

Previously, he had been 'ghosted' by a woman he'd had three great dates with before she dissolved into thin air, not answering his calls, texts, or messages on the site. She was still live on there and now and then, he would look, even though it pissed him off. Brian had said the young ones called it being ghosted. It had made him laugh, albeit at his own expense. So, no, he wouldn't be committing to any woman any time soon.

An email alert flashed at the bottom right-hand side of his laptop; a reply from Melody Dartford. Next Thursday was fine. She would put it in her diary. Nate clicked on his electronic calendar and did exactly the same, before returning to his internet dating. Next week was busy at work and for now, Nate would enjoy the last few remaining hours of the weekend.

Chapter 9: Melody

It had been a rubbish week at work, with Melody vowing to look for another job when she was mentally stronger. She fantasised about her last day at Crawford's Insurance and telling all the moaning, negative, nasty people who rang up shouting at her to go to hell with much stronger language. It made her giggle as she walked to her appointment at Lundie Therapy. She knew where the building was, about ten minutes' walk from her own place of work and opposite the Mexican fast-food takeaway that served amazing nachos. Strolling towards the office, she inhaled, smelling the tangy tomato salsa and zest of lime. Perhaps she would get something for dinner for her and Grace from there when she left. Well, if she left in a good mood.

Opening the double doors to the building, a face smiled at her from behind a desk. She smiled back and looked to the left, where a list of services was displayed on the wall, indicating the floor number they were located. Spotting Lundie Therapy, Melody returned her gaze to the receptionist, who was watching from behind gold-rimmed glasses.

'Can I help?' her jolly voice asked.

'Erm, yeah. I've an appointment with Lundie Therapy. Second floor, right?' She pointed to the wall.

'Yes. You can take the stairs to the left there. Or the lift. Mr Lundie's office is second right.'

Melody nodded and thanked the receptionist, opting to take the stairs. She travelled up them, two at a time, looking at the cold grey-white walls and the black plastic-coated handrail. She grimaced a little, feeling it was almost school-like and hoping that the therapist's office would be more welcoming and tranquil. Pushing open the door to floor two, she walked past an office before seeing Lundie Therapy. Clearing her throat, Melody knocked on the door twice.

Ten seconds later, the door opened. In front of her stood an attractive older guy with a warm smile. Tall, in good shape with greying hair and azure blue eyes, framed by a pair of round tortoise-shell-rimmed glasses. He reminded her a little of the actor, Daniel Craig. She said hello and held out her hand. Pleasantly surprised, Melody hadn't thought about what Nate Lundie would be like other than the Freudian-type image she had of therapists.

'Nate Lundie and you must be Melody Dartford?' he said with a firm handshake.

'Yeah... erm, nice to meet you.' She smoothed her hair with her free hand.

She felt a little flustered as Nate Lundie moved to the side and beckoned her in. His office was small but smartly decorated. A large leather chair and footstool sat opposite a yellow sofa with big, inviting cushions and a cream chunky woollen throw draped over the arm. A fur-type rug lay in front of the sofa and to the side, a small table with tissues, note paper, and a jug of water and glass.

'Take a seat, please.' He gestured to the sofa and Melody glanced at the wall opposite, painted a mushroom colour with an array of mismatched, quirky frames filled with quotes and images. A tall 1970s-style lamp sat in the corner.

'Nice place.' She nodded to the therapist and sat on the sofa, sinking in and immediately feeling more at ease.

'Thanks. Environment is important. It really affects our mood. Water?'

He poured her a glass of water. Watching his large, steady hand, she took in his comment. Christ, she only had to think about her own work environment and how it made her feel. Like battery hens awaiting their cruel fate, all the bodies in lines, headsets on, computers in front of them as they repeated the same monotonous bullshit hour after hour, day after day, month after month, year after year.

Taking a seat in the armchair opposite Melody, Nate turned his legs to point towards her. 'Thanks for coming along today, Melody. As mentioned in my email, this is a free consultation to explore a little about your current situation and so you can find out about what therapies I offer and ask questions.' He picked up a notepad from the side table next to him and smiled at her. 'Does that sound okay?'

After taking a sip of water, she cleared her throat. 'Yeah, great.'

He nodded and kept eye contact. 'So, do you want to tell me a little as to why you are considering therapy?'

His voice was gentle, kind, relaxing, and she leant back slightly into the soft sofa, putting both her hands around the glass, resting it lightly on her lap. A private person, on the whole, Melody found it hard to talk about her feelings. Moreover, she trusted very few people — not surprising given her past. This could be different. Nate Lundie was a professional. *Surely, he had heard everything and more from clients.* He wasn't there to judge, only support. Even so, she would go in slowly, tread lightly, just exposing her mind a little. She needed to suss him out. Trust wasn't guaranteed, even if she was paying for a service and she was sure — just like builders and car salespeople

— there were cowboy therapists out there.

Taking a deep breath, she began. 'Well, I had some difficulties as a child, more as a teenager and with help and my parents' support, I recovered.' She cleared her throat and sniffed. 'Then two years ago, my brother died suddenly.' Her eyes closed momentarily. It always hurt saying the words to new people.

Nate remained silent, his gaze on her. Kind but intense eyes behind his glasses.

'It was devastating, Felix's death. It ripped our world apart.'

He nodded and Melody tucked her long hair behind her ear before looking at the glass on her lap, the water bobbing slightly like the sea on a calm day.

'My parents, well, Dad really, is extremely overprotective. I get it but it's smothering. I've not grieved properly, I can't because Dad can't cope with me struggling and neither can Mum, but she's blocked it out, focusing on work. Dad thinks I will become really poorly like I did when I was younger.' Sighing, she glanced out the window. Two pigeons nuzzled on the ledge of a windowsill in the building opposite. Preening and cuddling, Melody smiled. *Everyone needs love. Every thing needs love,* she thought.

She glanced at the handsome therapist. He nodded for her to continue. Raising a hand to her mouth, she bit on her fingernail before speaking. 'Dad treats me like I'm thirteen.' She puffed out air. 'Sometimes, I still feel trapped by my adolescence. Then with Felix, well, I haven't processed it really.' She shook her head slightly and pressed her lips together. 'Last year, I met a guy at work. We fell in love but broke up two weeks ago. I'm gutted and now, I just know I need to start dealing with things.' Letting out a long breath, she straightened her back and took a sip of water.

Nate nodded, pen in his hand, although he hadn't made a single note, not taking his eyes away from her as she spoke. He removed his glasses, placing them on the side table, and returned his gaze to her.

'Okay. Well, first, thanks for sharing that. It's difficult to say how we feel. Sometimes, it's easier to say things to a stranger and easier again to a therapist, but equally, it can be harder. That unfamiliarity, fear of judgement. But we all need help at some point, Melody, and the right people never judge. So, thank you for telling me, it assists me to understand how I could help you.' A smile flashed across his face.

Nodding, she uncrossed her legs and put the glass back on the table as a tiny weight of relief jumped from her shoulders. For the next ten minutes, she listened to Nate Lundie explain his work, options, and goals, answering her questions as he spoke.

'So, hopefully, that all makes sense and you can go away and think about the next steps. Either therapy with me or any other reputable therapist, or simply digest and know where to come when you are ready. Here's a list of online resources and reading that may be useful.'

He handed her the flyer. She accidentally brushed his finger with hers as she took it and felt her cheeks blush from the brief contact. After saying goodbye, Melody walked down the stairs to reception and exited the building, going straight across the road to the El Cortez takeaway.

'Grace?' she called out as she entered the flat. Five seconds later, Grace popped her head around the lounge door, hair wrapped up in a towel, dressing gown on.

'Some kid spilt their ice cream sundae all over me!' She rolled her eyes. 'I spent my shift smelling like caramel sauce, whilst strategically placing an apron over stains.'

Melody laughed. 'This might make your day better.' She held up a large bag of food from the takeaway. 'Mexican food from El Cortez.'

Grace clicked her fingers and turned around in a dance. 'Oh yeah, mi chica!'

The pair gathered plates and opened their food. Spicy rice, nachos, chicken enchiladas, spicy chips, guac and salsa.

'This is why I love you,' Grace said, popping a chip into her mouth as she emptied them onto a plate.

They walked through to the lounge with the food, going back into the kitchen and returning with empty plates, cutlery, and water. Melody sat on the sofa as Grace sat on the striped rug, legs tucked under their coffee table, gazing at the feast, before spooning rice onto her plate.

'So, how did it go with the therapist?'

Melody crunched on some nachos sealed together with melted cheese and refried beans. She nodded, chewing her mouthful. 'Yeah, it was really good. Not what I thought it would be like, although I don't know what I was expecting.' She shrugged.

'He was okay to talk to?' Grace leant over and scooped some nachos onto her plate.

'Yeah. He was really nice. Easy to talk to.'

Grace raised an eyebrow. 'Easy on the eye, as well!' She winked and laughed.

Melody chuckled. 'Well, he certainly doesn't look like Freud!'

Grace clapped her hands together and tilted her head back. 'I'm pleased it went well. Will you go back?' She crammed some nachos into her mouth.

'I'm going to book in for two weeks' time, hopefully. I can book a block of six sessions, then he reviews. Which I'm pleased about, feels less of a commitment, given the price!'

Grace tapped her friend's knee. 'Sounds brilliant, hun. I'm really pleased. It's a big step and it'll do you good.'

Smiling, Melody nodded. She felt proud of herself for going to the assessment at Lundie Therapy. Ready to crack through her emotional iceberg, she had a feeling Nate Lundie would be the perfect professional to help her do exactly that.

The next morning, as Melody got ready for work, she looked at herself in the full-length mirror on the back of her bedroom door, turning to the side and flicking her hair from her neck. She was attractive; a size twelve with perky breasts and youthful skin, but being pale, her face sometimes looked washed out against her deep brown hair. She sighed, putting her black cardigan on before grabbing her handbag. As she did each morning, Melody glanced at the photo of what used to be her family in a wooden frame on her bedside drawers, swallowed her sadness, and left for work.

Her phone pinged and she looked at the alert. It was from her bank. Matthew had transferred the money for six therapy sessions with Lundie Therapy. It was far from cheap and she felt bad momentarily, then knew her parents could afford it. Plus, there was a flicker of anger in her that if her dad hadn't been so restricting and smothering after Felix died and even before then, she probably wouldn't need the therapy and may not have even needed the medication her GP still prescribed. She ran her fingers through her hair and tried to shake out the feelings.

It was her lunch break and Melody had walked from

Crawford's in King's Cross to St Pancras Gardens. It was under a ten-minute walk and unusually warm for the end of September. Sitting on a wooden bench, she ate her tuna salad wrap, feeling she was far away from the capital and the ever-constant rush of the city. Watching the birds, she observed the berry palette of leaves on the trees, the green in them almost gone as autumn crept in.

It had been another morning of monotony, but Melody had tried to be grateful for the few comments of thanks she had received from customers. There was a night out planned that Friday for someone's leaving party. It was someone she liked, rare at Crawford's Insurance. She thought about Brandon possibly going. He and his team were often invited to events as contractors. Maybe he would be invited, maybe he wouldn't. Sighing, she'd lost her appetite and put her half-eaten wrap back into her lunch bag.

Logging into her internet banking app, she saw the deposit from Matthew. Lundie Therapy required her to pay upfront for the sessions. Checking her emails for the payment details, she tapped them into her banking app. *One less thing to worry about,* she thought as the payment went through. She texted Matthew:

Got the payment, Dad. Thanks loads. I'll text Mum, too, and will see you after work. Xxx

She texted her mum, telling her the sessions were booked, and her mobile phone rang a minute later. It was Zoe.

'Hi, darling, are you okay?'

Hearing the clattering of cups, she knew her mother was calling whilst on her break.

'Yeah, I'm good, thanks, Mum. Are you?'

'Always, Melly.' She let out a small chuckle. 'I'm pleased you're going to therapy, darling. Your father and I do worry about you.' There was silence for a few seconds. 'I know your father can be intense, Melly, but he loves you, we both do. And I'm grateful that you are close to him.'

Zoe sighed and Melody felt sadness claw at her ankles. She had grown closer to her father since the house fire when there was a switch in the family dynamics. Matthew began to work shorter hours at the accountancy firm and was home more. But it developed into something that bordered on overprotection, before becoming an impermeable weed of suffocation after Felix died. Now, the loneliness and heartbreak she was sure her father felt, compounded by his marriage demise, made their relationship draining, despite her love for him.

'I know, Mum.' Melody sighed.

'And I know you prefer to talk to your father about things, but, well, I'm always here. I love you, Melly.'

Pressing her lips together, she looked at the leaves by her feet. It wasn't that she preferred to speak to Matthew, it was that she felt she had to, as part of his healing. And because, well, Zoe always seemed to be working and, in a way, blocked it all out. Her mum shied away from emotions, instead being practical, factual — much like her work. It was complicated, and Melody didn't want the responsibility of her parents' grief when she needed to manage her own. She thought about explaining to her mum, but it wasn't worth it.

'I love you too, Mum. See you Sunday.'

'Bye, darling.'

Melody inhaled deeply and breathed out slowly. She was doing the right thing, for her, for her recovery. Making herself happy. Her parents supported her, in their own ways. And she had to remember that Felix would never want any of them to struggle. Maybe if she got better, it would have a ripple effect on her parents, Matthew in particular. Nodding to herself, she put her bag over her shoulder and rose from the park bench. Perhaps things would be okay after all.

The week passed quickly and it was soon Friday — the night out for Melody's colleague's leaving party at a few bars in Soho.

The night before, Grace had helped her choose an outfit, saying she looked, 'Hotter than a polar bear in the Bahamas.'

Melody had rolled her eyes, laughing. Grace always knew how to make her feel better.

'You might even pull in that sexy little number!' She tapped Melody's backside as she walked past.

Looking at herself in the full-length mirror, turning slightly, she had to admit, she looked good; with curves in all the right places. Her mum always said she needed to smile more as a teenager. But, being unhappy means you don't smile much! However, things were changing and as she flicked her long hair, she smiled, hoping Brandon would be out for the leaving party.

Grace had got a staff discount at South of Here bar for the group from Crawford's. It was only a short walk from the office, so the team started there. Melody arrived at 7 pm, just a few of her colleagues were already there. They chatted about work, as people always did on work nights out. Sipping on her white wine, she couldn't help but feel the stampede of giant ants marching around in her stomach as she glanced at the door every few minutes, anticipating the possible arrival of Brandon. She had rehearsed what she would say; commenting that she was going for therapy. That she was sorry and understood his anger. That she still loved him and hoped in time he could forgive her.

Dave, one of her colleagues on the resolution team, came

over. Melody saw him look her up and down, and she narrowed her eyes.

'Alright, Mel? You look nice.' She smelt stale cigarettes on him as he came too close to her.

She tilted her head up and feigned a smile. 'Thanks, Dave.'

'I heard you broke up with Brendan from the IT company?'

Dave leant in and Melody got a whiff of the type of after-shave her dad would wear, mixed with the linger of cigarette smoke. She stepped back slightly, grimacing and holding her glass out as a hopeful barrier.

'Yeah. And it's Brandon, not Brendan.'

Dave tilted his head and swigged some of his pint. 'Well, his loss. Now, if you want some male company, you can always let me know.' He licked his lips and stroked her hand.

She pulled her hand back, thinking he resembled an oily lizard, watching its insect prey. She looked towards the door again.

'What do you say, Mel?' Greasy lizard Dave grabbed her shoulder.

She turned her head back to him, rapidly. 'It's fucking Melody, not Mel. And no, Dave, I would rather shit in my hands and clap. So, piss off!' She turned away and went in search of the toilets before she did what she really wanted to do, which was punch Dave in his sleazy face.

An hour later, it was time to move on to the next bar, where colleagues would continue to join the night. Saying goodbye to Grace, the group then headed to Soho, to a trendy bar called Coolin' Out. Walking with an older woman from the team, Melody still felt hopeful that Brandon may make an appearance. It was only 8:30 pm and Brandon often worked late, especially on a Friday, when everything seemed to go wrong before teams reduced for the weekend.

Ordering another wine in Coolin' Out bar, she made a conscious effort to avoid Dave, who was now sleazing over a newer member of Crawford's Insurance. Some of the team sat at booths, whilst others stood mingling in small groups. Melody took a seat with three other people from her team. They chatted about their weekend and bitched about work. Two of them went to get drinks, leaving her and a female colleague, sitting opposite.

'So, I hear your ex is seeing that girl from the canteen,' her colleague said casually, almost mockingly.

Melody's shoulders stiffened. 'What?'

'Brandon Steel. He's seeing the brunette who works in the canteen. It's well known.' There was a smugness in her colleague's voice that set the anger in Melody alight.

'And I can see you were dying to tell me,' Melody sneered.

She just shrugged and smiled sarcastically. Glancing to her side, her colleagues were deep in conversation and the two from their booth were at the bar, backs to everyone. Glaring at her colleague sitting opposite, she thought she was nothing but a spiteful, smug cow. Another mean girl who thought she was better than her. Picking up her glass of wine, Melody threw it directly in her colleague's face. Gasping, her colleague screamed and people close by, who could hear it over the music, turned to look.

'What the fu...'

'Oh, sorry. It was an accident,' Melody said calmly.

Colleagues came over. 'Is everything okay?' someone asked.

'No, it isn't. This bitch swilled me!' Melody's colleague was wiping her face on the sleeves of her top, the neckline of it saturated, as was some of her red hair.

'It was an accident. I got up and my foot caught in my bag

handle. I fell forward.'

'She's lying. She did it on purpose!' Her colleague was close to tears.

'I can only apologise. I'll get some tissues.'

Getting up from the booth and walking to the toilets, she had no intention of getting the spiteful cow any tissues, but it was good swilling the shit-stirrer, even if a second later she felt raging anger that Brandon had potentially moved on already.

Sitting on the toilet, Melody looked at her phone. It was 9 pm and she was losing hope of Brandon joining the night out, especially after what she just heard. She would simply have to get on with the night, trying to avoid the dickheads that seemed to gravitate towards her. Leaving the cubicle, she washed her hands and looked at her reflection. Her long hair curled around her face and shoulders. Pale skin with the remnants of some freckles, or sun-kisses as her dad always called them. She smiled to herself before reapplying her lipstick.

Heading to the bar where another group from Crawford's congregated, she squashed in to order a drink, giggling to herself that the £8.50 glass of wine price tag was worth spending to throw on her colleague's face. Waiting for a server, she glanced across the bar. On the other side, she saw Nate Lundie. She looked twice and a second later, he caught her eye. He nodded and smiled, as Melody lifted her palm from the bar and returned the smile. Her gaze remained on him for a moment before the bartender asked for her order, blocking her view of the therapist.

The bartender began pouring her wine. She bit her lip, feeling a little nervous but wanting to see Nate Lundie again. He looked good, even for an older man. Melody shook her head. She was tipsy and bruised from the gossip about Brandon.

Paying for her drink, the bartender moved away to the next thirsty customer.

Glancing across the bar to where he was, she noticed he had turned to his side. Only his profile showing, he was facing a woman, their drinks and bodies almost touching. He didn't look over, immersed in the conversation with a tall brunette, whose hair caressed her bare shoulder. And there it was again for Melody; a child stamp of jealous feet in her stomach. A feeling she didn't like, and a feeling that always meant something bad.

Chapter 10: Nate

It was Monday morning and as he poured milk over his cereal, Nate wondered where the weekend had gone. Spooning some of his breakfast into his mouth as he leant against the kitchen bench, he contemplated his weekend. He'd been smashed more times than a sex offender's windows lately and needed to reduce his alcohol intake and increase his fitness.

However, alongside dating and copious beers and rum, he had made a call to a local estate agent on Saturday and had arranged for them to come around on Wednesday evening to value the house. He was in two minds whether he would put it on the market, and would avoid searching for a possible property in a more rural location until he got a valuation. There was no harm in finding out what his oversized house was worth.

Friday night had been interesting. Nate had a second date with the woman from the dating app and ended up taking her back to his. They'd slept together. It was good. She was attractive, engaging, but something was missing, like a lost piece on a chess set that made it feel pointless playing. He tapped the back of the spoon against his lips. The missing something was the same thing that had been missing in most of the women he had dated. Most of the women since Annabelle Graham. Shit! He had let himself go there again. Annabelle was a train crash of thoughts. Doomed from the first stop.

Maybe his date felt their lack of chemistry. He rubbed his hand over his jaw and decided to give dating her a little longer.

Draining the milk from his cereal, he slurped the last mouthful and put his empty bowl and spoon into the dishwasher. Rubbing his tongue around his mouth to catch the last bits of his breakfast, he thought of Coolin' Out bar on Friday night and seeing his new client, Melody Dartford. She had looked so different. Black lace dress revealing a bounce of cleavage. Blood red lipstick on full lips that smiled at him. Wide doe-like eyes filled with the innocence of being a young woman.

Rubbing a hand through his hair, he tutted to himself for being unprofessional. Plus, she must have only been in her mid-twenties. He was old enough to be her dad. Shaking his head, Nate left the kitchen to brush his teeth before grabbing his lunch, laptop, and sports bag, ready for another week at work.

The charity spin-a-thon at his gym was in just over four weeks' time. He'd planned to up his classes, starting that evening. Money raised from the charity event would go to a local community centre that wanted to give their play area an update for disabled kids. Nate was keen to raise as much money as he could, and it was always good to set personal goals and challenges.

The work day went quickly, followed by the next few days. Soon it was Wednesday night and the estate agent was coming to value his property. Able to get away after his 3 pm appointment, he missed most of the rush-hour traffic home and was in plenty of time for the estate agent arriving at 5 pm. Driving in London was problematic, made more so by the continuous introduction of congestion lanes. But Nate loathed the Tube. Expensive, smelly, and full of space invaders, he preferred the stop-start traffic and parking charges — which were subsidised through his office lease.

The agent arrived, impressed with his property, smiling and

nodding throughout the viewing as if perusing fine gems. Nate mentioned the recent sale of his neighbour's home a few doors down and he made it clear he knew it was with that agent and how much it sold for. It was a pleasant house, but he felt his house had more desirable features such as a landscaped garden with porcelain tiling, as well as a newer built-in kitchen and en-suite. Suitably impressed, the agent looked around as he made notes, chatting about the market at present, before giving an estimated value and advising he would be in touch regarding the next steps.

After his morning sessions the next day, Nate had no clients in the afternoon until Melody Dartford. It meant a long lunch and then time to catch up on some admin before she arrived. A thought slipped into his head of her in the bar, looking vampish and alluring. 'Get a grip,' he said, rising from his chair and smoothing down his grey jumper. Most women looked great in make-up and body-hugging clothes. Deciding to walk to St Pancras Gardens, five minutes from his office, he grabbed his left-over stir-fry and headed to the park.

It was good to get some fresh air and although the autumn chill had landed in the capital, it wasn't raining, meaning he could enjoy the pocket of nature as respite in the bustling city centre. As a therapist, he loved to people-watch and sat, enjoying his lunch as folk milled around. Couples chatted, parents with children, elderly people holding hands. Friends, people walking or sitting solo; a mixture of folk, all with their own story.

Nate took his mobile phone from his pocket and looked at his messages. His date had texted, asking how his day was going. He sighed and rubbed the back of his neck, knowing he had been cool with her since the weekend. It wasn't deliberate and it was nothing to do with the sex. He just wasn't feeling the click he craved — that all-consuming desire.

Leaning back against the wooden bench, he wondered if he would ever feel that raging wildfire of attraction again. The desire that makes you crave a person so much that every nerve in your body feels like molten lava. The longing to immerse yourself in them, inhale them, devour them. An urge to always think of them, want them, need them. Two young people came skateboarding past at the speed most cars drive around housing estates. It snapped him out of his thinking, and he was grateful. With that, he placed his phone in his pocket and walked back to his office.

There was a knock at his door. It was 3:30 pm and as he opened the door, Melody stood, smiling in tight jeans and a floral blouse, under a biker jacket. She looked a lot less glamorous than the previous Friday and Nate was relieved. Of course, she was still an attractive woman, but he could dissolve that image of her deep blood-red lips and curvy body from his mind in order to be the professional he had worked so hard to be.

'Melody, great to see you. Come on in.'

Nate moved to the side and she entered his office with a returned hello. She took a seat on his sofa and relaxed her shoulders slightly. Pouring some water, he handed her it.

'How are you? Good week so far?' He sat down opposite, taking his notepad and pen from the side table before placing his glasses on.

'Yeah, okay.' She took a sip of water. 'I feel ready to start dealing with all the crap in here.' She tapped her head and gave a sad smile.

'Well, that's certainly positive. Sometimes, it's good to start at the beginning. It's a saying for a reason.' Nate pushed his glasses up his nose, and Melody nodded. 'So, let's attempt that and by starting with your childhood issues, we can try to understand and begin to process those that have impacted your adulthood.'

Melody swallowed and shifted slightly on the sofa before uncrossing and re-crossing her legs. It was always difficult for clients at first, and Nate appreciated that. Even people who liked to talk — sometimes liked the sound of their own voice a little too much — found aspects challenging. It was perhaps the way he delved and teased the thoughts, feelings, and behaviours out. But this was the only way they could work on them and ultimately, the only way that the client could move forward and have the autonomy to deal with any difficulties in the future. And so, she began telling him about her childhood.

Chapter 11: Melody

When he opened the door to his office, Nate's eyes struck Melody immediately. She wasn't sure if it was the light grey of his hair, the fact his glasses were off, or the dark grey of his jumper highlighting them, but his eyes were like magnets. She bit her lip as he invited her in and she took a seat on the comfortable sofa, clearing her throat as she did. The room smelt of ylang ylang and she inhaled, closing her eyes for a second before he poured her some water.

As he took the seat opposite her, Melody watched his ankle and foot, encased in a blue loafer, cross over the other as he picked up a notepad and pen. There was no wedding ring on his finger — so maybe the woman in Coolin' Out bar was just a girlfriend. As he mentioned the therapy, and starting at the beginning, she felt hopeful that it was the right time to address her feelings and challenges. She just had to ensure she focused on exactly that and not how handsome Nate Lundie was.

Let's start with childhood, he had suggested. Advising this would explain her coping mechanisms, both positive and negative, her development into adulthood, and how previous situations may have contributed to her life now. It made sense and she knew deep down that if she was going to benefit from therapy, she would have to be as honest as possible. Nate wasn't there to judge; he was there to help. She had taken the step to help herself and had to embrace it.

So, she began talking about her parents and older brother,

and how 'normal' life had been. Stable, happy, loving. She talked about childhood memories of grandparents and primary school. Nate made a few comments and wrote notes, asking about her emotions surrounding certain things. Melody felt relaxed and as she talked, the family nostalgia was soothing, even though she was often the irritating younger sister. When she shared her school days and friendship with Lily, along with falling out when they were eleven after Courtney joined the school, it still felt okay and positive. And despite not being friends for a while, Lily returned to her, temporarily at least.

Melody knew that she would have to tell him about being poorly when she was sixteen and that meant talking about Lily some more. But she couldn't say everything, no matter how comfortable she got with her therapist. If she did, she could end up in serious trouble with the police. Even after all these years. But she had time to think. Time to plan what to say to Nate that would both help and protect her.

The session had reached the end, and feeling a little lighter, she grabbed her Steve Madden handbag next to her feet and rose from the sofa. Putting her jacket back on, Nate stood opposite. She yawned, not out of boredom but of feeling relaxed, as if a layer of sadness was beginning to peel from her onion of trauma.

'Sorry,' she said, covering her mouth and trying to stifle a second yawn, as she pulled her trapped hair from her jacket collar.

Nate laughed, his symmetrical snow-white teeth flashing as he removed his glasses, showing those piercing eyes clearer. 'No need to apologise.'

Pausing slightly, she was hypnotised by his masculine appeal. 'Thanks. And thank you for… that.' Melody bit her lip.

'You're welcome. I hope you found it useful. We will pick up where we left off next week. Does the same day and time work for you?' He smiled, walked to his desk and picked up a business card to write the appointment on.

Her eyes followed him, glancing at his backside in his blue chinos. She bit her finger. Nate turned, waiting for a response. She nodded and after scrawling on the card, he held it out between his forefinger and middle finger. Gently taking it, Melody felt nervous being so close to him. She looked down as she took the card, then turned her eyes back up and they met his. Those striking blue eyes, like forget-me-nots. For a moment, she just stared at him until he coughed. Quickly smoothing her hair, she turned to the office door, feeling her face flush. He moved ahead and held the door open.

'Thanks, again. Erm, I will see you next week.' Melody held the business card up and smiled awkwardly.

'See you then. Have a good week.'

Leaving his office, Nate Lundie's business card gripped in her hand, she felt a fizz inside of her. She was going to her dad's for dinner. In the early days of their separation, Zoe would return to the house so the three of them could eat together — some normality in the graffitied mural of their family. Then, it stopped, with no explanation and Melody began meeting her mum one lunchtime a week, or going for Sunday lunch to a pub near her mother's apartment.

Leaving Nate's building, she looked over the road to El Cortez Mexican takeaway. Taking her phone from her pocket, she rang Matthew to see if he had already started dinner. He hadn't, so she picked up some food from the takeaway, excited to tell her dad that the therapy session had gone well.

Matthew's smile matched that of a kid at a funfair when

Melody told him that the session with Nate had been positive.

'Darling, I'm so pleased. I think this will really help you. And well, it'll get me off your back too.' He laughed, but it was full of sad tiredness.

She nodded. He was right, it would help them both. Matthew had aged so much in the last two years and his life had little joy. Instead, a fusion of worry and work. Melody wanted him to be happy. She wanted them both to be happy.

A few hours later, Melody was back home. As she took her jeans off and placed them over the white upcycled chair in her bedroom, Nate Lundie's business card fell out of a pocket onto the wooden flooring. Placing her hands in a prayer motion to her mouth, she looked at the card before bending to pick it up. Turning it over in her fingers a few times, Melody smiled to herself. She was dying to see him again, already.

That night, she struggled to get to sleep and was still awake when Grace came home, just after midnight. As usual, Grace was quiet, considerate. Melody clutched her quilt to her chest, grateful to have such a kind and caring friend in her housemate. The session with Nate had brought up the past. Thoughts she tried to suppress and conversations she certainly didn't want to have. She knew that next week, she would have to talk about her teenage life and that would include the incident that changed everything. Lying, her blanket pulled in tight to her, mimicking a cuddle she so desperately needed, she closed her eyes and was back. Back to school, over eight years earlier.

The best friends were both just turned sixteen and in their GCSE year. Only seven more months at school until they were free. Well, for the summer at least, before they both went to college. Lily had begun to see a guy in sixth form, Toby. Melody didn't like him. He thought he was God's gift and had a Peugeot car with some insanely loud subwoofer speakers. It wasn't impressive to her, but Toby acted like he was driving a Lamborghini and dining at the Ivy each weekend, as opposed to blasting Blue Monkey music from his ten-year-old, tiny Peugeot and munching on a McDonald's drive-thru meal.

However, Lily was besotted and she had to listen to her harp on about Toby at every opportunity, whilst biting her tongue. The truth was, Melody couldn't stand anyone else in their circle. It was Melody and Lily, Lily and Melody. Inseparable, in and out of school. Sisters from another mister, as they would say. Toby was disrupting this; acetone on the glue of their friendship.

She knew Toby didn't like her, but it wasn't for the same reasons she despised him. Toby wasn't jealous of her. He didn't need to be as Lily was smitten and he had the car and was seventeen as a top trump. No, he didn't like her as she was always around. And Toby knew that dating Lily meant Melody tagging along. Lily, caught in the middle, tried to make everything okay for the sake of her best friend forever and the so-called love of her life. She would nod and smile, pretending to be happy for Lily, whilst inside she was feeling a parasite of anger, jealousy, and inadequacy feeding on her soul — getting bigger and stronger each day.

'He's got a friend, Callum,' Lily had said one day, with excitement that made Melody seethe. She didn't want a boyfriend; she just wanted her best friend.

'He's at college.' Lily raised her eyebrows as if the thought of someone being at college was the winning lottery ticket for Melody's dating aspirations.

She had agreed to hang around as a foursome on the weekends. It was the only way she would get a night with her friend.

In his mobile disco, Toby would pick the girls up from Lily's on a Friday evening. They would go to McDonald's or drive to the park for a walk, or sometimes to the shopping centre. They would chat in the car and listen to music or park up and mooch about the area. Occasionally, she would sit in the back with Callum as Lily and Toby kissed for ages in the front. Lily sometimes giggling as his hands travelled to places Melody couldn't see. Callum would talk endless shit as she nodded intermittently, not listening to a word he was saying as she policed her friend.

'Why don't you just kiss him and see how you feel?' Lily had said one Friday as they walked through the local shopping centre.

Looking at a shop window, the mannequins in stupid poses wearing fancy dresses, she had clenched her jaw. 'Erm, because I don't fancy him one per cent.'

Lily laughed, and Melody didn't see the funny side. Callum was unattractive and he sniffed all the time, which made her gag.

'Aw, Melly, he likes you.' Lily had tilted her head as if they were talking about the last kitten in the litter that needed a home.

'I don't care. I don't like him,' she'd sulked, folding her arms.

'He's joined the gym with Toby. I reckon he will be buff by the summer.' Lily had put her arms out, flexing non-existent muscles, her eyes widened, trying to convince her friend.

Toby and Callum had been walking ahead, nudging each other and high-fiving as they guffawed. It made her lips curl.

'Good luck to him. I've seen more muscle on a chicken leg.'

Bursting out laughing, Lily had grabbed her friend. 'Eeeh, you are funny. But sometimes you look down your nose at people and it's not kind.'

She had rushed off and jumped on Toby's back, as she squealed in delight. Leaving Melody feeling like an axe had chopped through her middle. *You look down your nose at people and it's not kind!* How the hell could her best friend forever say something like that? Just because she didn't fancy Lily's boyfriend's ugly mate? Melody had wrung her hands together before making fists with them. Lily had changed. And it was since she met Toby. Toby had changed her and she was determined that his and Lily's relationship had to end.

As the weeks passed, Melody became more and more resolute that she had to split Lily and Toby up. She was starting to detest him and a flicker of rage would spark each time his name was spoken. Lily was constantly going on about Christmas and her and Toby's plans. Each year, it had been them making arrangements and now, she wasn't factored in.

It was two weeks before Christmas, and Melody had been thinking of her plan. Lily was very anti-drug after her cousin had been involved with drugs and gangs. Aware of this, Melody planned to get some drugs into the group. She knew the friend of the local shopkeeper's son had links to buy cannabis. She asked for his details and made contact from a phone box. Meeting him and giving a false name, she had used almost three weeks' worth of pocket money to buy the cannabis.

The Friday before the incident, Melody had made an unexpected effort with Callum, even flirting with him, much to Lily and Toby's delight. The following Friday, the group went to the local country park. After Toby parked his car, the four had got out and taken a walk in the frosty night — the greenery and ground coated in what looked like the lightest dusting of icing sugar. Surrounded by trees and minimal light, it was both creepy and comforting to see the dark shadows of clouds in the clear, crisp sky. Toby and Lily had strolled ahead, holding hands and play pushing one another. Walking behind with Callum, she'd chatted with him.

'You can tell you've been working out, Callum,' Melody had said, flicking her hair.

'Really?' he'd replied, eyes wide as a smile spread across his thin lips.

'Yeah. You look good.'

They had continued walking and she had tensed at the cold and the lies she was feeding Callum. 'Listen,' she'd said, moving closer to him, 'I have some dope. I thought it would be fun to smoke it.'

He'd turned to her, chuckled, and rubbed his hands together. 'Yeah, for sure!'

'Great. But Callum, I can't let Lily know it's come from me. She will be pissed off with me.' Melody had smiled at Callum and touched the back of his hand.

He had bit his lip and nodded. 'Erm, okay. I can say I got it?'

Like a bear into a trap, she'd thought, nonchalantly shrugging and giving him a big smile. 'Thanks, you'd be amazing for doing that. I think smoking it would be such a good laugh, but she will need some convincing and she's more likely to not have a go at you!' Melody had nudged him and giggled, flicking her hair again.

'Of course, anything you want.' He'd shrugged, staring at her.

She had hoped that Callum and Toby smoking dope would be enough to put Lily off her boyfriend. The pair caught up with Lily and Toby, and Callum retrieved the cannabis from his pocket that she had handed him, along with some tobacco, rolling papers, and matches.

'Look at what I've got!' he had announced, waving them in the air towards Toby.

'Now that's a party!' Toby had clapped his hands, then slapped Callum on the shoulder, laughing.

'We're not having any of that, Toby!' Lily had shouted, her eyes drilling into her boyfriend.

'Lighten up, babe. It's only a bit of green.' Toby had taken it from Callum's hand and inhaled it, making a dramatic performance of the sniff.

Lily had looked at Melody, who pursed her lips and shook her head, out of sight of the boys, who were studying their treasure. 'I'm not having any,' Lily had insisted, shoving her hands into her coat pocket.

'Just a little. It might loosen you up a bit!' Toby had elbowed Callum and they both laughed, knowing Toby was referring to the fact Lily was yet to have sex with him.

'Toby!' Lily's face changed. Her usual smile was replaced with a sneer and a little fear behind her soft green eyes.

Melody had watched, saying nothing.

'Oh, come on. It's just a little smoke. And it's almost Christmas.' He'd high-fived Callum and took some of the cigarette papers, getting ready to roll a joint.

'If you have any of that, I'm leaving.' Lily had pushed her shoulders back and lifted her chin.

'Lily, you need to remember we are young. We are *meant* to enjoy ourselves. Jeez, you would think you were a pensioner the way you go on at times.' He'd sniggered and nudged Callum.

In the dark night, illuminated by sporadic lighting in the country park, she hadn't need to see clearly to know her friend had red cheeks. Embarrassed by her boyfriend, who she had thought would always be on her side. At that moment, Melody hated Toby more than ever.

'C'mon Melody, we are going.' Lily had stormed towards her and linked her arm.

'Ah, don't be like that, babe,' Toby had said, glancing up only momentarily from making his joint.

'Yeah, chiiilllll out, Lily,' added Callum, which made Toby giggle.

'Losers.' Lily marched off, and had dragged Melody with her.

Inside, she had been cartwheeling with delight, linking her friend as they left. She'd been certain that the couple would split up. Drugs were a non-negotiable for Lily and alongside that, Toby had been a real prick about it. She had glowed inside as they walked and Lily ranted on about how angry she was. How much Toby had let her down and did he not care? Did he even know her? Unsure she could forgive him and she could never date a drug user. Melody nodded and said the right things as she had thought about their future; just the two best friends again. She had succeeded, but Melody had no idea that the next few hours would change her world completely.

Chapter 12: Nate

'So, you're really selling up?' Brian asked that evening when Nate was at his sister and brother-in-law's.

He nodded. 'Yeah, I think I am. The valuation from the estate agents is too much to not try. And the house is just too big for me. We bought that when we were younger, thinking we would have kids, and well…' Nate shrugged. 'I want to live somewhere a bit rural, but still have access to the city.'

'As long as it's not too far from us, eh?' Julie said, placing a large lasagne down on the table, crisped to perfection.

It was true, his house had been valued in excess of forty per cent extra than what they had paid. And despite having given Sarah a lot more than the half they bought the house for, following their split, it still meant that Nate would have a large sum for a smaller house, in a quieter, rural area, still near London. Maybe with a bit of land and he could eventually have his own practice on site. It was a bit of a dream, but why couldn't it come true?

The next day was Saturday, and he was at the gym, practising for the charity spin-a-thon. After speaking to a few people, including an attractive blonde, he realised he had yet to arrange another date with the woman from the app. They'd texted back and forth and said they would meet again, but it hadn't been arranged. In all honesty, Nate didn't want to meet again. There was a chemistry missing, as clichéd as it sounded. And perhaps she felt the same. Nate sniggered to himself as he looked in the mirror, doing weighted rows. There were too many beautiful women to commit further to someone who he just wasn't feeling.

It was soon the new working week and Nate had a busy one, with a new client and others that he would review to reduce sessions with or plan to close. The door was always metaphorically open to the clients he discharged. However, there was a sense of achievement for both parties when they were signed off and sent on their way to embrace and manage life. It was the ultimate goal.

On Wednesday lunchtime, he headed out for his break to St Pancras Gardens. He had made some chicken salad wraps with precision, ensuring the contents had been folded nicely into the flat bread, like a toddler tucked into a bed. The charity spin-a-thon was in just over three weeks, and Nate was cutting the alcohol and trying to eat more protein. He had bought some beef jerky, which he hated the sound of, but actually tasted quite nice, and had made some protein balls at home.

Sitting down to eat, he observed the peace and quiet of the park, surrounded by the hustle of city centre life. There was something so therapeutic about nature, and one thing he always advocated as a therapist was to get out into flora — a thing he had to put into practice himself. And a thing that moving further from the city centre would definitely provide, yet still near enough for work.

Leaning back on the wooden bench, Nate watched a couple walk past. Hand in hand in the crisp October air, they walked in sync. He smiled sadly; a pang of longing for something he wasn't quite sure he wanted. Opening his packed lunch box, a curious pigeon landed next to him, followed by a blackbird.

They tilted their heads, eyes boring into Nate as they made tentative movements.

A woman with a pushchair came barging past, and the birds took flight, leaving him to enjoy his food, unsupervised. After a bit of social media scrolling and demolishing his wraps, he opened the tub containing three protein balls. They resembled enormous rabbit droppings, but he knew they tasted good. Looking down at them, he made a hmph noise to himself and picked one out.

'Hope they taste better than they look.' A voice made him raise his eyeline.

It was Melody Dartford, and for the tiniest moment, Nate felt shy. He cleared his throat. 'They do and hello, Melody.' He smiled and she stared at him for a second before speaking again.

'Hi. Do you come here often?' She let out a flirty laugh and touched her hair.

He swallowed, slightly taken aback by the Melody outside of the therapy room. He chuckled and moved a little in the seat. Sitting down next to him, he could smell her fruity perfume; hints of apples and honey.

'Do you mind?'

Shaking his head, Nate spoke. 'Not at all. I try to come here a few times a week during my lunch break. It helps stretch my legs from sitting all day. And well, who doesn't love nature?' He tilted his gaze up to the sky for a second and inhaled. Looking back, her brown eyes were on him.

'Yeah, it's a lovely park and you would never think it was here, in the centre of the frantic city.' She glanced around the park. 'Are they nice?' Melody nodded at the protein balls.

'Erm, yeah. Take one.' He pointed the container towards her.

Taking one out, she looked at it in her palm, then raised her eyes back to Nate. 'Thanks.' Licking her lips, he watched, feeling slight discomfort but also a sense of intrigue. Taking a bite, Nate observed. *Was she deliberately trying to make it sexy?* he wondered as her lips burst through the protein ball. Nate stopped looking and bit his own in a much less alluring manner.

'Mmm. Wow, they are tasty.' Melody stared inside the half-bitten snack and wiped her lip. 'Did your girlfriend make them?'

Coughing, he covered his mouth, swallowing a little of the protein ball. 'No, I haven't got a girlfriend. I made them myself.'

'Oh. I thought… the woman in the bar the other week.' Her big brown eyes, like pots of melted chocolate, remained on him. Nate just smiled and shook his head. He wasn't going to elaborate on his relationship status.

'So, a health kick?' She put a leg over the other, then tucked her hair behind her ear with her free hand.

He tilted his head from side to side. 'Kind of. I try to stay healthy and fit most of the time. But I'm taking part in a charity spin-a-thon in a few weeks for Klubs for Kids. They are fundraising for a new playground that has more equipment for disabled kids.'

'Sounds brilliant. I've been meaning to do more exercise. It's hard with work and stuff, but I know it would make me feel better and help keep me in shape.'

Melody paused and bit her lip. Nate had a feeling she may have wanted a compliment about her physique. And usually, to a woman, or anyone, Nate would say something positive. He swallowed. The thing was, he found her attractive. Not just physically, but there was an intrigue about Melody Dartford. An edge, almost a thrill, that he knew would likely follow her into the bedroom. Tensing his jaw, he berated himself for his thoughts and replied as diplomatically as he could.

'You look fine, but exercise most definitely helps with mental health management and endorphin release, sleeping better, and a sense of achievement. So many benefits.'

She nodded and pulled at the sleeve of her coat. 'Well, I'd like to sponsor you. I can bring the money to the session tomorrow.'

'That's really kind, but you don't have to.' Nate turned to her and her eyes narrowed. 'But if you really want to, that would be greatly received.' His mobile phone beeped in his pocket. 'Anyway, I better get back. Enjoy your day. See you tomorrow.' Nate got up and as Melody said goodbye, he headed back towards his office, wondering if she was watching him walk away.

Chapter 13: Melody

'You're in a chirpy mood,' said one of Melody's colleagues that afternoon. And despite being in the job she loathed — mainly with people who made the underground population of the local cemetery good company — she was indeed in a chirpy mood. And it was down to bumping into Nate Lundie on her lunch break. Sitting close to him on the bench, she could see the firm shape of his thighs and the wrinkles around his magnetic blue eyes that only made his face more attractive. His full lips as he bit into a protein ball; sharing his lunch with her.

There was a chemistry, Melody felt it. *Surely Nate did too?* Now she knew he went to the park sometimes on his lunch break, she hoped to see him outside of their appointments. However, the therapy had to be her focus during her sessions. Melody had to process her cargo of emotions and tomorrow, in the appointment, she had to talk about the incident.

Walking up the stairs the next day for her therapy session with Nate, she quickly checked her pink lip gloss in her pocket mirror and sprayed perfume. She had worn a sheer blouse for work and undid one button before she left, leaving a slight peek of her cleavage. Paired with a black midi skirt that showed the curves of her hips and a black biker jacket, Melody knew she looked smart and a little sexy. Lizard-like Dave had given her a, 'Phowarrr.' And whilst she didn't appreciate his pervy acknowledgement, it was a level of validation that she looked attractive.

Reaching the top of the stairs, she walked along the corridor to the second door and knocked. He opened it, smiling with a hello. Nate was wearing a blue polo shirt and chinos. The polo shirt showed his toned biceps, the colour, highlighting his eyes.

Did he look me up and down there? Melody thought as she returned the greeting and followed him into his office. Pouring some water, he asked how her week had been, not acknowledging the park yesterday. She took a seat, thanked him for the water, and picked up her bag. Taking out her purse, she handed him £50.

'That's for the spin-a-thon.'

His eyes widened. 'Thank you, Melody, but that's too much money. I can't take that.'

She smiled and shook her head gently. 'Please, I want to. You, they, are worth it.'

He grinned and she saw a slight dimple emerge on one of his cheeks. Damn, she really wanted to kiss him.

'That's very kind. The charity will be so grateful. Thank you.'

Melody pushed her chest out slightly as Nate took his seat and repeated, 'So, your last week?'

Telling the truth, she told him that the last week had made her think and realise it was the right time to unpack her emotional baggage.

'Excellent,' he said, placing his glasses on. 'Last week, you talked about early childhood and the formative years of friendship-making, school, your older brother, and parental roles. Tell me about your teenage years and when you first became aware of your mental well-being and changes.' He opened his notepad and crossed a leg over the other.

Taking a sip of water, Melody rubbed the back of her neck with her free hand. She placed the glass down on the side table and took a deep breath. She hadn't talked about the incident for seven years since she left Hopewood. Shifting slightly on the yellow sofa, his gaze remained on her. Clearing her throat, she explained how at the age of sixteen, Lily began a relationship with Toby, who was older and in sixth form. It was the year of their GCSEs; an important year for their future and both had planned to go to college, even doing the same A-Levels.

'We hoped to study to become primary school teachers.' Melody looked down at her lap. She let out a weak laugh. *And look at the shitty job I've got now,* she thought to herself as she took another sip of water. 'But that all changed. For me, anyway.'

Talking about the night in December at the country park, she omitted the truth about who sourced the cannabis. Years may have passed, but Nate Lundie had some level of duty of care. She knew that from his website and the information he shared at the assessment meeting. Safeguarding or something, and it meant that even though it was eight years ago, well, he could still tell someone and that would no doubt get her into a lot of trouble. Plus, she had paid the price enough already.

She rubbed the side of her neck and saw his eyes follow her hand. Deliberately, she left it there for a few more seconds, sliding her fingers over her skin before continuing.

'Callum got some cannabis and pulled it out of his pocket to cheers from Toby. Lily wasn't impressed in the slightest and after a bit of an argument, she wanted to leave. Of course, I wouldn't let her leave alone. The country park led onto a shopping area but it was dark and late, and well, not safe.'

Nate was listening, nodding, pen poised. He remained focused on her, and she thought how attentive he was. Melody also thought how gorgeous he was and shook her head slightly, trying to focus back on the session and the help her dad was paying for.

'We left and went home. Lily came to stay at mine and I made us hot chocolate when we got in.' She tilted her head and looked to her left, out of the office window. 'Lily used to love cinnamon sprinkled on the top of her hot chocolate and she said I was the only one who got the amount right.' Melody bit back sadness and fury in equal measures.

'She slept over and it was lovely having my friend to myself. Lily was angry about Toby. Even though she loved him, she couldn't go out with a drug user, not after what happened to her cousin, who'd almost died and had a brain injury from taking drugs.' Sighing, she looked Nate straight in the eyes. 'But it was amazing to have her back. That closeness that we'd had all those years. Just us.'

He nodded, and she knew he understood her. Nate Lundie really got her. Closing her eyes for a second, she inhaled. Regurgitating the past was hard. It was harder still that in some ways, Melody felt she held on to the pain and resentment — like an old, ugly tattoo, inked on a regretful drunken night — despite her time in Hopewood.

'The next morning, we both had missed calls, but we'd slept in after talking all night and our mobiles were on silent. Mum came into my bedroom and woke us, panic in her voice. She sat on my bed, wringing her hands and glared at Lily with watery eyes. She was like another daughter to Mum and Dad.' Putting her hand to her forehead, she swallowed. 'I'd never seen Mum like that before. She just blurted it out; Toby and Callum were dead.' Melody covered her mouth to stifle the cries.

Nate's eyes softened, and it made her feel comforted. He cared about her, she could tell. Turning her eyes to her trembling hands in her lap, Melody continued speaking, gaze down. 'They'd smoked all the cannabis over a few hours, then Toby had driven them home. But they never made it. His car came off the road and ploughed into a tree. Toby died pretty instantly and Callum died a few hours later from his injuries in the hospital.' She blurted it, spitting out the words before she began to cry.

He leant forward, reached for the tissues on the side table and handed them to her. She took one as he spoke. 'I'm so sorry you both had to experience that at such a young age. And a tragedy for Toby and Callum and their families.'

Another comfort from him, and Melody wanted Nate to hug her in his strong arms. It had been so long since she relived all of this, with another person, anyway.

'It was. Lily felt some level of blame. For leaving, for arguing with him. And of course, Toby and Callum's parents were distraught and said some stuff in the heat of the moment.' She clenched her jaw, shaking her head slightly. 'My parents were hysterical, didn't want me anywhere near people they didn't know and Lily…'

Melody wiped her nose. She was trying to remain composed, not wanting to look like an upset, blotchy mess in front of Nate. She still grieved for Lily, for their friendship, and she never forgave Toby for all of it, despite it being her who got the cannabis in the first place. It was he who started the dominoes of her and Lily's friendship to topple and fall.

She wrung her hands together. 'Lily couldn't cope. She dropped out of her GCSEs and stopped leaving the house. She didn't even want to be around me, her best friend. I reminded her of that night.' Puffing out air, her brow furrowed and she picked at a painted fingernail. 'As if it were my fault,' she said loudly, anger projecting in her voice.

Nate remained focused and didn't flinch, fully listening and absorbing her words.

'Her dad was offered a transfer at work to Manchester, so the family went to try and start afresh. And she didn't say good-bye.' Dropping her head, plump tears plopped onto her black pencil skirt. Those tears felt as painful as they had eight years ago when Lily moved to Manchester and told her via text message that it was best they were no longer friends.

The therapy session left her feeling like she had jet lag. She got the Tube home and napped on the sofa before waking and making dinner. Grace came in before midnight and Melody was watching TV, sitting on the sofa, fleece blanket tucked over her.

'Hi, lovely,' Grace said as she entered the flat and heard the TV on. Taking her shoes off and dumping her handbag, she walked into the lounge, smiling, pizza box in hand. Grace was always happy. One of life's positive people.

'Hi. You okay?' Melody said flatly with a strained smile.

Grace nodded. 'I have pizza.'

She sat on the striped rug by Melody's feet and placed the pizza box on the coffee table. Opening it up, she took a slice and rammed it into her mouth. 'I'm starving. I went straight from uni to work and didn't get a break.'

She turned the TV off, placing the remote on the armrest of the sofa and got up. 'I'll get us a drink.'

'Help yourself.' Grace pushed the pizza box towards Melody as she returned to the sofa, a glass of water in each hand.

'I'm trying to be good. Actually, I was thinking of joining a gym.' She looked at the pizza, caramelised onions mixed with chicken and what looked like a peri-peri or tikka flavouring.

'Even more reason to have pizza if you're joining the gym.' Grace laughed and tapped the pizza box. Melody took a slice.

'How was therapy?'

Her face softened as she thought about Nate, not realising her thoughts had transferred to her body language.

Raising her eyebrows, Grace spoke again. 'What's with the smile?'

'Oh, nothing. It's just that it was really useful. Emotional. *Very* emotional. But Nate, he's just amazing.'

Grace swallowed the mouthful of pizza she was chewing on and took a swig of water. 'Oh, yeah? *Amazing*, is he?' She started laughing, her blonde ponytail of hair swaying slightly.

Melody touched her collarbone and felt herself flush.

'Do you fancy your therapist?' Grace put her pizza down and turned fully to Melody. 'You do! You fancy your therapist!' She clapped her hands and laughed.

'Grace! Stop it!' she huffed, giggling a little.

'Oh my gosh! You can't fancy your therapist!' Grace tilted her head from side to side and lifted her slice of pizza again. 'Although, actually, he was pretty fit for a dad!'

Melody picked at a bit of chicken on her pizza, not making eye contact with her friend. 'He's so lovely, Grace. I know it's more than just a job for him. He cares about people. I've always felt like a patient, you know.' She glanced at Grace, who nodded slightly as she tapped her friend's leg.

'Like I need pills to make me happy. Doctors who've just expected me to live with feeling sad, even though my emotions are anchors in the sea, keeping me from moving. I haven't had proper therapy for over seven years, and back then, it was them in control, not me. This feels different. *I* feel different. *He's* different.'

Grace shrugged and grabbed her friend's hand. 'Well, I think that's fantastic, hun, and I'm proud of you. If the therapist is doing such a good job already, it's only going to get better. Just don't ogle him too much.' She sniggered, and Melody rolled her eyes.

The next day was Friday, and Melody decided to walk to the park on her lunch break. In truth, she had thought more about Nate than she had the content of yesterday's therapy session, and she couldn't decide if that was positive or negative. She wasn't naïve or stupid, and knew that he could have a girlfriend and that he also had a professional boundary. However, she wouldn't be having therapy forever, so if he was single, perhaps...

Heading to the park, she passed the chain shops, hotels, and eateries of the capital. It was the start of November and the London air was cold. Hugging her red scarf around her neck, she watched folk rushing by. A mix-up of people, going about their daily lives amidst the backdrop of buskers and homeless people begging. Walking quicker than usual, she wanted to get to the park and hoped that Nate would be there. Having no idea what days he went to the green space at lunchtime, she figured that they would bump into one another again at some point.

In a city as big and busy as London, it felt almost fate to her. That perhaps Grace had brought them together for more than therapy — for healing, for love. Biting her bottom lip, she smiled to herself. She dipped a hand into her black leather Steve Madden handbag and pulled out her lip gloss, coating her full lips with it, before dropping it back into the bag. Nate was a great therapist and the sessions were helping, but she wanted him to see her as more than a patient, or client, as he called the people he saw. Melody felt that sounded like being hired by an escort. Grinning, she ran a hand through her hair.

Getting to know him outside of the therapy room was her

real desire. The therapy was precisely that, and it was about her. She couldn't exactly ask if he was in a serious relationship, or his favourite bar, or even how he took his coffee, in a session where he was being paid to help her work through her emotional obstacles and improve her mental health. As she waited at the pedestrian crossing, she realised Nate was doing so much more in the sessions than supporting her mental health. He was giving her confidence, helping her to get over Brandon, and was igniting a new desire in her: for him.

Approaching the entrance of St Pancras Gardens, she glanced around, searching for him, then berated herself for being so silly. So childish. In all honesty, she wasn't even sure if he found her attractive. But the thoughts remained. *Had he looked at her for a moment longer than normal? Had his eyes travelled over her body? Had she seen the shyness of a natural attraction that he was trying to hide?* Melody didn't know, but she suspected. Certain there was a chemistry that he couldn't deny.

One thing she was sure of was that Nate had taken up permanent space in her mind and that when she thought of him, her thoughts were more of a sexual nature than a therapy nature. She bounced a little in her step as her eyes moved around the park. One amazing thing about seeing him was that she had almost stopped thinking about Brandon. At first, she was desperate to get back with him, now Brandon just felt like an immature Mr Right Then.

Nate carried himself like a man. A mature man who had life experience, focus, kindness, and who had that confidence of knowing who he was — the ultimate attractiveness. She guessed he was in his mid-forties, only a few years younger than her dad. But Nate had that film star suave, and after looking at images of Daniel Craig for hours, she was dying to mention that he reminded her of him. Of course, it had to come at the right time. Perhaps towards the end of their sessions, or when she was certain that he found her attractive as well. The problem with Melody's new feelings was, that if he didn't reciprocate her attention, it could all come painfully crashing down.

Chapter 14: Melody

It was Wednesday evening and Melody had been to see her dad, updating him about her therapy. Omitting the fact she was attracted to Nate, she had told the truth in that Nate Lundie was a great therapist and she was feeling positive and confident on working through her past issues. Her reiteration of progress to Matthew over the last few weeks had already resulted in the reduction of his anxiety and need to check on her. It pleased her; she didn't want her dad to struggle more than he already had. He was fraught with grief and, because of the past, had worried about her for eight years. She couldn't change what had happened, but she could change the future for herself, her dad, and her mum.

Her session with Nate was the next day. He hadn't turned up at St Pancras Gardens the Friday before. Melody had left in a foul mood and was quiet the rest of the afternoon at work. Returning to the park the following Monday, again, he hadn't been there. Unable to get to the park on her lunch break on Tuesday, she had met her mother for lunch at a sushi place near Russell Square. It had been nice for her to share some positive news about her therapy and to see relief on her mum's face.

Zoe was calm, practical. Even when Felix died, she mechanically went through the death admin and process, showing only flashes of emotion. But Melody knew she was loved by her mother and that Zoe would do anything for her, even if a lot of the time her love was shown through money. They'd ate sashimi, maki, edamame, and miso soup as they chatted and she left her mum feeling uplifted.

Melody returned to the green space once more that lunchtime and again, Nate didn't turn up. For all she knew, he went at a different time on each visit, and there she was, scurrying through the city centre each day, desperate to get to a bench near to where they had previously sat. She would have to drop it into conversation at her therapy session to work out his pattern. Melody gritted her teeth. It wasn't practical for her to go to the park each lunch break, chasing something she may never catch. Plus, it was going to get colder and, although unusually dry for the time of year, she would not sit in a park in the pissing down rain, waiting for her jackpot to possibly appear.

That evening, arriving home from seeing her dad, she showered and put her loungewear on. Letting out a sigh as she sat on her bed, Melody grabbed her laptop, resting it on her knee. Deciding to Google Nate and see if anything came up, she typed his name into the search engine. Lots of results appeared. Tilting her head from side to side, she knew that this was not unusual, as this would include anyone in the world with his name. Adding UK into the search box, she began scrolling down the first of the many result pages.

Searching for him on the usual social media platforms, Melody couldn't find Nate Lundie anywhere. She had briefly searched for him the week after the initial assessment at Lundie Therapy. Knowing professionals sometimes change their name on Facebook, she tried a few different versions of his name, including Nathaniel and spelling Lundie, Lundy. To no avail. Instagram and X proved a non-starter also. She even checked TikTok, knowing that it was as likely to find him on there as it was that she would become prime minister.

Then she found something. A Facebook business page. Clapping her hands together, she clicked on the Facebook link. Lundie Therapy's page came up. There wasn't a photo of Nate, just a logo for his business, the same logo as displayed on his business card. She perused through his page as she sipped a cup of tea. There was nothing of great interest — a few advertising posts and one or two reviews. There wasn't anything posted since July and looking over the previous posts, it was clear that it wasn't used frequently. She followed the Facebook page, just so he knew she was supporting, and then clicked back out of Facebook, returning to the Google search results.

Pulling her crocheted blanket up a little further over her legs, she scrolled down the first page. A LinkedIn profile for Nate Lundie was the sixth search item. Melody had never actively used LinkedIn, although she had an account. She'd had a profile for years when she was thinking about her non-existent career. She knew it was more focused around work, careers, and professionals. Although she had employment, it certainly wasn't a career she wanted thanks to her rubbish GCSE results and subsequent inability to do her A-Levels as planned.

Clicking on his link, Melody stared at his profile picture. He looked gorgeous. His hair, slightly blonder than it was now, but still with a medium sprinkling of silvery-grey that illuminated his eyes. His hair flopped a little to one side and he smiled in the image; a natural smile that showed his hint of a dimple. His magnetic eyes weren't framed by his glasses and he looked slightly tanned in the photo, as if taken in the summer or after a holiday in the sun.

She quickly picked up her mobile phone and visited LinkedIn via her web browser. Finding Nate's profile, she clicked on it and took a screenshot of his photo before returning her gaze to her laptop and clicking back on the Google search. There was a newspaper article featuring him. Melody read over the story about a charity he used to work at as a therapist, sharing details of some funding award they had received. There was a small picture of the team, including Nate.

Another article came up on the search about a school, from around ten years earlier. Scrolling down, it became apparent that he used to work at there. Melody frowned; she never thought of Nate being anything other than a therapist, but of course, they had never talked about his current life or his past. She rubbed her forehead. It impressed her that he had worked in other professional fields. He was clearly a very intelligent man.

As she put her laptop to one side, she picked up her mobile phone and went to her photo gallery. She opened the photo of Nate from his LinkedIn profile and edited it, cropping it to make his image bigger. She looked at the screen, the photo of him staring back and touched it, biting her bottom lip. Yes, Nate Lundie was an intelligent man, but he was also extremely handsome, and Melody Dartford was becoming increasingly attracted to him.

Chapter 15: Nate

'It's definitely going on the market,' Nate said that night to Julie on the phone.

'Well, I think it's a good thing. It's too big and surely it must remind you of the past, the bad stuff?'

There was a pause. He scratched his head as he leant against the kitchen bench. The truth was, it did. But it reminded him of the good past and the terrible past. When he looked at the grey and white floor tiles in the kitchen, he was reminded of him and Sarah putting them down and the night celebrating with prosecco, a takeaway, and making love. The good years, before he strayed.

The flirting he instigated with random women meant nothing. Sexual fantasy, the thrill of desire. It was wrong, but it never became anything, not until Annabelle. And now, those ridiculously expensive porcelain tiles reminded him not only of Sarah, who he'd promised to love and lied to but also of Annabelle Graham and the subsequent demolition of his marriage.

'Nate?' she asked, checking he was still there through the silence of his thoughts.

He cleared his throat. 'It does. And perhaps I've been clinging to it when I don't even want it.' He sighed and rubbed his chin. 'It feels time.'

'Does this mean Brian and I can help you find your dream house in the countryside? Perhaps with a shepherd's hut that we can come and stay in when we want to explore the quieter life, outside the city?'

Nate laughed. 'Absolutely!'

Another thing he had done that week was to call it off with the woman from the dating app. He felt bad, but it was best to stop it now, for both of their sakes. Plus, he had his eye on Anita, a fit blonde at the gym and he was open to continuing to date without pressure. It was two weeks until the spin-a-thon and Nate was at the gym that evening — hoping to see her.

First, there were a few clients scheduled that day, including Melody Dartford. After lunch, he made some notes and sent emails before there was a knock on his office door at 3:30 pm. He caught himself looking at his reflection before walking to answer it. Opening the door, she stood, wearing a red wool coat that brought warmth to her pale cheeks. Long, brown hair, slightly curled, framed her face. She wore lipstick that made her mouth look full. *Kissable*, he thought before scolding himself.

'Melody. Hi! Come on in.' He moved to the side, gesturing her in with the wave of his arm.

She smiled. 'Hi. Thank you.'

Watching her walk past, he smelt perfume. The same fruity scent that he now associated with her. Nate wanted to close his eyes and inhale her. Again, he berated himself for being unprofessional. As usual, she headed towards the yellow sofa and Nate poured her a glass of water. He took his seat opposite. Standing about a metre and a half away from him, she peeled her wool coat off slowly, seductively, watching him observing, like a punter in a strip club. She revealed a dress that was just about acceptable for workwear but had a tightness across her chest that left her breasts desperate to burst out the v-neckline. Moving in his seat, he wondered if she was doing the slow motion, almost striptease, on purpose.

His mouth felt dry. Clearing his throat, he spoke as she sat. 'How's your week been, Melody?'

She nodded. 'Okay. I have been trying to get out on my lunch break to the park. You know, the one I saw you at?' She tilted her head and held his gaze, a loose wave of hair falling over her collarbone.

'Good. Nature is a natural medicine.' He took his glasses from the side table and put them on before picking up his note-pad and pen.

'Do you get a regular lunch break time to get outdoors?' she blurted, almost frantically.

'Not as regular as I would like.' He laughed. 'So, last session, we finished with you telling me about the tragic incident involving Toby and Callum, then Lily subsequently moving to Manchester.' He noticed Melody was picking at a button on her coat that she had placed beside her on the sofa. 'It would be good to start from there and explore your feelings around Lily moving and what happened next regarding your management of the situation.'

Melody kept her eyes down on her coat but nodded. Nate observed how she rapidly went from assertive temptress to frightened child.

'When Lily left, I thought my world would end. I never had a sister, and she was the nearest thing. But as well as that, she was my best friend. Her not wanting to keep in touch was like she pulled my heart out and threw it into acid.'

He watched her as she wrung her hands together and swallowed.

'It all got worse. I was inconsolable. Not only had she gone, but the families and friends of Toby and Callum... they just wouldn't stop.' She sniffed and glared out of the window.

'Constantly wanting to talk to me about that night. Asking questions after questions.'

Nate noticed her jaw stiffened and she continued speaking, staring out of the window, unblinking.

'Comments. Nasty comments, blaming Lily and me. And I had to take it all. Not Lily. She fucking didn't. Just me.' Her shoulders pushed back as a sneer crawled on her face. 'I couldn't concentrate at school as I couldn't sleep. Classmates shunned me and blamed me for Lily leaving. I got bullied or pitied. I wanted everyone to just leave me alone.' She blinked and shook her head rapidly as if waking or coming out of a trance. Nate kept a straight facial expression. After taking a sip of water, she continued.

'Then it got too much before my exams and one student said it should have been me who died.' Melody's jaw protruded, and she looked past him. 'I punched her in the face and broke her nose. I was suspended from school and two days later, I lost my mind.' She chuckled at the last part as if it were a scene from a comedy film.

'What happened, Melody?'

Inhaling, she glanced at the ceiling, tapping her feet. Then, with no facial expression, she looked Nate straight in the eyes. 'I tried to set the house on fire with me inside when my parents were out and Felix was at football. It got me a six-month stay in Hopewood Park Psychiatric Hospital.'

Chapter 16: Melody

After therapy, Melody went to see Grace at South of Here bar. She was on shift, and although Melody knew she wouldn't be able to talk much, the thought of being alone was as appealing as squeezing her size six feet into a size four shoe. Her mum would be working as usual, and visiting her dad would mean she'd have to wear a fake smile. Grace was a perfect, safe choice.

She began the short walk to the bar. There was a drizzle in the air, that kind of wet mist that soaks you rapidly. Pulling her umbrella out of her handbag, she opened it and covered herself. King's Cross was busy, as it came to the end of the 9-5 working day. She walked, wondering about the stories of the people passing her. *Are the people alone lonely? Are we all just walking around with a suitcase of problems and emotions, each of us carrying luggage of a different size and weight?*

Sighing, she quickened her pace, just wanting to see a familiar, friendly face. Reaching the bar and pushing open the heavy door, she wiped her feet on the huge coir entrance mat. Looking around the dimly lit space, she spotted Grace behind the bar and walked towards her.

'Hey, what a lovely surprise,' she said, leaning over the bar and squeezing Melody's arm. 'You okay?'

She swallowed down her emotion; a nasty-tasting tablet of rage and sorrow and shrugged.

'Hard session?'

'Yeah.'

'Sexy Nate make it any easier?' Grace winked and smiled.

It made Melody laugh, and that was one of the many reasons why Grace was her best friend. *Screw Lily,* she thought.

'A little.' She smiled weakly. 'Can I just hang around here for a bit?'

'Of course, hun. I'll get you a bowl of chips with my staff discount. I've got my laptop to do some study on my break, if you want to sit in a booth and use it?' Grace tilted her head.

Melody checked the battery on her mobile phone. Just over twenty per cent, that wouldn't entertain her for long. She sighed, nodding.

A few minutes later, she was set up in a booth and logged onto Grace's laptop. Staring at the screen, she wasn't sure what she was going to do. Checking her emails and socials for a bit, she thought about the charity spin-a-thon Nate was doing. Perhaps she could go along and watch? After all, she had sponsored him £50. Surely there couldn't be more than one of these events over the next week for a children's charity? She typed it into Google. As she went to click search, Grace appeared at the booth with a bowl of chips and a drink.

Looking at the screen as she placed them on the table, she raised an eyebrow. 'What's that?'

Melody shook her head lightly. 'Ah, nothing. Just Nate mentioned his gym was doing a charity spin-a-thon and, well, I was curious.' She dipped her fingers into the bowl of chips and took one out, popping it into her mouth and breathing out quickly, as it was too hot. 'Thanks for these.'

'So, you're either really serious about joining a gym or you want to go and watch your sexy therapist in his cycling shorts!' She began laughing.

Melody rolled her eyes. 'I'm just curious!'

'Yeah, right,' Grace said, winking before she walked away, back to work.

Clicking, the search results came up. Third down, after two sponsored sites, was an article from the local newspaper. She followed the link to the page and it explained about the spin-a-thon and how the money raised would be spent. It was taking place at Fit for Life, a local gym, in Stratford, about four miles from their flat in Walthamstow. Feeling an instant boost, she picked up some more chips. Perhaps she could go and watch the spin-a-thon and then join that gym. Maybe Grace would go with her to the charity fundraiser?

Melody searched for the local Fit for Life gym site. On the website, it mentioned the spin-a-thon. Next Saturday, from 2-6 pm. Further down the page, it said about drinks locally afterwards. She bit her lip. This could be the perfect way to speak with him outside of the therapy room, where the professionalism could be relaxed. She could get to know him — and try to find out if he was attracted to her.

The next day was Friday and the weekend off work for Melody. After work, she went to see Matthew to update him on her therapy. Both her parents asked each Thursday evening by text message and she knew they meant well, despite it being slightly annoying. Maybe one day she would have children and appreciate the protective instinct that never dissolves. Her dad, in particular, was just a heavier coating, like wallpaper that had been painted over so many times that it begins to distort and appear messy.

Melody knew she had to be gentle with her father and that she was his entire world — especially since her parents' marriage had ended. When she became impatient with him or overwhelmed with his snatching of her independence, she tried to remember what the fire did to them all, and the subsequent sectioning of Melody. The pain of helplessness, blame, and guilt that her parents were submerged in for a long time, became a million times worse when Felix died. They just didn't want her to deteriorate again and Felix's death had been and still was an enormous risk.

Melody had managed in her own way until recently when she knew she had to deal with it and everything else. Her behaviour manifested in unhealthy ways. Ways that made her feel jealous of people who had the things she wanted, or made her feel a rage inside that would spray out like a hosepipe watering the arid ground in summer. She didn't withdraw and cry, become quiet or distant. When Melody was struggling, all she could think about was punishing people who made her pain worse. Anger became a fuel in her that was dangerous. She knew that and despite them never admitting it, she was sure her parents knew that as well.

The week passed quickly and it was soon Thursday again. Melody had only been to the park once that week on her lunch break as the weather was dreadful; enough rain for the local birds to have several mini ponds to swim in.

It hadn't stopped her from thinking about Nate and the chance to see him outside of the office that Saturday at the spin-a-thon. She had chosen her outfit for work that day with the precision of a surgeon. Clothes, shoes, accessories, and make-up. Deciding on a tight, almost see-through sky-blue T-shirt and figure-hugging jeans that made her backside look round and grabbable. With that and her ample breasts pushed through her slightly transparent top, Melody knew she would give Nate a rush of blood.

She curled her long hair and added some gold earrings. Packing her make-up in her bag that morning, she put a jumper on for work, that she would remove before her therapy session. Placing her fingers to her mouth, she started daydreaming about the session with Nate.

Was she imagining their chemistry? It was so hard to decipher. All of their encounters, apart from one and a brief sighting in the bar, had been in his office — where he was professional. Even so, she was sure she picked up on some signs during their time together. A lingering look, a slight movement of his body towards her or mirroring her. A lust in his eyes or when his lips pressed together. *Was it real or her wishful thinking?*

Either way, she knew what she felt was real and regardless of anything else, it had done the job of taking her mind off some of the shit she had been through. The sessions obviously brought things up — they had to and would continue to. How else could she unpack her suitcase of trauma and put the items in the bin? Or neatly fold them and keep them in good condition rather than screwed up, damaged, and unloved?

Her time in Hopewood Hospital had felt like a blur. It had been six months of monitoring, assessing, reviewing, and planning. Talking, listening, repeating. She was only sixteen and 'celebrated' her seventeenth birthday there before being discharged. At first, all the doctors, nurses, and therapists had merged into one. Psychiatric nurse after psycho-therapist, psychologist, counsellor, consultant. An endless list of professionals that seemed longer than a seven-year-old's Christmas list. Names, faces, all swirling in a sea of despair, each trying to be her life raft.

The police charged her with arson and the CPS reduced the

punishment with the mitigating factor of her mental health, from a custodial sentence to a community order that included her sectioning. It could have been worse. Melody had nightmares still to that day and despite never intending to hurt her family, she couldn't fit back together all the pieces that came apart and led her to that catastrophic incident, even after eight years.

Her sectioning was an intervention. As she adapted and started to get help at Hopewood, the chaos and labyrinth of her mind became easier to navigate and manage. Then a discharge plan was decided, she was medicated and assigned a community psychiatric nurse with regular reviews. In truth, no one knew what it was like. Melody orchestrated pity. Some people blamed her. But on the whole, it was sorrow, misfortune, and hope that she would be okay. Because they didn't know the truth. They would never know the truth; that she caused the death of Toby and Callum and subsequently lost her best friend forever.

Chapter 17: Nate

Checking his emails, there was one from the estate agent at Move Now, sharing the draft advert of Nate's home. After some last-minute back-and-forth decision badminton in his mind, the property was going on the market. Leaning back in his Eames-style chair, the house looked impressive on the website, with a notable asking price that would allow him to buy a small cottage with a large garden plot, outside of London in the countryside. It was Thursday, and viewings would likely start next week. Saturday was the spin-a-thon and he intended on getting drunk afterwards with the group from the gym, then lying in bed most of Sunday.

His work week had been busy, and at the session that day, Melody had mentioned she might 'pop in' to see him at the gym. He felt both excited and apprehensive as soon as she said it. She arrived at the therapy session looking very attractive, and he had struggled to not look at her breasts under the palest blue T-shirt.

As she came into the office, they greeted one another as usual. She removed her jacket as Nate filled her glass with water, chatting small talk. When he reached up to give her the glass, he noticed how tight her top was — the material stretching to capacity over her large breasts. He was certain the temptress saw his eyes travelling over her inviting chest. A smile flashed across her face as she pushed her shoulders back further.

Clearing his throat, Nate felt flustered. Not sure what kind of bra she was wearing, he could see the shadow of her nipples, coated in the pale blue top like a second skin. He averted his eyes, feeling his cheeks warm, but wanted to look and touch her for the full hour. And something about Melody Dartford's smile, before she began to talk and the tone turned serious, indicated she knew that he would have that exact reaction.

Despite his temptation, he had listened to Melody during the session, as she explained her time in the psychiatric hospital as a sixteen-year-old. Even without being a father, Nate understood the turmoil that would have caused for her parents and the severity of concern that their adolescent child was so mentally unwell.

'The truth is...' she began, her eyes down to the floor, 'that I don't know what I wanted to happen that day I started the fire.' She sniffed and looked up, unblinking. 'And even with all the professionals and the medication, I still often feel rage in me, like I did that day. That fire has never fully gone out and sometimes I think I could do something like that again. That I *want* to do something like that again.'

Nate nodded. It was common to think like that, but something about the way Melody looked when she said it unnerved him. Almost like there was a door behind her eyes that closed, locking part of her away. An uncontrollable part. He swallowed, thinking that the room was saturated with emotion and he wasn't focused, sharp. Too busy thinking with his genitals. They talked some more and he suggested they broach the subject of her brother's death in the next session.

'We have two more sessions before we can review, so it would be good to bring things to more recent times now I understand your past, your trauma and mental health management.'

She sipped some water and nodded. Turning almost child-like, she spoke with a whine to her voice. 'Does that mean our sessions will end?' She twirled hair around her finger.

'Not necessarily. We will assess and see where you are at. I usually make a plan after session six and discuss it with the client. Some people need more, a lot more, perhaps on a less frequent basis, such as fortnightly. Some people feel that they have processed and have the tools. It's a joint decision.' He smiled and she mirrored it, tilting her head and pouting slightly.

Wanting to end on an optimistic note, he asked about the positive relationships in her life now, trying to look for good coping mechanisms and support. She mentioned her flatmate, along with her parents. Melody talked about her mother, Zoe, who she commented was emotionally strong, tough, and ploughed her energy into work at a local law firm — a distraction from grief. She had grown more distant from her mother since her brother died and subsequently, her mother left the family home. Melody admitted that she had always been a daddy's girl, and was close to her father, who was over-possessive — and had his own clear mental health issues, in Nate's view.

Deciding to leave it there, given the heaviness of their session, he wrapped up the hour and nonchalantly referred to what she would do at the weekend as he closed his notepad and took his glasses off.

'I might pop and see how the spin-a-thon is going. See you getting sweaty.' She smiled and her tongue touched the outside of her top lip.

Nate definitely wasn't imagining this. With that and her nipples practically visible through her top, he was certain she was trying to seduce him or tempt him to seduce her! He felt a wave of nerves, but floating over it was the tiniest thrill. Laughing nervously, he put his hands on his thighs before rising from his chair.

'Well, luckily there are about eighty people taking part, so I won't be the only sweaty one.' Nate glanced at her quickly as he rubbed the back of his neck.

She pressed her lips together and put her jacket on, pushing her chest out as she placed her arm into the sleeves. He swallowed, his mouth feeling parched.

'But you're the only one I will be watching.' She giggled and turned towards the door.

Nate let out a deep breath, saying nothing. He followed her to the door and opened it, not knowing what to say, given her last statement.

'Well, see you.'

She walked out and turned, looking over her shoulder at him. 'Yeah, you will.'

And with that, Melody Dartford left and Nate Lundie shut his office door, returned to his seat and muttered, 'Shit' under his breath. He ran his hands over his head and sighed. It was Annabelle Graham all over again, but this time, he absolutely couldn't let anything happen.

Chapter 18: Melody

As she got the Tube home that Thursday, Melody was certain Nate Lundie wanted her. And she knew she had to have him. Walking from the station to her flat, anger marched alongside her. *Why had she wasted time with stupid little boys like Brandon? Immature men with shit attitudes, and no actual idea how to treat a woman.* Anyway, none of it mattered now she had Nate. Well, she *almost* had him.

A few more sessions of therapy. After that, she could get to know him without the professional boundaries that he was clearly trying to uphold whilst blatantly wanting to grab her and show her what a real man was. She giggled to herself. It was just a matter of time, and she was prepared to be patient. In fact, she was prepared to be the best patient!

On arriving back at the flat, Grace was home, cramming for an exam she had the following day.

'How's it going?' Melody asked as she pulled her slippers from under the sofa and put them on.

'Shit.' Grace let out a groan and threw her head back against the sofa. 'I've just got to get through tomorrow and then one essay to submit before Christmas break.'

Melody rubbed the top of her friend's head. 'You can do it. I'll make dinner. Pasta?'

'Perfect, thanks.'

After putting the food on to cook, she brought some juice in for the pair.

'We could celebrate on Saturday night by going out to Covent Garden?'

Grace looked up. 'Aren't you going to the spin thing to watch Sexy Nate?'

Melody grinned. 'Yeah, but you could come and they are going for drinks after.'

'Christ, you've got it bad!' Grace laughed. 'I can come out for one, but I've picked up a shift.' She tapped a pen on her revision notes.

Shrugging, Melody nodded. 'Yeah, that's great.'

Grace straightened up and grabbed her friend's hand as she stood by the coffee table. 'Hun, I'm so pleased you are in a better place. And therapy is clearly working. But be careful, yeah? I know you fall fast and hard. And well, it's just not going to happen with him, is it?'

Not waiting for an answer, Grace turned her eyes back to her notes. Melody remained on the spot for a second before going into the kitchen, steaming more than the pasta boiling in the pan, and wondered why Grace would be so negative. It was a good job Grace was studying as she ate because Melody didn't want to speak to her. Instead, she made an excuse to eat in her room, saying she was going to watch a show she had downloaded. After her pasta, she looked through her wardrobe for a few possible outfits for Saturday, feeling determined she would get her man and her happy-ever-after with Nate.

Saturday morning arrived and Melody was excited to see Nate at the spin-a-thon. Although not as keen for Grace to come with her after her comment on Thursday evening, she was still pleased to not be going alone. Given the event was at a gym, then drinks afterwards, she opted for high-waisted leather-look jeans and a vest top, with her biker jacket. She would wear a cropped cardigan in the gym, changing to her jacket and adding some heels, lipstick, and heavier eye make-up for the drinks.

As Melody drank tea, she wondered if Nate was prepared and if he had been thinking of her. She thought about what he would look like in his gym clothes. If his legs would be as muscular as she imagined. Grace was right in one way, she did, 'have it bad' for him.

The friends caught the bus along to the gym, arriving at 4:30 pm. Melody wanted to go for the start, but Grace wasn't prepared to watch, 'A load of sweaty strangers cycling for four hours,' knowing the snacks would be electrolyte powder and protein shakes over vodka and cocktails. Walking into Fit for Life, it was like a nightclub. Music boomed out and the lighting was UV strips in the dark warehouse.

'To be honest, it could be a nightclub if they served alcohol,' Grace said, twirling around.

Melody laughed and twirled around herself, more to look for where the spin-a-thon was than dancing in the nightclub-like gym. There was a large room to the right, with a glass front.

'That must be it,' she said. They walked towards it and a PT came over.

'Here to support the spin-a-thon?' he asked.

'Yeah.'

'That way. You can probably tell.' He smiled and walked off.

'Phwooar. If the PTs all look like him, maybe I will join this gym as well,' Grace said, looking behind as they walked.

Entering the spinning room, the music and heat were intense. 'You're joking, aren't you? I'm gonna melt quicker than a lit candle in here, hun.' Grace laughed and fanned her face with her hand.

She was right, it was stifling and as an instructor blasted out commands at the front and supporters stood around the side of the hall, Melody glanced at the rows and rows of bikes and wasn't sure she could stand the heat long enough to find Nate amongst the 'Tour de London'. Someone in a Fit for Life uniform came and handed them a drink of something in a sports bottle. They gratefully took it, unable to make out what the person was saying over the heavy bass of the rock music.

'It could be the piss of a hundred men and I would drink it right now,' Grace screeched in Melody's ear, opening the bottle. 'Mmmm, it's not piss. Or if it is, it tastes nice.' She elbowed her friend and cackled.

Melody chuckled and took a sip of the drink, hoping the liquid and being in the space a few minutes would help her acclimatise to the sweat box they had entered. She glanced around the room, trying to spot Nate as her eyes adjusted to the UV lighting. There must have been fifty people on the bikes, with many others in gym clothes sitting in a row of seats and congregating at the side of the hall.

'Where's Sexy Nate?' Grace giggled at his nickname.

'I can't see him.' She continued to search across the hall. 'Oh, wait a minute, there he is, I think.' The man who she thought may be Nate was standing chatting with a group of people in sportswear. She assumed they were cycling in some sort of shift pattern. He turned from the side to the front and took a drink. It was him, and Melody felt the flutter of nervous excitement in her stomach. She smoothed her hair.

'Let's get a seat over there.' She pointed to a few chairs amongst three rows of people.

Grace nodded and followed, picking up a flyer for the gym on the way. Melody kept watching as a bell rang and people began dismounting the bikes. Nate and the group he was with walked towards the bikes. Reaching a bike where a woman dismounted, he high-fived her. Melody could just about see from the distance and the dark lighting that he was smiling. Biting her inner lip, a snap of jealousy consumed her as she observed him, desperate for some acknowledgement.

Nate cycled for forty-five minutes. Melody's gaze remained on him most of the time, but he didn't look around the room. Instead, focusing on the instructor and the gigantic screen at the front of the hall which calculated the group's current mileage. Grace played on her phone, the odd giggle here and there or pointing it towards Melody to look at some silly meme.

The bell rang again, indicating a cyclist change over. The woman he high-fived earlier came bouncing back over like a perfectly presented Tigger, despite the activity. Not a hair looked out of place and her bare arms were sculpted like she was made of ice. Gritting her teeth, she rose from the plastic seat, her backside feeling like the hard resting place had murdered it.

'I'm going to say hello. Come with me, so I look less weird.' She glanced at Grace and offered her hand to pull her up. Grace complied and they walked around the side of the hall to reach where Nate and some other cyclists were resting and talking to supporters.

He turned as they approached, almost instinctively. A quick smile flashed across his face as he wiped his brow with a flannel.

'Melody. Hi. How are you?' His smile returned, and Melody brushed her hair off her shoulder.

'Not as hot as you!' She giggled and he moved slightly on the spot.

'And Grace. Nice to see you again. Both of you.' He glanced

at Grace and back at her. 'Thanks for coming down. It's pretty intense, isn't it? The pressure is on to get to the target.' He pointed to the screen and the women followed his finger, then returned their gaze to him.

'Ah, pressure is for tyres!' Grace said and Nate laughed.

Melody smirked, feeling a little put out that Grace made him laugh. *Was she flirting with him?* Surely not.

'It's a great gym. I might join.' She looked at him and kept a straight face.

He nodded. 'It is great and some good joining offers.'

Did he want her to join?

'Wait a minute, I'll get one of the PTs. He can tell you the current deals.' He nodded to them before turning and walking away.

'He does sweaty, *very* well!' Grace winked at her friend.

'Yeah, he does. And those legs. What I wouldn't give to wrap mine around them.'

Grace nudged her friend. 'You scruffy mare. Seriously, how old is he, anyway? I mean, he's got grey hair and that.'

Melody shrugged. 'I don't know. I don't care. He's like the most delicious layer of cream on a homemade cake.'

Melody turned to Grace and they both began laughing, then noticed Nate and another guy walking towards them. He introduced the PT before shaking his bottle and raising an eyebrow, then walked towards a table with replenishments. Watching him walk away, Melody couldn't help but look at his legs and notice what amazing shape he was in, regardless of age, before the PT's voice brought her back into focus, asking about their current circumstances. She listened and both she and Grace answered his questions, but all Melody could really think about was having a drink with Nate later that day.

Chapter 19: Nate

The day of the spin-a-thon arrived and Nate was as prepared as he could be. Sitting at his white dining table on one of his four grey velvet chairs, he ate steak and a four-egg omelette. He'd made a batch of protein balls, slightly different to his last lot after losing two hours of his life to recipe videos on YouTube. Happy with the money he had raised so far, his total included £50 from Melody, who told him she would come and watch the event. Closing his eyes for a second, he tried to shut his mind off from the image of her breasts against her T-shirt.

'What are you playing at?' he said aloud, shaking his head. He had checked his records and she was almost twenty-five years old, but still young enough to be his daughter and he imagined her father wasn't much older than him. *Although he probably won't look as good as me,* he thought, smirking. Still, it was wrong, unprofessional, and he needed to stop thinking about a client sexually. It was the first time it had really happened in his career as a therapist. Well, the first time he wanted to act on it. Puffing out air, he rose from the dining table and walked to the dishwasher, placing his dirty plate inside.

Collecting the container of protein balls and two gym bottles, he placed them inside his gym bag that lay on the bottom, carpeted step. Straightening up, he thought about the house going on the market that next Monday. Running his hands across the wooden, carved bannister, he sauntered upstairs, and a sad smile crept onto his face as he recalled the hours of work put in to get the bannister just right. How Sarah tried to help, but she hated woodwork, only liking the musky, powdery smell of the earthy material. Nate had stripped, sanded, and carved the bannister before varnishing it. All done on the evening, after work. But it was beautiful, a work of art and as he reached the top, he ran his hand over the final spindle and felt lonely in the big family house. Sighing, he rubbed his palm across his eyebrows and walked into his bedroom. Taking his gym clothes from the bed, he changed and returned downstairs with his trainers and a bag of clean clothes for after the spin-a-thon.

Arriving at the gym, he entered reception. People were congregating just past the foyer, bottles in hands, the pulse of adrenaline-filled music in the air. The spinning instructor ushered them to the hall and into pairs next to a bike. Nate rushed as casually as he could — which he was aware probably looked like he had insects in his underwear — over to a bike where Anita was; the striking blonde he had been saying hello to for several weeks.

'Hi, Nate,' she greeted him, smiling. 'You wanna go first, or shall I?'

He glanced at her top, showing her toned physique. 'I'm happy to, but, of course, ladies first if you would rather!'

She let out a giggle and Nate ran a hand through his hair and flashed his white teeth.

'You go ahead.'

The spin-a-thon started ten minutes later and everyone gave it their all. The pairs cycled in forty-five-minute sessions. It didn't give him much of a chance to talk with Anita, but she was going for drinks afterwards, so that would do him. On his second break, he was sharing the protein balls with some fellow cyclists. Turning around, he saw Melody and her friend who had collected his business card, walking towards him. Slightly taken aback, even though he knew she was coming, Nate said hello and Melody made a flirtatious comment. It gave him a buzz, knowing that a young, attractive woman was flirting with him. Quickly, it turned into more of a sting, acknowledging she was a client and he *had* to stop such thinking. There was an hour left of the spin-a-thon. Once finished, people were getting changed, before heading to the bars in Covent Garden to celebrate.

'Where are you all meeting for the first drinks?' she asked, tilting her head, whilst he ate the protein snack.

He swallowed. 'Survivor Bar. They have a happy hour.' Nate raised his eyebrows.

She leant in slightly. He could smell her intoxicating fruity perfume mixed with mint from her breath. The music blasted a little louder after the instructor announced they were into their last sixty minutes. She moved closer, the space between them smaller. Her hair brushed against his bare shoulder, and he felt a pang of desire.

'I think that will make me very happy indeed,' she said, before leaning back and biting her bottom lip.

Nate swallowed. *Christ, she was sexy and she knew it.* He chuckled, trying to make it into a joke when he knew it was another layer of flirtation, blown towards him like dandelion seeds. The PT walked over, bursting through the dam of sexual tension, with two membership forms attached to clipboards. Nate puffed out air and made his excuses to leave. He was doing the last cycle in about ten minutes and needed to change his focus from the temptress that was Melody Dartford.

Chapter 20: Melody

'Could you have been any more obvious?' Grace laughed as they took a seat and began filling in their gym memberships. Melody smirked and looked at her form.

'I'm only doing the week free trial. I haven't got time to join a gym, not with my finals in the spring. But after that...'

She wasn't listening, saturated by the scene with Nate playing over and over. She had been so confident, so assertive, and he had liked it. Melody was certain of that. *I want him so much,* she thought to herself as she looked across the room to where he was getting onto a bike. Her lip curled as she noticed the slim blonde flicking her hair around him.

'Yeah, okay. Well, it's worth trying for free.' Her gaze remained on him as she spoke, before the music blasted again, making her jump. 'Shall we hand these in and go for a drink before everyone else arrives?'

Grace clapped her hands together. 'Hell, yeah.'

Melody signed her name at the bottom of the gym registration form. 'Let's go get our faces on. I might use one of the lockers to save ramming my shoes and cardi into my bag.'

The pair rose and as they left the hall, she glanced towards Nate's bike, but he didn't look. Shrugging to herself, she would have plenty of time to talk and flirt with him later. After applying more make-up and changing shoes, they were ready to go to the bars in Covent Garden, starting at Survivor Bar. Melody put her shoes in a canvas bag, along with her cardigan and popped a pound coin into a locker on the gym floor. She pocketed the key. Grace nodded in approval, before linking her friend and clicking her fingers as they walked away.

Arriving at the bar twenty minutes later, the friends ordered drinks and some small plates of food to share. Tucking into the pitta and hummus as Grace sank her teeth into one of the mini chicken kebabs, Melody talked about the gym and how she felt it would help her well-being.

'I guess seeing all those fit men won't hurt, either. Especially a certain someone?' Grace raised an eyebrow before taking a sip of her vodka and lemonade.

She grinned. 'He's so fit, isn't he?'

Grace tilted her head from side to side as she chewed on some food. 'He is, *but* he's your therapist, hun. And he could be in a serious relationship. Plus, isn't he a bit old?'

Taking a deep breath, Melody could feel the flare of anger wafting low in her stomach. *Why did Grace have to piss on her rainbow?* 'Well, he won't be my therapist for long. Our six sessions are almost up. I think even just one or two after that will be enough.' She looked at the table and prodded a fork into a few chips. 'And he's not married and clearly not serious with anyone else. He wouldn't have been flirting with me or that blonde bike bitch.'

She said the last three words through gritted teeth and, although not meant to be amusing, Grace sniggered.

'And so what if he is bloody older? Does it really matter? My ex-boyfriends have been my age and look at that, it's never worked out and they've all been arseholes.'

Grace shrugged as she ate some pitta. 'True. I just... well, you need to be careful. You fall hard, Melody and that makes you open to being hurt.' She reached over to her friend's hand, but Melody moved it away.

'I'm not a child, Grace,' she said, glaring across the table. 'I've been through enough to cope, okay?'

Shaking her head, Grace put the palms of her hands up. 'Jeez, okay. I'm just being a mate.'

They ate in silence before a server came and broke the tension, checking everything was alright with their food.

'Let's just have a good few hours before you go to work. We haven't been out in ages.' She smiled at Grace.

'Yeah, good plan. Although I can't have any more of these.' She pointed to the drink, then made a silly face as she slurped some through a paper straw.

An hour and four vodka and Coke's later for Melody, people from the spin-a-thon arrived. She didn't recognise many, having been so focused on Nate but saw the gym staff amongst the crowd. Nate waved, then turned back to the group. She observed him in a black jumper that clung to his muscular physique. He didn't have a layer on underneath, the V-neck showing a patch of the top of his tanned chest, despite it being November. Melody felt the urge of desire biting at her ankles. She looked at Grace, who giggled, almost reading her friend's mind.

They gave it a few minutes before walking over to the group. Nate squeezed through the crowd and said hello. His body language was slightly stiff, as if he was unsure of how to greet them in a neutral, sociable place, now that he wasn't sweaty and in gym clothes. He offered to buy them a drink, which they accepted, Grace opting for Diet Coke, before he was highjacked with new people arriving. Melody and Grace talked to some of the group as happy hour became happy hours in Survivor Bar. Grace soon had to leave for work.

'I've had a great day, hun.' She hugged her friend. 'And it's been lovely to see you so happy.' Grace held her out, grasping her arms. 'I've always got your back. No matter what.' Pulling her in for another hug, Melody closed her eyes, grateful she had a friend like Grace. Although part of her wondered if Grace would feel the same if she knew the full truth of her past and even recent behaviours.

'I'll see you to the door then I'll pop to the toilets to top up my make-up.'

Saying goodbye again, Grace left in an Uber. Walking into one of the gender-neutral, self-contained bathrooms, Melody put her arms on the small sink and leant forward, looking in the mirror above it. She sighed. *Was Grace right about Nate? Was she setting herself up for more hurt?* Taking out her deep red lipstick, she coated her full lips with it, wiping a bit from her teeth. She smiled in the mirror, rehearsing for when she saw him again. Going over her eyeliner, she caught sight of her youthful skin — not yet wrinkled with the years of age, sun damage, and laughter lines. She snorted. Perhaps she would never get those laughter lines. Her life hadn't exactly been a blast, well, not in the funny sense, anyway. She used the toilet before washing and drying her hands and spraying perfume on her neck, chest, and thick, curled hair.

Closing her eyes, she played backed her and Nate's interactions in her mind. The glances, the lingering eyes. Was she imagining it? No. He knew she liked him, and Melody was certain he liked her back. He just didn't want to act on it in the therapy room. Of course he didn't, he was a professional. But he wanted her. She knew it, just like she wanted him. And Melody always got what she wanted, one way or another.

Chapter 21: Nate

The spin-a-thon had been a success and it was looking like a large amount of money had been raised for the playground at Klubs for Kids. Adrenaline made the hair on Nate's arms stand on end and he felt like he could do it all again with the sheer rush of achievement. However, now it was time to celebrate.

The group entered Survivor Bar for congratulatory drinks. Travelling there, Anita had been talking to another man, which narked him slightly, but not enough to pop his balloon of euphoria. Glancing at the bar, he then gazed around the room for Melody and Grace. They sat at a table on bar stools. Melody was staring at him and tilted her head. Her cardigan had gone, replaced with a biker jacket and more make-up. His eyes went to her chest, a low-cut vest, with a curl of her long, dark hair tickling her collarbone and resting on the material of her top.

Raising a hand to wave, the women moved towards the group, and he wanted to kiss the soft, inviting skin of her neck as she approached. Looking confident, carrying herself with an assertiveness that Nate had rarely seen in someone in their mid-twenties, and had only once seen in a woman under twenty. He rubbed his hand over his mouth and chin.

'Want a drink?' he asked as they reached the group.

Taking their order, he squeezed into the queue at the bar and let out a massive breath. *What's the worst that can happen? She's an adult?* Then he condemned himself. *You're her therapist, for Christ's sake,* he thought, as he tapped his debit card on the bar. *If* something happened, Nate would just have to stop being her therapist. He had a code of ethics, which if on thoughts alone, would already be breached. If he went near Melody Dartford, it could be catastrophic. There was something in her; a potential to cause damage — like the risk of speeding down a country lane. So why did he keep thinking about it? And why did he have a feeling she knew exactly what she was doing? He puffed out air as he carefully collected the three drinks. Not that anything was going to happen. It couldn't.

The night went on, everyone celebrating and relaxing after the gruelling exercise. Remaining in the same bar, some people left after an hour or two, including Melody's friend and some spinners with family commitments. Anita talked to one guy from the gym, but he was determined to at least have a good flirt. Watching for an opportunity, he kept one eye on her and one eye on the rest of the group, mainly Melody, who was chatting with a male PT.

In each direction, both of the women were being chatted up. Nate couldn't deny he felt a gnawing jealousy, snapping at him like a dog waiting for the post to arrive. Anita was attractive, smiley, and toned. Melody had a menacing sexiness that could only mean trouble. And she was troubled. He sniggered, feeling tipsy and just had to keep himself in check, especially with Melody. The guy talking to Anita sloped off. Nate took advantage and shimmied over to her casually.

'Any aching muscles yet?' he asked, tilting his head.

'My shoulders feel a little tense. I think they will be sore tomorrow. But this'll help!' She held up her glass of white wine and took a sip.

'Well, if you ever need a massage…' Nate raised an eyebrow, then laughed. 'Sorry, that was really lame!'

Anita nodded, but a grin spread across her face. 'It was, but, well, maybe.'

He felt smug then the guy who had been flirting with Anita returned with two drinks in his hands. Glancing around, he saw Melody in his eyeline. Her unblinking eyes were fixed on him. Staring, she stood still, like a statue in Madame Tussauds, unmoving. And as their eyes met, his heart raced for a few seconds and he felt a sensation less familiar to him: anxiety. Making his excuses to get away from Anita and her drinks provider, he ventured to the toilets. Slowly walking inside one of the self-contained bathrooms, he felt a slight push behind him. Spinning around, Melody stood in the doorway.

'Just checking you're okay?'

She looked how he could only describe as intense. But with her thick, dark, curled hair and red lips, she also looked like a sexy vampire — and at that moment, he desperately wanted her to bite him.

'Erm, ye…yeah,' he stuttered. 'Just need a piss.'

He stepped back as she stepped forward and shut the door behind them. In the self-contained bathroom with him, he knew there could only be trouble. But as she stepped forward, so did he. His heart pounding in his ears louder than the music in the bar as desire drowned any thoughts of rationality. Standing inches apart, Nate went to speak. She placed a red-nail-painted finger against his lips and the same finger from the other hand onto her own lips.

'Shhh,' she whispered, with a look in her eyes that made him want her more than he had wanted a woman in years. She took her fingers away and Nate scooped his hand around her neck and pulled her to him, kissing her frantically. Devouring her as she placed her hands firmly around his hips. She bit gently on his lips, sending thunderbolts of pleasure through him. Every nerve in his body craved her and he knew it was Melody in control. She giggled as she pulled her mouth away and reached for the belt of his trousers, her mouth open, eyes wide. Nate groaned, yearning for her touch. Then someone banged on the toilet door.

'Hurry the fuck up in there, man,' a drunk voice slurred.

His hand went to his forehead before he shook his head violently. 'Shit. Aghh, God, this can't happen. This can't *ever* happen!' He turned away from her, his hands interlocked and flat against the back of his head.

'C'mon, man, I'm growing a monkey's tail out here!' came the impatient voice from the other side of the bathroom door.

Nate tilted his head to the ceiling. His heart thumping with the urge for her, but his head telling him there was something poisonous about it all. He was clammy and felt dizzy, intoxicated by lust. She grabbed him from behind and he felt the hot poker of longing.

'It's wrong.' He spun around to face her, as she released her hold, frowning. 'Melody, I'm so sorry. This can't ever happen. We can't... I shouldn't...' He pulled his hand over his mouth and chin.

'It's okay,' she said quietly, twirling a chunk of her hair.

'Are you shitting for the Guinness World Record in there, mate?' The voice shouted again.

'Two fucking minutes!' Nate roared back. 'I'm so sorry. Please...'

'It's okay,' she repeated, glancing at the floor before opening the door and stepping out.

'Oh, I see. Lucky bastard,' the guy outside the toilet said as he winked at him and slapped his arm.

He stood for a moment, watching her walk along the corridor, back to the group, and thought he definitely wasn't lucky. And now he was certain that Melody Dartford was trouble. Nate left the bar following the incident. It was after 10 pm by that point and many people had gone home, so it looked less obvious. Melody was ordering a drink, her back to him. He said a quick goodbye to a few people and dodged out the door like a snake sloping through bushes. His head spinning, he made whimpering noises as he dashed through Covent Garden.

What the hell had just happened? And how could he have let it happen? He let out an aghh as he paced towards home and dug his nails into his scalp. She was a client and a vulnerable one at that. True, she didn't present outside of the therapy room as vulnerable, with her bold lipstick, assertive words, and confident body language. But she was obviously a disturbed patient. She had witnessed trauma, been scapegoated, and there was something else in Melody Dartford that Nate knew had yet to surface.

In the therapy sessions, her voice and demeanour changed when she talked about her troubled past. Almost robotic and childlike, with a coldness in her usually warm chocolate-brown eyes. Her jaw would clench and her body stiffen. Protection? Anger? He didn't know, but he knew there was a disturbance in her that hadn't been processed. He'd seen it before, of course, and was using therapy techniques to assist her. However, the disturbance wasn't settled, remaining in her, and it was creating a sensation in Nate that was more than anxiety and less than fear.

Until tonight, when the boundaries had been broken. He had overstepped the line, compelled to her like a moth to a light. The surging urge of desire, captivating him. Capturing him. And he succumbed. He had fucked up and it was damage limitation now that meant he would have to find Melody another therapist at least, and he could be struck off, at worst.

The past flashed into his head and he clenched his eyes until they almost hurt, trying to push it out. A car tooted, making him grab his chest as he strayed too close to the kerb. Leaning against a lamppost for a second, Nate tried to steady himself. Too much drink and desire, and now damage had been done. As he took deep breaths, he was unsure if the bile in his throat was due to alcohol or anxiety. Rain fell and he turned his face up to the sky for the cool drops to cover it, soothing his burning panic and regret.

Melody Dartford was attractive, sultry, assured. He felt she knew what she was doing, despite her age. And that was the problem. She wasn't just his client, she was a young woman. If word got out, not only would his career be over, and his reputation ruined, but people would shake their heads, appalled. And they would comment that it had happened again.

Waking after the worst night's sleep he could recall in a long time, Nate pushed his head into his pillow and grimaced. His first thought was *what the hell had he done?* His mouth was dry, his lips cracked, and his head throbbed. He'd woken through the night, sweating, experiencing the nightmare of years ago. Falling back to sleep in a drunken, desperate state, he'd slid back into the dream, unable to escape the lava from the volcanic eruption of his past. Of Annabelle Graham.

It had begun seven years earlier when he worked at Richardson College. Teaching sociology and psychology A-Level, both teachers and the students were under pressure to get excellent exam results — the best exam results in the area were what was expected. After all, they were a college with many students who were children of doctors, barristers, and CEOs. The pressure was on, as it increasingly was in education. Some students needed more support than others, regardless of parental occupation, and often, Nate and his colleagues in different subjects were asked to privately tutor students. Annabelle Graham was one of them.

Just turned eighteen years old, Annabelle was a capable student who could get good grades if she applied herself. Wanting to go to Oxford University, he knew she would need top grades from her A-Levels and that meant extra hard study in sociology and psychology. When her father, Ian, got in touch with the college about extra tuition, Nate had the capacity to help. The Grahams were friends of Nate's sister, Julie, and her husband, Brian. Their son, his nephew, had gone to school with Annabelle and Julie had recommended the extra tuition to Annabelle's parents.

It was late November, and the students had coursework to submit that would count towards their results. Exams the following May and June would dictate their overall grade and, for Annabelle — and the vast majority of the students — it would determine university offers. Nate began tutoring Annabelle for an hour on her lunch break once a week. This meant it was of no cost and could be done during his work day.

She was a polite, friendly, popular learner. The type of student who showed commitment, respect, and wanted to learn. Annabelle would come to the Thursday lunchtime session with a positive attitude and endearing humour that included her showing Nate an animal meme each week before the session started. She was tall, willowy, with light brown straight hair that she would tie up during the sessions in a messy bun, revealing her long, slender neck, as strands of hair would slide from the bun, tickling her décolletage.

Annabelle would wear her clothes in a way many women forget to, with an air of not caring what people thought. Perhaps an age thing, perhaps because she was simply naturally beautiful. Her pale collarbone would jut out of her top as she leant across the table whilst he explained a theory or approach. Her face close to his, Nate would sneak a peek at her; unblemished with age and lack of sun damage. Chocolate sprinkles of freckles across her forehead and small nose.

She would wear lip gloss that made her lips look sticky, like sweets that had been encased in their wrapper too long, pulled out, leaving a residue on the plastic covering. The gap in her teeth when she smiled would never change without dentistry, but it made her face even more of a work of art. Nate didn't notice these things. Not at first. He was her teacher. A professional. At first.

After hard work, Annabelle had submitted her coursework with confidence and in January, the focus became the upcoming A-Level exams. By this time, Annabelle was going out drinking more with friends and her parents worried her studying would slip. They asked for more tutoring, which meant an evening visit to her family home. Nate didn't mind, it was authorised by the college and he could charge for the sessions.

He continued to tutor her on a Thursday lunchtime and visited her home at 6 pm on Tuesday evenings. The memes continued to start the session and sometimes they chatted about Netflix shows, or Annabelle would play a little of a song she had been listening to, or mention where she had been partying. She'd ask his opinion on music, media, travel, and life — something that, as a teacher, he didn't get asked often as it was about the students. Nate felt Annabelle saw him as a person, as well as a teacher, and it felt good. He felt human and not just a robot in a role.

'Nice earrings,' he had said one day, nonchalantly, as she breezed in like a tall, pretty, vibrant sunflower. Dangling from her earlobes were Moroccan-style silver earrings with red and purple gems. It reminded him of his trip to Marrakesh with Sarah, and the array of jewellery, colourful ornaments, and rainbow bags.

'I got them from the craft market in town. A treat to myself after I broke up with my boyfriend.' She bounced down on the seat and her blouse moved slightly, showing a peek of a bra.

'Oh, sorry,' Nate had replied as he opened a textbook.

She had shrugged. 'No need for apologies. He was a dick and really immature, despite being twenty-five.' She'd tilted her head slightly and put a pen to her pink iridescent lips that shone in the room's light, like polished silverware.

Nate nodded and had laughed. 'Yeah, us guys take a lot of years to mature.'

'Well, my next boyfriend will be older. No messing around with these pathetic boy racers and clueless men-babies.' Her gaze had remained on him as she bit her lower lip.

Nate had felt himself blushing and cleared his throat. 'So, we talked about Bowlby's attachment theory on Tuesday night. Have you had any thoughts about it?'

That day, in cold late January, was the beginning of the end of Nate's teaching career. And as the next six months unfolded, his career wasn't the only casualty.

Chapter 22: Melody

Melody arrived home by Uber at 11 pm. Following their encounter in the toilet, Nate had disappeared and after hanging around for another thirty minutes, she had said goodbye to the remaining group. Grateful for the silent taxi driver, she replayed the scene over in her head. Nate had clearly left feeling conflicted. She knew he wanted her, desired her. His attraction to her wasn't just in her mind. It was real. *They* were real. She just had to make sure their first kiss wasn't their last.

Thanking her Uber driver and entering the flat, Melody took her heels and jacket off. Pulling her hair around to her face, she inhaled, trying to find the scent of him on her body. His hands grabbed at her hair as he hungrily kissed her. The passion, the longing coating her skin as he held her. Melody had *never* been kissed like that. She'd followed him to the toilet. She had to. The night was going quickly and she knew it was imperative that he acknowledged her and experienced her outside of the therapy room. Nate needed to see her as a woman. A sexual being and not some nut-job. She didn't want him as her therapist. She wanted him as her lover.

Her legs had trembled as she followed him and she was grateful for the many shots of vodka that had released a few inches of her belt of restraint. Her boldness had surprised him as she entered the bathroom. But she'd seen it, the desire in his eyes. The arousal and his craving for her — hungry, like a starving wild animal circling its prey. As he stood looking at her, she had never found him more attractive. Then they had moved closer and he had lunged at her, kissing her frantically, like the world was going to end. It was fervent, delectable, as their lips fused in sexual sync. He'd groaned, grabbing her hair and touching her neck and she had held him, feeling his toned torso beneath her hands, knowing they each had an appetite that needed satiating. It would have gone further had some drunken idiot not brayed on the door. Then a switch flicked in him and the therapist came back, reprimanding himself for crossing the boundaries.

Putting her head back against the hallway wall, she was drunk, but desperately wanted to get in touch with Nate. His business card had his work mobile number on, which she knew differed from his personal one, as she had seen the two phones during her therapy sessions. She could email him; he may have it as an app on his personal phone. But despite the urgency to contact him, like the desperate need for oxygen when swimming underwater, Melody knew she had to plan things when she was sober. However, she couldn't wait to tell Grace.

An hour later, Grace came home. Melody was asleep on the sofa, a fleece blanket covering her. A plate with a discarded corner of toast and a half-drunk glass of water lay on the floor. Grace was exhausted and after hovering over her snoring friend and making sure she was okay, grabbed a glass of water and headed straight to bed.

The next morning, Melody woke on the sofa. Clicking her neck, she let out a groan, moving on the furniture that wasn't long enough for her body. Her lips were almost stuck together as she reached, bleary-eyed, for the glass of water on the floor, gulping the remaining liquid with gusto. Pushing her shoulders back, she sat up and rubbed her face. Feeling the crustation of mascara from not washing her make-up off the night before.

Yawning, she arched her back for her poor posture during the night. Her bladder was screaming for release, but getting up from the sofa was proving challenging, with a distinct lack of energy and a wave of nausea threatening to overpower her. A minute later, she knew that not moving would mean peeing on the sofa, so she dragged herself up and shuffled to the bathroom. As she relieved herself, Melody remembered she and Nate had kissed. More than that, they had the most sexually charged dalliance of her life!

As she came out of the bathroom, Grace was exiting her bedroom. 'Morning, sleeping beauty,' she said as she tied her dressing gown belt.

'Morning,' she croaked, placing her hand on her forehead.

'Good night?' Grace yawned as she walked towards the kitchen.

'Like you wouldn't believe.'

They poured some cereal and a glass of orange juice each and sat at their tiny dining table that could only accommodate two. Permanent placemats covered the scratches and cup stains. Melody took a gulp of juice, then grinned at Grace.

'We kissed. Nate and me kissed.'

Grace's eyes widened, and she put a hand to her mouth as Melody smiled and clapped her hands together.

'OMG! Tell me everything!'

And Melody did, to jaw-dropping, squealing, and gasps from her friend.

'Jeez, I can't believe it. I mean, how unprofessional is he!' She blew out air.

Grace was right, but she didn't like the comment. This

wasn't about professionalism; it was about chemistry. Unavoidable magnetic attraction. They were meant to be together, and professionalism wasn't even part of the equation. Melody straightened her shoulders.

'Well, clearly our attraction to one another is more important and overrides any client and therapist set-up. I'll just stop seeing him for therapy.'

Grace was silent for a second.

'What?' Melody asked.

'You don't think he does this all the time, do you?'

Melody raised an eyebrow. 'Of course not,' she snapped. 'Can you not be happy for me?'

Grace reached over and tapped her friend's hand. 'I am happy for you. Obviously, I am. I'm just being the sensible one and even though you might need a relationship or a good night with a hot man, you also need help with your grieving and managing, hun. That's all.' Grace smiled.

Melody knew she was looking out for her and if Grace knew about her previous stay in the psychiatric hospital, never mind the reasons why, she might be even more concerned.

'You can't just stop doing therapy. That's not how it works.'

She puffed out air and shook her head. 'Grace, I think I, of all people, know that. Don't patronise me.'

'Oh, c'mon, I'm trying to help. Listen, I'm pleased for you *if* this works out with Nate, but he might regret it. I doubt it, cos you're gorgeous.' She smiled and Melody returned the smile. 'But if it progresses, you will have to find another therapist. And if it doesn't, you'll have to decide if you can have therapy with him still.'

'He'll just recommend me to someone else so we can drop the therapist/client relationship and start seeing each other.'

She shrugged, before spooning the last of her cereal into her mouth. She had almost convinced herself that she and Nate would become an item. 'Plus, he's got a lot more to lose if he doesn't do what I say.' Melody sniggered and Grace giggled, shaking her head. And the truth was that she meant every word.

Chapter 23: Nate

Lying in the bath, Nate spent over an hour letting his muscles and mind soak. Every ten minutes he pushed his foot around the plug release, letting a little water run out before stopping it and then using the same foot to kick the hot water tap on, topping up his giant, boiling pan. He desperately wanted to talk to someone, but knew no one would understand and not judge.

Julie was the closest option. She'd never wavered in her support about Annabelle Graham, even at the cost of hers and Brian's friendship with the Grahams. And although Julie loved Sarah like a sister, he would always come first. After their childhood and Nate protecting his older sister and their mother from their abusive dad, the siblings had an unbreakable bond. But this, well, it was almost history repeating. He closed his eyes, letting the hot water surround his body, and Annabelle came back into his mind.

The month after Annabelle had mentioned splitting up with her boyfriend, there had been a few suggestive incidents. At the time, he laughed them off or minimised them. He had been flattered by the attention, if the truth be told. Life at home with Sarah was fine; he loved his wife and found her incredibly beautiful. But it was boring, flat and without fizz, like a bottle of lemonade deprived of its top. Their life was mechanical, predictable, safe. Sarah was his best friend, his comfort blanket. But their comfort with one another meant slippers and cups of hot chocolate, over passion and spontaneous sex.

Annabelle's attention and presence began feeding his ego, fattening it up like a growing puppy that would eventually turn into a savage dog. He had started noticing her, really seeing her. The beautiful, carefree innocence young adults wear with ease. Her energy, glow, body. She'd asked him if they could change the tutoring to a Monday night, saying she was starting a gym class on a Tuesday evening.

Her parents both worked late a few nights a week, but they didn't mind not being there, as long as they could transfer the money and with agreement that he updated them on Annabelle's progress. Not sure if she was doing it so they would be alone, Nate hadn't cared. He was already addicted to Annabelle before they had even touched.

Two weeks later, he had gone to her house for their first tutoring session alone. She'd answered the door in a cropped T-shirt and denim skirt. Following her inside, they'd chatted small talk as he shadowed her to the dining room, where they usually sat. Instead, she had walked through to the kitchen and jumped on the breakfast bench. He'd lingered behind, wondering if she was going to get them a drink. But Annabelle had silently stretched her hand out to Nate — eyes wide and a grin on her pretty face. He'd taken her hand, stepped towards her, and she'd grabbed his other hand, placing it under her skirt, in between her legs. Nate had shuddered with arousal and they'd kissed and made love there in the kitchen.

His first hit of the drug that was Annabelle Graham became an addiction that he couldn't get enough of. That he needed to function, to survive. But like all drugs, it created destruction and six months later, once Annabelle had left college, passed her exams and had been offered a place at Oxford University, they were caught by Ian Graham who had assaulted Nate and reported him to Richardson College.

The college had launched an investigation, despite Annabelle and Nate both claiming that their relationship didn't start until she left the college and was an adult. It was a lie. Despite being eighteen, she had still been a student at the prestigious college, but they had both known that they couldn't tell the truth. Nate had resigned before he could be pushed out, even though there wasn't the evidence the authorities needed. It had ruined his career at Richardson's, his career in education, and his marriage to Sarah. In the end, he had lost Sarah and Annabelle and, to that day, he wasn't sure which made him sadder.

Eventually, he got out of the bath. The water wasn't soothing his conscience, drowning his emotional turmoil, nor had it made anything clearer. That same feeling of panic he felt for months seeing Annabelle, then during the aftermath of being caught out, plagued him again. That was the thing with excitement, with something slightly sinful. The allure of the wrong, the buzz of the do-not-cross line, the adrenaline of danger. It had always been in Nate: thrill-seeking. And Annabelle had been the drug he needed as well as the bullet that maimed him.

Now, sitting on his black leather sofa in his loungewear, he stared at the second hand circulating on his clock and tried to let rationality, sensibility, and professionalism win the tug of war in his mind against the greedy animal of lust wanting fed. This time, it wasn't age that would make people gasp, even though Annabelle was an adult before anything happened.

It wasn't that Nate was married. It was that Melody Dartford was a client. A patient in the medical sense of mental health support, and therefore, regardless of presentation outside of the therapy room, she was vulnerable. He knew that from her backstory, that hadn't all been told to him yet. She had a history of being sectioned under the Mental Health Act and a diagnosis. That was enough to know. And the power dynamics of patient and doctor or client and therapist — however it was badged up — was critical to care and support. Professional boundaries, conduct, safeguarding. Nate knew it all, he was registered with the British Association for Counselling and Psychotherapy (BACP). He hmphed, shaking his head. It was likely he could lose that registration, just like he lost his teaching career. Putting his hands to his head, he sighed.

What the hell had he done? He'd had sexual contact with a client, for God's sake. And even though it was only a kiss, it would have gone further. He had wanted it to go further. Nate slammed his fists into the sofa by his sides. Melody wasn't innocent in this, despite her mental health issues. She knew exactly what she was doing. She had seduced him. He wasn't prepared to, couldn't shoulder all the blame, all the responsibility. He was wrong, no doubt about that. But Melody was also wrong and she had persisted, teasing him. And he'd resisted, he'd remained professional. Until alcohol clouded him last night.

Closing his eyes, he pressed his lips together, trying to digest and rationalise what had happened and the impact on his future. It was her who had followed him and locked them in the bathroom. But he had kissed her first. No board would give a damn about the detail, just that it happened. That a therapist had sexual contact with an existing client. Even a past client would be bad enough. Sniggering to himself, he said aloud, 'At least you're not married this time.' Only it wasn't funny. None of it was funny and he had to find a way of harm minimising the situation pronto.

A few hours later, Nate logged on to his laptop. Checking

his emails, there was one from Melody. He had expected it, given she didn't have his personal number and their prior communication had been via email. He'd wanted a few hours to try to get things a little more lucid in his head, but his mind still felt like tins of paint had exploded in a room. Amongst the usual spam messages attempting to shaft him a little more was her email.

Hi Nate, I hope you got home okay last night. Anyway, I've been thinking about you, us. We need to talk.
Melody
X

'Shit,' he said aloud, as his hand rubbed across his forehead. Even a bloody kiss at the end. And what the hell was 'us?' He grimaced as acidic bile accumulated in his throat. Rising from his sofa, he opened the lounge window and gulped in the cold winter air. He would have to reply, but this needed some serious consideration to avoid any escalation. And Nate did not want to get into conversations about passionate kisses in toilets on his work email address.

Going to make a cup of coffee, although he really wanted a rum, he ran through options in his mind of what he could send as a reply. Something that wouldn't get Melody angry, or upset, or lead her on. Something neutral but not cold. A promise to talk about it, in person. Nate put his palms down on the kitchen bench, steadying himself as he took a deep breath.

The kettle clicked and he poured water over a spoon and a half of instant coffee, adding in a dash of milk. Taking the spoon out of his cup, he watched the water swirling lightly until it settled. Mesmerised and out of the moment for a few seconds until reality booted him up the backside. Carrying his coffee back to the lounge, he placed it on his glass side table and sat down. Grabbing a teal velour cushion, he rested it on his lap and placed his laptop on it. Looking at the screen, he puffed out air and began to write a draft.

Hi Melody, I hope you're feeling well this morning. 'Go in caring,' he said, nodding to himself.

Sorry, I didn't get a chance to say goodbye last night. I was drunk and felt terrible. 'Leave it open, admitting nothing,' Nate said aloud.

~~*It shouldn't have happened.*~~ 'Needs to be said in person in case she reacts badly.' Nate pulled at his bottom lip and jaw with his hand. He had to be careful; sensitive but protect his own arse.

We should talk. At the session next week. Or we could meet tomorrow lunchtime in the park?

He was conscious of her being a paying client and using up possible therapy time with their sexual episode deconstruction. He also didn't want to sound like he was asking her on a date, but the park would be neutral ground. He would apologise and explain he was drunk, didn't know what he was doing. That it was really all a blur, despite him being able to recount every second, every sense. Then he would offer her a refund; a full refund of her sessions so far, and those outstanding. Nate tapped his lips. He could recommend a therapist, a friend of his who he trained with and who was much more professional than him. He groaned and pushed his head back into the cold leather of the sofa.

Yes, he would suggest that. If Melody was adamant that she wanted to finish therapy with him, there were only two sessions before a review and he would discharge her, saying he had no capacity — doing it gently to not piss her off. And he had to get out of his head that he wanted her. To have sex with her so badly that his skin felt on fire. He *had* to quell those thoughts, those emotions, and desires. Nothing good could come of it. He frowned, gazing past his laptop into space. Melody was vulnerable and, in a haunting way, Nate knew in the pit of his stomach that she was also dangerous.

'For fuck's sake!' he shouted, running a hand over his blond-grey hair. Looking at the laptop, he re-read the email.

Hi Melody, I hope you're feeling well this morning. Sorry I didn't get a chance to say goodbye last night. I was drunk and felt terrible. We should talk. At the session next week. Or we could meet tomorrow lunchtime in the park?
Thanks,
Nate

It felt colder than he intended and, in reality, he wanted to tell her to come round so he could take her to bed. But he knew, without a doubt, that she was a no-go area. He had to stop it from escalating. He closed his eyes, gritting his teeth. Christ, it had already gone too far. Like a lake with one of those metal signs warning people of crocodiles. Nate knew he couldn't go near her again and that if he did, she would sink her teeth into him, and, like a swimmer in a lake filled with crocodiles, he wouldn't make it out alive.

Chapter 24: Melody

On the sixth attempt at constructing an email to Nate, Melody felt happy with it. Emailing felt too formal, given the conversation subject. However, she had limited ways to communicate with him. Melody knew she couldn't just turn up next Thursday at their session as if their only interaction outside of the therapy room had been a quick sighting in the local supermarket. Tapping her feet on the rug in front of her sofa, she had spent the last hour writing, editing, deleting, and re-writing an email that sounded friendly, mature, and that wouldn't scare Nate away.

She was certain he wanted her. However, she didn't know if he would pursue their sexual attraction or if he woke up that morning feeling guiltier than a priest caught paying for sex. Melody was frightened, scared of rejection and hurt. She couldn't help the way she was; falling fast, investing emotions, becoming almost possessive of people. And it wasn't just boyfriends, it was friends. She didn't want to share, and she wanted to be someone's favourite, but didn't everyone? Cherished, spoilt, number one — like she had always been to her parents, even when Felix was alive. She shook her head, berating herself and read the draft email.

Hi Nate, I hope you got home okay last night. Anyway, I've been thinking about you, us. We need to talk.
Melody xxx

She grabbed her messy bun before removing two of the kisses. Maybe three looked a bit desperate, but one made him know she didn't regret their kiss, perhaps. Clicking on the send icon, she sighed and then shut her laptop down. She could check for replies later on her mobile phone. For now, she would try to sleep. Waking two hours later, Melody felt more tired than when she lay down. She got out of bed and walked into the lounge, where Grace was studying.

'Got you a present,' she said, getting off the sofa and rushing to the kitchen.

Yawning, Melody sat down. Grace returned thirty seconds later with a Terry's Chocolate Orange, one of her favourite sweet treats. Melody knew it was because Grace was aware she had upset her earlier that day with her negativity around Nate and the kiss. Leaning up and taking the chocolate, she thanked her friend.

'You're not getting any, mind,' she joked.

Grace shrugged. 'Got my own, didn't I! How you feeling?'

'Pretty rough. Think I'll just watch rubbish TV and have a bath tonight when you're at work. And dip this in a cup of tea.' She passed the chocolate from hand to hand.

'Sounds like a good idea. You contacted him?' Grace asked tentatively.

'I emailed a few hours ago. Not had a reply yet.'

The pair were quiet for a minute.

'Okay, well, I'm going to get on with my studying in my room. But if you need me…'

Grace stroked her friend's hair before heading to her bedroom, leaving Melody looking at the chocolate and wondering if and when he would reply. She didn't have to wait long, seeing an indication of new mail ten minutes later on her mobile phone. Clicking on the mail icon, she felt her hands shake. It was from Nate. Her heart beat fast in her throat as she read the brief message, imagining his gorgeous face in her mind.

She read it four times before taking her eyes away from the screen. Melody couldn't decide if the email was good or bad. He hadn't put a kiss on it, which pissed her off, but perhaps it was because it was emails and, well, kisses were usually in text messages, maybe. She drank the dregs of a can of pop and looked at the email again. He apologised for leaving without saying goodbye to her. It made her smile and she had the image of him standing in the bar — he'd looked so handsome.

Melody put her finger to her mouth. In the email, he suggested meeting the next day at the park. *Surely that's a good sign?* She wanted to ask Grace her opinion but didn't feel ready to share his message yet. Perhaps he was just playing it cool or was embarrassed about being drunk. Nate wanted her, she was sure of that. They just had to work out a way to be together.

Chapter 25: Nate

The new week had come around and Nate returned to his daily routine of work. Seeing some regular clients on Monday morning, he struggled to concentrate, Melody plaguing his mind. His emotions had been up and down all weekend like the pirate ship ride at a fair, along with that sinking feeling in the stomach that being on the ride gifts you. He'd distracted himself the day before — no longer feeling hungover, just feeling the quagmire of worry — by giving the house a good clean and minimising clutter. Not that he had a lot, but the first viewing for the house sale was that evening and he knew there would be more coming in the next week. Melody had replied to his email the day before.

Hi Nate, yes it would be good to chat tomorrow. I can be there at 12:15? Thanks,
Melody
x

Grateful for the shortness of the email, he had responded with a brief, see you then, message. Now, as time was ticking close to twelve, he wanted to meet her, like he wanted to visit the dentist for a root canal. Despite the distinct lack of appeal, Nate knew he had to do it. He had to tell Melody that they had no traction and offer her alternative support if needed.

On his way out of the door to his building, he bit back

nauseous as he walked to St Pancras Gardens. Nate felt tension and anxiety in every step and his back gathered sweat, despite the cold weather. It wasn't even fully her fault. His past haunted him still. It used to be constant. A grieving for Annabelle, for Sarah and his old, normal life. But the yearning, the heartbreak, the loss he felt for Annabelle was like something he had never experienced. And the pain had scarred him. He doubted he'd ever be truly over it and knew it impacted on his relationships with women. Even practising his own rehearsed advice to clients wasn't enough to completely lay Annabelle Graham to rest.

Melody had ignited some of those feelings. Nowhere near the fire of Annabelle but the lust, the hunger, a spark. Despite her being a woman he craved to devour, Nate didn't want the dangerous excitement, and he certainly didn't want the career-shredding consequences. He clicked his neck from side to side and rolled his shoulders. Approaching the park entrance, he breathed in the crisp air and strained his eyes to see as far as he could.

Further into the park, he reached the area where they had sat on the bench. She was sitting on the same wooden seat. His stomach dropped and his heart beat faster. Yet, he couldn't help but smooth his hair and straighten his posture; torn between what was right and wanting, needing the forbidden. Getting closer to her, she turned her eyes his way and smiled. Nate smiled back, a pleasant, not over-the-top smile. Taking a deep breath, he was almost at the bench. She looked gorgeous. Her hair was in loose waves, curled around her face, bouncing on her shoulders. Pink lips and white teeth smiled at him.

'Hi,' was all she said.

'Hi, Melody.'

Nate sat down, his legs felt wobbly. He bounced them

momentarily in case she noticed. She wore a checked wool dress under her open coat. Thick tights clung to her shapely legs. Calves encased in black boots. He got a waft of her apple scent and wanted to bury his head in her hair and neck.

'I've been thinking about you.' She turned her body slightly towards him.

He felt a bolt of discomfort along with urges that he was battling. He simply nodded, saying nothing.

'Saturday. The kiss. It was just so… powerful.' She touched his leg, and he automatically stiffened, making her remove it as her eyebrows furrowed.

'Melody. We can't do this. *I* can't do this.' He placed his hand on the back of his neck.

Her eyes widened. 'So, you do have a girlfriend?'

Nate shook his head. 'No. But that doesn't mean I can…'

'Let me guess, "It's not you, it's me?"' she sneered.

'Melody. Listen, you're extremely attractive.' His eyes were on her and she smiled. 'But I am a therapist and *you* are my client. I've already breached protocol. It's unethical.'

She shook her head. 'You make it sound like I am some animal you are testing on. *You* kissed me, Nate. I know you wanted to and I know you enjoyed it.' She tilted her head and seductively bit her lower lip.

He had to think with his head, but it was bloody difficult.

'I made an error of judgement and I'm so sorry for that. And I hope you can forgive me for crossing boundaries.' He noticed her nostrils flaring. Clasping his hands together, he continued. 'I value you as a client and I think you are an incredible woman. But you are a client and that means nothing can ever happen again.' He breathed out, feeling perhaps he was getting the control back.

She clenched her jaw. Her eyes fixed on him. 'So, I stop being a client and then, well, we can…'

Nate interrupted, 'Melody, we can't be anything. It's inappropriate and…'

'Are you saying you don't find me attractive?' she said loud enough for people on the next bench along to glance over.

He swallowed. 'No, I mean yes, I do find you attractive. You're a beautiful woman. But, it's unethical.'

'You keep fucking saying that. Like I'm some dirty secret that can be swept away.' Melody's voice shook. She looked at her lap and took a deep breath. 'I'm sorry. I like you and I felt a connection between us, since before we kissed.'

Anxiety bubbled in Nate's throat. He had to play this carefully. He did fancy her. Of course he did. And in different circumstances, he would have undoubtedly taken her to bed and had a fling with her. But now, in the reality of the last few days, he didn't want Melody anywhere near enough to risk his career — he just had to keep reminding himself of that when the brain in his trousers argued otherwise. There were plenty of single women who weren't his clients. Who weren't vulnerable and volatile like her.

'So did I, Melody. But you must see that I can't act on it? That anything between us would be a non-starter, a no-go area?'

Looking up from her lap, Nate saw tears in her eyes and felt like he had bitten off a baby chick's head in front of its mother. He instinctively grabbed her hand, then scolded himself for going to comfort her, knowing she may read into it more. Squeezing it and smiling at her, he let go again.

'Look, it really isn't you. I have a registration with BACP. It's my professional conduct. I've already over-stepped…'

'So, you've done it already. It doesn't matter. I won't tell. We don't have to say anything until after you've discharged me from practice.'

The willingness in her eyes was like that of a pleading child, and Nate saw a glimpse of the endearing side of her outside of the sexual vamp. But it was still one of her many vulnerable sides, and he simply did not fully trust her.

'Melody, we can't. And I'm not sure that I should continue to be your therapist.'

She grabbed his hand and a tingle shot through him. 'You can't just abandon me.'

Nate grimaced slightly at the dramatic use of the word.

'I've told you things. Really personal things and you need to help me manage. I need you to help me deal with Felix's death. You can't just desert me. It'll make me ill again.'

Gently pulling his hand away, he touched the outside of her upper arm — usually a safe, non-threatening place to have contact with someone.

'You won't become poorly again, because you've come so far. You don't realise how strong you are. How resilient.' Clichéd shit was pouring out of his mouth as he held her gaze. He knew she needed help, highly likely more than two more sessions, and for that, he felt bad. However, every instinct in him felt he needed to crawl out of this pit of snakes as soon as he could with no more bites.

'So, I don't even get my last two sessions?' She wiped an eye and inhaled deeply.

'I don't think it's a good idea, do you?' Nate could feel himself softening toward her. She did need help. Perhaps after making it clear nothing could happen, he could finish the two sessions. His mind had been made up on the way to the park and now he felt guilty and responsible as her therapist.

'I'll not even mention Saturday. Please, just try?'

He rubbed his forehead. Shit! Ultimately, it was he who kissed her. Perhaps he could get through another two sessions then sign her off. Keep her sweet in a way and he'd just have to rein in his sexual thoughts and remind himself that nothing good could ever come of it. She wasn't Annabelle and ultimately Melody wasn't worth any extra problems in and out of work.

He puffed out air. 'Okay, let's see how it goes on Thursday, as you may not feel comfortable and I can't compromise your well-being any further.'

A smile spread across her face. 'Thank you.'

Nate nodded. 'Right, I'll see you Thursday. I have to pop to the chemist.'

He didn't have to visit the chemist, but he needed to leave the situation. Getting up from the bench, he smiled at Melody. 'See you Thursday. Take care.'

She nodded and smiled back. 'See you then.'

Nate walked away without looking back and the pirate ship ride began swinging back and forth in his stomach again.

Chapter 26: Melody

Melody sat shaking on the park bench, unsure if it was from anger or anxiety. *How could he just reject her like that?* She knew Nate was attracted to her; he even admitted it during their conversation. She clenched her hands into fists. Why was he so cold and assertive in his rejection? After all, he kissed her first — grabbing her, snatching at her mouth, consuming her with passion. Taking a deep breath, she closed her eyes tightly and tried to replay their conversation. *Perhaps Nate was just scared. Maybe he would come around, especially once she was no longer his client.* Melody felt a little sprinkling of hope.

Tapping her thumb and forefinger against her mouth, her thoughts were interrupted by a young child running past screaming as his mother pushed a baby in a buggy a little behind. He was chasing the pigeons and she couldn't help but sneer at the child, wondering why parents let their children scare animals. As the mother passed, Melody gave her a look of disdain, before there was quiet again and she could re-focus on Nate. She wouldn't mention their conversation today or the kiss, or anything of the sort on Thursday. Instead, she would assess what he was like with her — his demeanour and comments.

She wouldn't push it, ask, plead. No, she would play it cool, mature, in control. Hopefully, that would help smooth over any anxiety Nate felt about his professional conduct and all that unethical rubbish he kept spouting. They were meant to be together. And it would happen, she was sure, even after the last thirty minutes. She just had to be patient; not a great skill of Melody's, but she had to persevere. She couldn't give up on her and Nate.

Rising from the bench, she felt clouded in confusion and wanted to go home, to rest in silence and think about her next steps with him. Instead, she had to return to work to be spoken to like shit by the public — moaning about their premium or inability to claim — for the rest of her shift. It began to rain as she left the park. She fastened her wool coat and, taking her umbrella from her bag, put it up. As she walked back to work, through busy King's Cross, Melody felt she was submerged in a rain cloud, even with her umbrella covering her.

On her arrival back to Crawford's, she headed to the kitchen to make herself a cup of tea, before she would take her seat back with the battery farm chickens in the rows of identical office booths. Her team leader, a rat-faced woman called Selina, who thought the £1,000 a year extra in her salary made her Deborah Meaden, came into the staff kitchen. Selina looked at her, then at her watch, before returning her gaze to Melody as she made her drink. Tapping a spindly finger on the face of her cheap timepiece, she raised an eyebrow.

'Your break is over, Melody. Chop, chop.'

She clapped her hands as she spoke the last two words, which made Melody want to 'chop, chop' her with an axe.

'Piss off, Selina!' she snapped, glaring at her scrawny face, much to the amazement of her colleague, whose mouth dropped open, with no patronising words coming out this time.

Melody walked past her, leaving the tea bag in her cup, in fear that a moment longer in the company of another arsehole at Crawford's Insurance would make her explode. The rest of her shift passed quickly, much to her relief, and it was soon home time.

Arriving at the flat, Grace wasn't at work, so Melody could update her on the conversation with Nate. Knowing Grace may be slightly critical, Melody also acknowledged that Grace was the person she could confide in the most. She couldn't tell her mum or dad, unable to even imagine how they would react. It certainly would involve her dad upping the paranoia and continuous communication to an unmanageable level when it had just about felt normal — well, normal for Matthew.

'I hate seeing you upset.' Grace squeezed her hand as they sat at the kitchen table. 'You deserve to be happy with the right guy.'

Melody sniffed. 'It's so complicated for him and I get it. I just really like him.' She sighed.

Grace nodded and passed her some kitchen roll. 'I know. And I'm certain he likes you, but it sounds like he's frightened about his reputation. I mean, if he was reported for getting into a relationship with a client, couldn't he be like struck off or something?'

Leaning back against the hard dining chair, Melody shrugged. She hadn't thought about that; Nate being struck off for malpractice or being unethical, or whatever the hell it was in his field of work. She hadn't acknowledged that even though he had a registration as a therapist, that sexual relations with a client could lead to him being de-registered, losing his business.

No, she hadn't really thought about that consequence. However, she now knew she had an extra card to play. The ace up her sleeve, if he didn't come around, or became nasty. And Melody was never afraid to use certain methods in desperation. In fact, it was a skill of hers.

That evening, Melody visited her dad. He made chilli and the pair sat together eating, talking about work, and her progress in therapy. Of course, she had omitted some of the truth. As she talked, Matthew nodded, his eyes wide with enthusiasm and a proud smile on his face in between asking questions. She felt terrible, but simply couldn't tell her dad the truth. He would be devastated and worried. Plus, she already felt bad that Matthew was paying for the sessions that had now moved focus to lust and a game of persuading Nate they could be a couple, rather than the psychological intervention and support it was meant to be.

Matthew had even re-joined his local darts team with a few old mates. He'd been a member before Felix died and it had been his social life, playing locally against teams across London. It was a massive step for Matthew, and Melody knew it was because her dad felt she had some stability and he didn't have to carry such a heavy weight of worry for his only child.

'Sounds like it is all going well, love,' Matthew said as he scooped up some chilli onto a slice of garlic bread.

She nodded, chewing a mouthful of food before replying, convincingly, 'Yeah, it is, Dad.'

Melody failed to update her father on another incident — a written warning work had issued her after she had told rat-face Selina to piss off. The day after she blasted her in the staff kitchen, she had been asked to attend a meeting with a manager called Glen, whose office always stunk of sweat. He'd sat across from her, a table separating them as if he was a member of parliament, not a manager who people never actually saw as he was working from home so often.

Glaring at Melody with beady eyes and a nose that looked damp like a dog's, he'd spoken in his nasal, high-pitched voice, asking her to explain herself. She'd listened to his whine, nodding intermittently as he'd commented about 'unacceptable behaviour', and 'code of conduct'.

'To be honest, Glen, it was my brother's birthday yesterday. You may remember, he died. So, I was struggling and have felt very upset and alone. You might also know I am on anti-depressants and getting therapy so well, I feel fragile.' She'd looked down and clasped her hands together. 'I shouldn't have said that to Selina, but she was hardly sympathetic to my situation and, as a manager, I think she should know what's going on with her team. She should ask in welfare meetings and I haven't had one for at least six months.'

Melody had to focus on not letting the smug smile dance across her face. Okay, she had lied about Felix's birthday, but the rest was true. And well, she had a protected characteristic, and work should accommodate that.

'I see. I'm sorry that you have all that going on, and that you haven't had a recent welfare meeting. I will see that you have one in the next few weeks.' He had made a scribble on his notepad. 'I do, however, have to give you a written warning for your behaviour, but I will accompany it with some notes for HR.'

'I understand.' She'd shrugged, annoyed but feeling like she had taken some control back and Selina would get a bollocking, so it was worth it.

'I hope the therapy goes well,' Glen had said, with a quick smile of his thin lips.

'Thanks,' Melody had replied, before leaving, pleased to exit the stagnant room.

An hour later, she left her dad's, grateful for an easier night than she had predicted and happy her dad was beginning to enjoy life a little more. Matthew would never not be anxious about his daughter. It was a parents' role, Melody knew that. Ever the protector. However, there was, added to this, the history of Melody's psychological state. Matthew, Zoe, and Felix had witnessed the decline in her mental health in the months after Toby and Callum died, and Lily moved to Manchester.

Her family had watched her dwindle. They had powerlessly seen small chunks of her fall off as the weeks passed. Her colour fading without knowing her deadly secret — that she had provided the drugs that led to their deaths. Melody's family had been helpless spectators. Then the fire occurred and she was sectioned, and the criminal charges followed. Her parents had to live through the trauma of what could have been, trying to desperately understand why their daughter could do such a thing. To comprehend the danger, the desperation, the depression. And failing, unable to get answers. Then the world cracked again when Felix took his own life.

Worry and loss had never left her parents. It was there, strong in her father. A dullness in his eyes that held a dark shade of concern. Knowing that it could happen again. She could be poorly again. Their other child could die. A response, a circumstance, a consequence. Felix's death had been a trigger for a possible relapse. It didn't happen to the extreme this time, but something else could cause it. Cause the sink of Melody to be topped up a little too much — for the tap to turn on, water to gush out, and a catastrophic flood to follow.

Chapter 27: Nate

After the chat with Melody, Nate felt a little more focused. It was unpleasant seeing her upset and he never wanted to hurt a woman, but it was impossible, despite the battle with his desire. He had to keep reminding himself that there were many more women out there. Beautiful women who would not be a risk to his career. Melody had a temporary infatuation with him because, well, like many people he came across in his practice, they were searching for something missing. Most found it through therapy, within themselves. Some didn't. But Nate knew he was not her 'something'.

Two more sessions were all he had to get through. Then she would be a closed client. Nate genuinely wanted to help Melody recover and manage her mental well-being, but sleeping with her wasn't part of her recovery. And risking his career further was certainly not part of his agenda. This was a lesson he would ensure he learnt. The first time around with Annabelle should have been enough, given the fallout.

On Thursday, at her penultimate session, he would talk to her about more coping mechanisms and the death of her brother. They had been covering the elements of dialectical behavioural therapy in their sessions, which Nate felt was a gentle yet effective form of therapy for someone with Melody's past trauma in her youth and current obstacles. He had decided that he would provide more worksheets and information for her to take away. The last session would be summarising, looking at triggers and responses. He would ensure she had tools to support her, including community resources and online support.

On Monday evening, a young couple were the first people to view his property. Opening the door with a smile, he welcomed the pair in. They explained they were planning on a family in a few years' time and wanted a house large enough. As expected, they were impressed but made no secret of the fact it was well over their budget. After saying goodbye to them and shutting the solid wood front door, Nate shook his head.

There was another viewing later that week with the estate agent claiming he had further enquiries and was awaiting more communication. The house was a high asking price, but worth it and fair, given the sales in the area. He hadn't yet looked at possible future properties for himself, absorbed in the drama of the last few days. However, he would be happy to rent if needed until he found his perfect country escape and boy, he craved escaping more than ever.

Thursday arrived and Nate felt like he was going for a job interview — his gut, a cement mixer churning sand and concrete. He knew Melody had a level of unpredictability and instability, her record showed that. He just had to placate her, watch what he said, and keep his hands off her. During the week, he had deliberately avoided going to the park at lunchtime, not wanting to bump into her. Outside of the therapy room felt more tempting, more dangerous, and even without alcohol, Nate wanted Melody. His desire, the dragon in him he was forcing not to breathe fire. He just couldn't act on it, no matter what.

Sitting in a trance, he placed his hands on his lap and stared at the pictures on his office wall, head back in his armchair.

Annabelle came into his mind. Julie had said she was working for Amazon. It felt like a lifetime ago. After the fallout, all contact had ceased and the relationship between the Grahams and Julie and Brian was irreparable. Annabelle, being a young woman, moved on, meeting men her own age. He had to try to glue back the smashed crockery set that was his marriage. But it didn't work and he gave up wanting to try — grieving for the thrill of Annabelle.

Nate had seen her occasionally over the following years. Sometimes, she hadn't seen him. Driving, or in a supermarket, or on the Tube. Or maybe it wasn't even her; just random people, the image in his mind imprinted onto their faces. Her ghost, a mask worn by strangers. But one time, in a bar as he sat with another date, he saw Annabelle. He'd got up, making an excuse to go to the toilet and approached her, his heart racing, mouth dry, wondering, could they try again? She hadn't seen him, and as he got closer, a face appeared next to her shoulder as a man embraced her from behind. She'd closed her eyes and tilted her head to touch his, two bodies almost melting into one. Her smile said it all, and she turned to face the man, then kissed him. Nate felt like secateurs had chopped at his heart and he left the bar, and his date, returning home, wounded.

A knock startled him and he puffed out air, getting up and clicking his neck as he walked to open the door. It was Melody, with a faint smile on her face. Not the sexy, alluring grin she wore so well, but a pretty, meek smile.

'Hi,' she said as he moved to one side and she entered his office, mechanically going towards the sofa.

'Hi,' he replied, casually wiping his sweaty hands on the legs of his chinos.

He poured some water and took the seat opposite her.

Melody was wearing a mustard roll-neck jumper, no flesh on show, but still, the curves of her body were obvious as she took her coat off. Her feminine frame that Nate admired. Paired with black jeans, tucked into flat boots, she crossed one leg over the other and sipped from the glass.

'How are you?' he asked, looking at her with his head leaning slightly forward.

She shrugged. 'Okay, I guess. You?'

Nate shifted a little in his seat. 'Yeah, good, thanks.' He flashed a strained smile and cleared his throat, wanting to get straight into the session and guide the conversation around Melody and not 'them'. Taking his glasses from the side table, he continued. 'So, this session, I think it would be useful if you talk about your brother's death and feelings around that. Obstacles, impact, support. Then we can look at some more coping tools, including some DBT handouts I have for you.'

Melody relaxed back on the sofa and nodded. She was quiet, duller, and Nate knew it was his fault. But he had a job to do and needed to focus on that.

Chapter 28: Melody

Melody had spent three full days thinking about how she would act, and what she would say to Nate at her penultimate therapy session that Thursday. She had left work at the end of her shift and rehearsed it all again — for what must have been the hundredth time — as she walked to his office feeling almost bereft. In her mind, she was trying to blur the edges of how attracted she was to him. However, she knew that when he opened the door, no amount of preparation would stop her heart from racing.

She had considered the options and after much deliberation, planned her next steps. Driving her car to work, Melody had parked at the car park she knew he used — from a conversation about the Tube and his discount permit through renting the office. Not knowing what type of car Nate drove, she had left the house super early for the anxious drive into the capital, and had secured a space on the ground floor of the parking lot, near to where permit spaces were reserved. The charges were outrageous, but he was worth it; they were worth it.

Melody had looked at the photo from his LinkedIn account, saved to her mobile phone's camera reel, at least fifty times a day. Zooming in on his handsome half smile and his eyes that felt like she was floating in the ocean. She had studied him: each line and crease of his face. The mole on his left cheek, the dimple on his right.

She had spent hours concentrating on the photo, willing

him, with some form of desperate telepathy to ask her on a date. Praying he'd kiss her again, tell her he'd made a mistake and they have to be together. Willing him to open his office door to her that day and for them to passionately embrace. Him, holding her with his strong arms, needing her.

As she got nearer to his office, Melody just wanted to grab him and yet all she could manage, when he opened the door, looking devastatingly handsome, was, 'Hi.'

Nate stood with a grey knitted jumper on that, despite its loose fit on his torso, still clung around the shapely muscles of his upper arms and lay like a second skin across his toned shoulders. Paired with some blue chinos and grey desert boots, she could smell woody hues with citrus as she passed him slowly and headed to the yellow sofa.

He handed her a glass of water. *Was that a slight shake in his hand?* Sitting opposite, she couldn't keep her eyes off Nate's. Those forget-me-not blue irises sparkling against his pale hair. Putting his glasses on, he began talking and she couldn't absorb any of it — like water running through a sieve. At the end of his speech, he paused and rubbed the back of his neck, waiting for her to say something. Instead, she just leant back into the sofa and nodded. When it became obvious she wasn't going to speak, Nate filled the silence.

'So, let's start with your brother and his death.'

He sounded cold, especially for someone who had kissed her with such electric passion. But Melody had to conform, play the game until she could well and truly get the ball back in her own court. So, she told the truth and spoke of the shock, the denial. The subsequent increase in the already stifling overprotection from her father, preventing her from processing her grief healthily.

Her mother, burying her head after burying her son — almost unable to speak his name. Then the subsequent separation and her mother moving from the family home. She mentioned feeling both oppressed and concerned about her father and mother. Until recently, where the curtains had begun to part and shards of light were beginning to shine through for her dad.

'Obviously, I haven't said anything about last weekend to him. That would send him into panic, which would impact me.'

Nate swallowed and looked down momentarily.

'But he's becoming more normal again.' She laughed and tilted her chin up before rubbing the blanket that lay across the arm of the sofa. 'Normal for him, which he has never been since before the fire.'

He listened and Melody felt good talking, even almost removing the underlying sexual tension that perfumed the air. As the session ended, she rose from the sofa and slowly put her coat on, not wanting to leave. Rising from his chair, Nate glanced at her. His eyes scanning her, Melody bit her lip, pleased that he was looking at her in *that* way. Walking slowly to the door, she hoped his eyes would remain on her.

Turning, she saw his cheeks were flushed. 'Okay, well hopefully those worksheets prove useful and we can talk about them next week along with some summary pieces, triggers, and coping scenarios.' He scratched his neck and leant close to her, opening his office door. She inhaled him and could almost feel the heat from his body.

'Yeah, see you. I hope the rest of your day isn't too busy.' She giggled a nervous laugh, not knowing what else to say.

'Done now for the day. Just a few bits of admin to do once I get home.' He nodded, smiling the most awkward smile she had seen on his face.

'Bye, then.' She walked through the door and turned.

'See you.'

Shutting the door on her, Melody cried silent tears. *How could he just ignore it? Her? Them?* She took the stairs and exited the building. Melody knew she had fallen in love with Nate and was certain, under the hard layer of armour, he could fall in love with her. They had something, it was undeniable. She only had one week to make him see it. She needed a plan. Standing with her back against the bricks of the building, she clenched a fist and wiped her eyes with the other. Watching a seagull land across the road, pecking at a takeaway container with gusto, she thought of how close they had been as she left. The lingering look as she had put her coat on. His body language speaking louder than any words.

She tapped her mouth. He'd said he was finished for the day after their appointment. Going home to email or whatever. Smoothing down her hair, she sniffed up and walked to the car park. At least she wouldn't have as long to wait, remaining in her car for him returning to the car park, and hopefully see what car was his. It could be hard to spot him leaving, but he'd have to slow down for the barrier. Melody had secured a good enough space to possibly see him leave, then she would follow him home.

Laughing aloud, she began rushing to get to her car to execute her plan. However, she wasn't laughing at the plan that may or may not work. Melody was laughing at the fact Nate Lundie thought he could outsmart her and deny his feelings. He underestimated her and she would show him he needed her, wanted her — even if it required firm persuasion.

Chapter 29: Nate

The therapy session with Melody had been strange. Nate was pleased she hadn't brought them up and instead, had focused on the purpose of the session, as well as being relatively open to talking and exploring coping tools. It was strained, undoubtedly. Sexual tension clung to the air, like grease from a cooked breakfast, as his mind wandered to thoughts of kissing, touching, having sex with her. But only thoughts. They could never be actions and he had to keep out of her shooting range.

Nate couldn't lead her on and had to ensure he didn't do or say anything that could compromise his professionalism further, or give her a reason to fizz. She was volatile, he had no doubts about that. In a way, it made her sexier. An edge, an unpredictability. That was great in the bedroom, but not when it came to developing an obsession and the potential ruining of his career. And he felt Melody most definitely had that capability.

He was tense throughout the session. His shoulders stiffer than usual, more conscious of his eye contact. Wanting it to be over, especially after she'd mentioned her father early on. Nate already had him down as a bloody nightmare, given what she had claimed about his overbearing shadow on her. Compassion in him knew he was grieving, but her father sounded oppressive, suffocating, and controlling.

He was certain that Melody's overprotective father's ways did nothing to help his daughter move through her mental health issues. Flippin' hell, it sounded like her father needed a good amount of therapy himself. Nate was relieved when Melody commented he knew nothing about their kiss. He could do without some mad dad putting in a complaint. And as for her mother, she sounded cold and dismissive.

She had talked and he had listened. Yet, his mind walked in its own direction as he snuck glances at her curvy frame and pretty face, clean of heavy make-up. *It can't ever happen. It can't ever happen,* he repeated over and over in his head, as he felt his thoughts drift to fantasy. He was his own worst enemy when it came to pretty women, but she was the black widow spider, waiting to strike. Nate had to keep his guard and his trousers up and not let manipulative Melody get her hooks into him.

As the session drew to an end, Melody put her coat back on, her pert breasts pushing out as a mustard sleeve slid into it. Then, as she walked to the door, he stole a look at her round arse and shapely legs. He would have to go on a date that weekend, something to occupy his mind and satisfy his desire.

There was an awkward moment as they said goodbye. Nate saw longing and sadness in her eyes and he felt a punch to the throat. But he couldn't reassure her. Couldn't make her feel needed, or act out what he really wanted to do, out of therapist mode. She left, and he puffed out air, running his hands through his hair, feeling drained. Deciding he would make a call to take his mind off the last hour, he rang a client, then tidied his office before finishing for the day.

Twenty minutes after Melody left, Nate grabbed his bag and laptop and locked up his office. Taking the stairs, he arrived in reception and said goodnight before exiting the building. It was cold and dark, the petrichor scent of rain rising from the ground as he tried to avoid puddles for his suede shoes. A few minutes later, Nate reached the car park. His car was parked on one side of the ground floor, in the permit area.

With the hopeful selling of his house at some point, he anticipated a move from his city centre office to a more rural location over the next few years. *That's if I keep my registration,* he thought, laughing sarcastically. The parking costs and rents in the city had exploded and were unlikely to ever return to reasonable rates. Small businesses were increasingly being priced out and Nate had to consider this along with any possible long commute as part of a relocation plan. However, for now, it wasn't even on his radar — getting through the next few weeks unscathed from Melody Dartford, was his priority.

Walking along the footpath, he entered the ground floor of the multistorey car park. He stopped for a moment to find his car keys that weren't in his jacket pocket. Tapping his chino trousers, he located them. Moving towards his white Audi, he clicked his keys, opened the boot and placed his laptop and bag inside, before getting in his car.

Leaving the car park, there was a car in front of him messing around with the card slot to raise the barrier. Nate felt impatient and was about to exit his car and ask if he could help when the orange plastic arm slowly rose like a drawbridge and the car left. He drove up to the barrier and got through, his permit on their recognition system. The road outside of the multistorey was busy; rush hour city centre traffic in full force. He was used to it, but it was another reason for an eventual office move — to reduce the commute time.

Arriving home forty-five minutes later, Nate was happy to not have a house viewing that evening, although he did have to tidy a little for a viewing tomorrow that the estate agent had arranged. Taking off his jacket and boots, he dumped his bags at the bottom of the stairs and walked straight into the kitchen, feeling the cool porcelain tiles through his thin socks.

Opening his American-style fridge, he grabbed a bottle of San Miguel, took a bottle opener from one of the kitchen drawers and flipped off the lid, leaving it on the countertop. Gulping quickly, he let out a satisfied sigh after he swallowed that first mouthful of cold, fizzing, malty hops. He closed his eyes for a moment, holding the chilled beer as the coolness of the floor tiles soothed him from his feet up and the refreshing beer from his mouth down.

Walking to the lounge, Nate plonked down on his black L-shaped sofa, feet up, and drank some more of his beer. Placing his head back against the cushion, he closed his eyes for a second. It was time to get back on the dating site, take his mind off Melody, and arrange some fun for the weekend.

Chapter 30: Melody

Melody sat waiting in her vehicle on the ground floor of the car park. She glanced at her watch again. It had been over twenty minutes that she had been staring at the entrance looking for Nate. *Perhaps there was another entrance, or he wasn't parked here after all.* She slammed her hands against her steering wheel and let out a groan. As she ran through the options of bumping into him again after her next session, she felt the clawing of despair inside her. She couldn't lose control, couldn't lose him. Not now that she knew he wasn't just a quick kiss on a night out. Melody was in love with Nate. They were meant to be together: her happy-ever-after.

Moving a little in her seat, she sighed and then saw him, walking next to the entrance and exit barriers. Clapping her hands together, she watched him pause for a moment, ducking down slightly, like a soldier in a trench — knowing he wouldn't see her, but just in case. Nate began walking again and she followed him with her eyes, stretching up a little as he snuck out of view. She spotted him again. The boot of his white car was open, and he placed his belongings inside before shutting it and disappearing around to the driver's side.

Starting her engine, she left the lights off. The car park was busy and noisy enough for him not to hear or notice an engine starting, but the lights would illuminate her and gain attention. She would wait until she saw him at the exit barrier before following. A thunderbolt of excitement shot through her, and she bit her lip. Her plan was devious but necessary as she needed more leverage.

Following Nate home and finding out where he lived meant she could use that knowledge, if required. Aware he lived somewhere in Stratford — he had mentioned it when referring to the spin-a-thon — Melody hoped she would not lose sight of his car in the stop start traffic of the city centre and its outskirts.

A white car pulled up to the barrier, behind a blue one, which was taking its time to get through. She was thankful for the delay, able to see that it was him driving the white Audi. Another car got in line behind his, so Melody crept forward, just as Nate's eyeline would make looking as far back to her difficult. She turned her car lights on and manoeuvred around behind the red car separating hers and his. He pulled away and Melody willed the car in front to go through the barrier smoothly.

It did and she followed, despite her hand shaking as she placed the card into the slot on the side of the barrier, impatiently waiting for the rising of the barricade. It jerked up and she shot out of the car park and slipped straight onto the road that would lead out of the city centre. She saw Nate's car, two in front, the red car still behind him. The traffic lights were on stop, so Melody moved in her seat, squinting her eyes to try to get some of his car registration. She saw a YR at the start, but nothing more. Still useful in case she lost him and had to search for his car on this journey or a future one.

The lights switched to green and the traffic moved. Her skin sweaty, Melody was anxious to get through the lights behind him before they flashed to red again. She was tailgating the red car. A shitty move, she knew, and one that she had been on the end of many times with impatient drivers. *Desperate measures,* she thought to herself as her knees bounced. Melody got through the lights and continued following. Thankfully, he couldn't drive fast in the congested city centre. Eventually, they reached the motorway. He switched lanes towards the second slip road and she tailed, hanging back.

Another set of traffic lights stopped them just off the slip road. Groups of young people waited at the crossing, laughing and joking. The lights changed to green and traffic began churning along again. Nate kept in view, but now there were a few cars separating them. He joined the motorway at the next junction. Melody shadowed, before he took the first exit and she copied.

He continued down a high street, filled with cafés, bars, boutiques, and charity shops. She slowed down, only one car separating their vehicles. Easing off the accelerator, she kept a safe distance in her undercover operation. Her palms were sweaty as she gripped the steering wheel like she was protecting a bar of gold. A car at the next junction prevented her following immediately and she cursed at it. Then able to manoeuvre, she turned left and caught sight of Nate's white vehicle. It pulled into a parking bay, indicating to Melody that this must be his street. She hung back, putting her hazard lights on and hoping few cars would pass as she was causing a temporary blockage in the terraced street, that had a line of vehicles parked on each side.

Finger to her mouth and her breathing shallow, she observed him get out of his car, walk to his boot and, after collecting his bags, click his central locking. Her lips dry, she rubbed her tongue over them watching him rush across the road and down the footpath, past a few houses, oblivious to the covert operation. He travelled up a short path to a dark front door that he opened before he walked in, shutting it behind. Melody let out the breath she had been holding, and a smile crept across her face. Result!

She sniggered to herself. Perhaps she could become a private investigator and tell Crawford's Insurance to fuck right off? She was determined and resourceful and felt a buzz from discovering where he lived and feeling that little bit closer to him. But it was better than that, there was a *For Sale* board in his front garden. Melody began driving down the terraced street slowly, stopping just past Nate's car to take a photograph on her phone of his car registration, before continuing on her way. The houses were stunning, all uniform in presentation with the odd difference of a tree in a garden, paved areas, different coloured doors, and one that stood out more than others as it was on the sales market. Luckily for her, that was Nate Lundie's house.

Driving home, Melody felt the cloud of despair dissipate slightly. Knowing where Nate lived gave her options. His house looked enormous, and she knew he didn't have a girlfriend. He'd confirmed that in the park on Monday. He had also mentioned not having kids in conversation during their therapy sessions, meaning he must live there alone.

I bet he gets really lonely, she thought to herself. He wouldn't be lonely for long; he would have her. Driving towards home, her body warmed up with the love she felt for him. Her blood was like the sweetest hot chocolate being pumped into her heart as she thought about how life would be as Nate's girlfriend, living in a big house with him. She would cook for him, baking cakes and bread from scratch. And she would have her own dressing room, filled with white, antique-style furniture including a tasteful dressing table and baby pink stool. She could give up the job she hated and re-train. Eventually, she would become a mother to Nate's babies and the house would be filled with their gorgeous family.

She smiled to herself, feeling a rush of excitement. An angry toot snapped her out of her fantasy, and Melody jerked. Stationary at traffic lights, they had changed to green, with her vehicle remaining at a standstill. She looked in her rear-view mirror to a man holding up his hands and shaking his head. *Prick,* she thought as she put a hand up and accelerated.

She desperately wanted to share her news with Grace, but it didn't sound good in reality — Melody following her therapist home. She could rationalise why completely in her own mind, but explaining it to Grace may be harder. Instead, she would just say that he was slightly flirtatious during the session and she knew he fancied her, but she behaved and perhaps that would make him want her more. It would keep things open for when she won him around, without making him sound like an unfeeling bastard. She didn't want her closest friend to think badly of him, not since her intention was for them to be in a relationship. And with Nate being part of Melody's life, he would be part of Grace's life, too.

'So, you're okay-ish?' Grace said over a cup of tea as Melody updated her.

Wrapping a piece of brown hair around a finger, she leant against the grey countertop in their kitchen. 'Yeah, I feel there's a chance. I think as soon as I'm signed off as a client, we can chat and see what happens. Maybe have a date, you know. Something normal.'

Grace nodded, picking up a ginger nut biscuit and dunking it in her tea. Melody knew she wasn't convinced, but she didn't want to get into it.

'Well, I love you, always. Regardless of men and jobs, and

you stealing my cereal.' She poked her friend's upper arm in jest and winked.

Melody laughed and tilted her head. 'I love you, too. Even though you snore louder than any other human or animal I've known!'

Now it was Grace's turn to laugh. 'Let's have some dinner, eh? How about cereal and toast?'

They sat on their sofa and ate Grace's cereal, followed by slices of toast, covered in peanut butter as they watched a trashy reality show. Melody was going to see her dad tomorrow but she was also going to Fit for Life, her membership had been processed early that week and with Nate crammed on all the shelves in her mind, the gym was another opportunity to potentially see him.

Matthew would also be pleased about her joining a gym for her health and well-being, given he was beginning to enjoy his exercise and socialising. Although Melody wasn't sure to what extent darts provided exercise, except for a few steps to the bar. Grace also suggested a Pilates class on Sunday morning that they could try together.

After a quick induction at the gym the next day, Melody went to her dad's. He'd made sausage and mashed potato, smothered in gravy. Hungry from the gym, she tucked in.

'Dad, your cooking is getting better all the time.' She smiled a sad smile, acknowledging that Matthew's cooking had only improved because Zoe couldn't cook for him.

He nodded in agreement as he swallowed a mouthful of buttery mash. 'You've looked pale the last few times I've seen you, love. Are you getting enough sleep?' Matthew put his cutlery down on the orange placemat and focused on Melody across the wooden dining table.

Melody sipped some juice, desperately wanting to tell her dad that no, she wasn't sleeping and, in fact, everything was awful. She feigned a smile. 'Yeah, I'm fine, Dad.'

His warm eyes remained on her. 'You're not. I know my girl.'

She nodded. 'I'm pale cos it's freezing, Dad, and even though I have your dark hair, I got Mum's pale skin!' She let out a laugh, aimed at convincing her dad everything was okay.

He swallowed. 'You'd tell me, wouldn't you, if you were struggling?'

Melody squeezed his hand. 'Of course I would, Dad, but I'm fine. Now what's for pud?'

Matthew grinned and got up, reaching for her empty plate and stacking it on his. 'Go in the lounge and I will bring through some of Auntie Glynis' cake.'

She followed his instructions, feeling safe that she had dodged an interrogation. After zesty lemon cake with vanilla frosting, and an hour of listening to the news and putting the world to rights, Melody got ready to leave.

'Has Grace finished university for Christmas now?' Matthew asked as she put her trainers on in the hallway.

'Yeah, she's all done. She's worked so hard.'

'Bring her round on Tuesday for tea. I'll get us all a takea-way.' Matthew kissed his daughter on the cheek.

'Great, yeah, she'd love that. I'll check she's not working and we'll be round at the usual time.'

Matthew nodded. Melody hugged him then he watched her walked down the drive, get into her car, remaining, as usual, at the front door until she was out of sight.

That night, she went to bed feeling less anxious than the previous nights. Opening her bedside cabinet for hand cream,

Melody saw her medication, lying in its blister pack. She took the strip of tablets out and turned it over in her hands. She had stopped taking her prescription dose of anti-depressants. It wasn't something she had discussed with her GP, not wanting to bother him and actually, getting an appointment was harder than getting a part in a Hollywood film these days. Plus, Melody knew her body and her mind more than anyone else and the therapy had helped, well, until the kiss.

She had grown as a person; Nate had even said so. And Grace, her mum and dad knew she was doing okay, managing. So, why would she want to remain on the tablets that she didn't need, even after a shitty week? It proved she could manage, didn't it? Her last session with Nate would be the ultimate test.

Melody had a plan, she just had to be brave enough to execute it. And after tonight, she had a plan B. If things didn't work out the way they played on a reel in her head next Thursday with Nate, she would jump to the next level to show him she loved him. To prove to him that they were meant to be together. And for that, she needed to ring the estate agent.

Chapter 31: Nate

Despite his best efforts, Nate hadn't been able to secure a date that weekend but had been mildly entertained by message exchanges with some women who held a little potential. Instead, the viewing of the house on Friday night felt promising and he had visited Julie and Brian on Saturday evening. On Sunday morning, he headed to his regular spinning class, needing the surge of energy that exercise always provided him with.

He hoped Anita might be there. To possibly catch some conversation with her, he travelled to the gym earlier, doing some stretches and parking his backside on his usual bike as he waited for the class to start. As he cycled gently, conserving energy for the brutality of his forty-five-minute regime, he scrolled through his dating app to see if anyone new had joined. It was addictive, even if it didn't give him the buzz he craved.

Bodies walking past the spin room glass doors kept catching Nate's eyes, and he looked up intermittently. Taking a sip from his water bottle, he glanced out into the gym. He coughed, almost choking on his water as some spilt down his leg. Wiping his mouth, he observed Melody sauntering past with Grace, both clutching a mat.

Shit! He had forgotten they had joined the gym on the day of the spin-a-thon. They hadn't seen him in the spin room, but of course, she knew he was a regular at the gym. Nate ran a hand through his hair. This could become very awkward. Two minutes later, the instructor burst through the door, forcing him out of his Melody mania and back to reality with an influx of chatter.

Anita didn't turn up for the spinning class and Nate snuck straight out after the session had finished, knowing Pilates was an hour and that Melody and Grace would still be in the hall. Despite his urgency to leave unnoticed, he was curious to see her, after capturing a glimpse of her in tight gym leggings and a vest that hugged her ample breasts. Scolding himself for letting his dirty mind go there, he rushed out of the gym and to his car, driving home to the calmness of his sanctuary.

Monday morning arrived and Nate was grateful he had a busy week at work, which included his last session with Melody. He was relieved. *After Thursday, she will be the one who got away. Or more like I'm the one who escaped,* he thought to himself, laughing aloud but still with a shudder. If he saw her at the gym, he could manage that. Nate wouldn't be rude. He would just try to avoid her, for both their sakes.

Plus, last night, he had spent some time looking for houses outside of the city, in more rural locations. There was a lot of choice, with homes and decent-sized gardens or land in quiet towns or villages, with the tranquillity you see in a magazine. It gave him a boost, knowing there was a plan for him in a new place, not too far from his connections and family. With viewings booked in from the estate agent that week, Nate felt a move could be sooner than he had expected.

Once he moved location, he'd change gyms. Despite having made friends and routine at Fit for Life, a relocation would mean too far to travel. He would meet new people, make new friends, and exercise local to wherever he moved to. It meant that regarding Melody, any discomfort that felt like running in shorts two sizes too small, would be temporary. She would get the message, eventually, and it was for the best — for them both.

Nate had avoided going to the park at lunchtime for over a week. It helped that the weather was rubbish. However, he missed the fresh air. Even the wet, cold fresh air. As the week went on, he decided to go to St Pancras Gardens on Wednesday lunchtime. The early December air was biting but after putting on his winter coat, gloves, and a beany hat, he ventured out to the park following a hard session with a child-neglect survivor.

As he approached, he tentatively walked into the green lushness and strolled in the opposite direction of the bench area he had sat on with Melody those two times. Luckily, she was nowhere to be seen and Nate could stretch his legs for half an hour before returning, refreshed, to his office. Today was an early finish for a viewing of the house that evening, which he hoped would distract him from thinking about the last therapy session with her the following afternoon.

Chapter 32: Matthew

Matthew was pleased when his daughter mentioned therapy. Although he had faith in their family doctor, he knew she would wait a long time for specialist support. He could see her coming undone, like he had for what felt like years in a cycling pattern. Each day, noticing his child trying to walk through setting concrete — seldom a crack of flexibility in the struggle. Then, when his precious daughter split up with Brandon, well, it was another issue that dissolved her stability.

Of course, he would pay for her therapy. Zoe had offered, but Matthew insisted. Zoe liked to throw money at things, paying most of Melody's rent. It was her plaster, her stitches to try to fix everything and everyone who was wounded. Although it helped on a practical level, Matthew had a deeper concern for his child's well-being and he wanted to offer her that support through the therapy.

After all, he didn't get the chance with Felix; who took his own life with no warning signs — or perhaps they just didn't see them and it haunted him daily, threatening to blind him with guilt. He'd pay ten times over, with money and his life, if he could go back in time. But he couldn't and therefore, he had to do what he could to help his daughter.

Neither Zoe nor he could survive if she declined again. Estranged but still connected by the shackles of loss, guilt, regret, and the crippling weight of protecting the only living child they had. Standing in the kitchen, he rubbed his mouth as tears gathered in his eyes. He closed them and two tiny water pockets trickled down his cheeks as he thought about the past. His son, their loss, but also the dissolving of Melody all those years ago — those horrendous nine months that still cursed them.

Matthew blamed himself, even over eight years later. It had to be his fault. How could he have not realised his baby was struggling? His own child, walking on the thinnest tightrope of sanity. Until she slipped, fell, crashed to the ground, and almost died. At the time of the incident eight years ago, Matthew had refused to believe the possibility suggested by the psychiatrist and police that, when starting the fire, Melody may have wanted not only to die herself but for her family to die with her. It was incomprehensible.

Placing his hands on the kitchen countertop, Mathew took two deep breaths and tried to steady himself. The past was a dark, haunting place that robbed him of his own sanity, as well as his daughters. He wondered, far too often, if her illness had planted a seed of despair in her older brother, that grew. A toxic growth, seeping poison into Felix's mind and soul, until he couldn't take anymore. Felix had adored his sibling. The irritating younger sister until she got to the age where he wanted to protect her from harm and look out for her. Matthew pulled his hand over his mouth and walked to the sink, lifting a clean glass from the draining board and filling it with water. He gulped and gasped as if he was submerged in the liquid he was consuming.

Melody may have been an excellent actor as a teenager, able to dupe her parents, tell white lies, deceive them. But after the incident, Matthew made it his life's mission to study his daughter and know her every reaction. An almost telepathy in order to protect her. Vowing that never again would she feel the crushing vice of despair. He had developed a mental encyclopaedia of his daughter — lessons learnt about her over the years. And the Melody manual he had created, now indicated she was struggling again.

The family had worked hard to help her get well, and she had, on the whole. Everyone has a wobble now and then. But then Felix died without warning, and Melody went numb, mute, cold. Or perhaps her alarm bell was ringing to ears that couldn't hear. Tilting his head back he said an almost inaudible, 'Sorry.' An apology to both of his children in case his focus on his daughter for the six years before Felix died may have led to him not seeing his firstborn suffering.

Melody had blocked out her emotions. Matthew and Zoe knew it was to not worry them and because they, too, were crippled with an indescribable pain. Then Zoe left and Melody almost changed roles, protecting her father; looking after him. Shamedly, Matthew let her. Cut open and bleeding to death from the loss of his son, then his marriage, and he let his daughter care for him — another guilt he carried.

Knowing that a therapist would help her process the loss of her brother in a safe place, where she didn't have to think about her dad, Matthew was supporting the sessions. He also knew they would expose the past, but Melody needed this exhumation. And now, added to the issues, was a recent break-up. Matthew had high hopes for the therapy sessions and it seemed in those critical weeks, they were making a noticeable difference.

She'd found her own help this time and that was encouraging, empowering. The therapist required six sessions paid in full. Matthew had reassured his daughter that she could have as many sessions as she needed. Those first few weeks after her initial therapy appointments, Matthew felt like he had her back. The sun in his daughter was unmasked, shining through her smile. Her laugh was lighter, her eyes showing softness instead of a seriousness not meant for a person in their twenties. She had returned a little — not quite the girl who was fifteen before life changed forever. Even so, his Melly was knocking down the walls that encased her.

He tapped a cup off the kitchen countertop as the kettle boiled. A cyclone of thoughts changing direction. Perhaps he was overreacting. Shaking his head, he rubbed his lips. No, something was wrong; his daughter was slowly freezing again. Matthew knew her like she didn't even know herself. Pouring water onto his tea bag, he glazed over until the scalding liquid pooled on the bench.

'Shit,' he said, grabbing the dishcloth and soaking up the water. No, he wasn't overreacting. He recalled his daughter showing him the therapist's business card when first mentioning it as a possibility. A sleek design with a small image of a brain. Linton Therapy or something like that. He couldn't quite remember but knew it was in King's Cross area and the therapist was male. Hopefully, the professional would help his daughter to work through her obstacles.

Moving through to the lounge and sitting on the sage green sofa in the home he had shared with his family before destruction moved in, he leant over and placed his cup on the G-Plan side table. Pressing his teeth together, he sucked in air. His knowledge, the parental connection, made Matthew know all was not right with Melody for the last two weeks. He was working through her routine, patterns, links, activities, and people she came in contact with to explore any triggers.

Last Friday, he had deliberately suggested Grace came along for dinner the following Tuesday, using her finishing the university term as an excuse for a catch up. His aim was to speak to Grace alone and ask how Melody had been. He needed answers and knew if there was a problem, Grace would struggle to hide it.

Maybe the therapy was bringing things up. Things she was finding difficult. His instinct told him it was something more serious. He had learnt to read the book of Melody word for word over the last eight years and something was wrong. A page had a rip in it, a scribble, causing a mess on the usually legible words. And Matthew was determined to find out what it was.

It was Tuesday and Matthew had planned to speak with Grace alone when she and Melody visited that evening. They arrived, full of the bounce that he always wanted to see as a permanent demeanour for his daughter. He hugged them both as they entered the hallway before gesturing them in as he congratulated Grace on finishing the university term.

'Only six more months to go, Grace, then it's graduation!' He clapped his hands.

Grace nodded. 'Yeah, I've just got to pass first.' She laughed as she slid her shoes off.

They walked into the lounge — the wood-burning fire providing welcoming warmth. Sitting on the sofa, Matthew sat on the matching green armchair and caught Grace glance at the photo of Zoe, Felix, and Melody on the side table. She turned her eyes to Matthew, catching his gaze and gave a weak smile of sadness and pity.

'So, what do you fancy eating?' Matthew looked at his iPad in his hand, scrolling on Just Eats. 'Your choice, Grace.'

'Pizza?' Grace said with a shrug.

'Oooh yeah. Perfect!' said Melody, smacking her lips together impersonating eating.

Matthew scrolled for a second, then passed the iPad to them. 'There you go, pick what you want and then, Melly, you can put the kettle on.'

Melody rolled her eyes playfully. 'That's okay, as I already know what I want. Chilli chicken with extra sweetcorn. Mmmmm.' She rubbed her stomach as she rose from the sofa before walking to the kitchen, closing the lounge door to keep the heat in.

It was the opportunity Matthew needed to chat with Grace. Rising from the armchair, he perched on the end of the sofa where Grace sat.

'Grace, I just want to quickly ask, while she's busy…' he glanced to the closed door, separating the kitchen and lounge. He could faintly hear his daughter opening cupboards and the chinking of cups. Looking at him with wide eyes, he felt she already knew what he was going to say.

'I'm worried about Melly. I know when things aren't right. Despite all the female intuition lark, I know my daughter in a way even her mother doesn't know her.' Matthew was aware he sounded desperate. He was desperate and he felt a crescendo of emotion just thinking about her struggling. Life was cruel and Melody, like everyone else, wasn't immune from the harsh bastard life could be — her twenty-four years had already evidenced that.

In many ways, his daughter was formidable. Still managing after a traumatic adolescence, a psychiatric hospital stay, the devastating loss of her brother, and then her parents splitting up. She'd kept going, never gave up; like a flower growing in concrete. But while he still had blood in his veins and his heart beat, he would forever protect her — something he couldn't do with Felix. And Matthew simply could not change the fact that worry pumped through his body with his blood.

Grace pressed her lips together and nodded. 'I'm a bit worried about her, too. I'll call you to talk properly tomorrow on my break at work. What time do you finish?'

'I leave work about quarter-past five, so preferably any time between then and half-seven, when I play darts. But I can still answer if needed.' Matthew spoke quickly, conscious time was running out before Melody would return.

Nodding, Grace smiled at him. 'I'll ring around six, on my break and I'm certain everything will be okay.'

Matthew squeezed her hand and, thanking her, went to help his daughter bring the drinks through. A minute later, they returned.

'Your dad tells me he's playing darts again?' Grace said to Melody, as she handed her a cup of tea.

'Yeah, they'd missed you. Hadn't they, Dad?'

Matthew nodded. 'It's good to be back. Although they sink more beers than a group on a stag weekend!' He chuckled then took a sip of his coffee. 'And it's good you're doing some exercise, Melly. Good for the endorphins and all that.' He tapped a finger on the side of his head.

She smiled, but Matthew knew that smile — the one of pretence, and worry screamed inside of him once again.

His mobile rang just as he placed his plate in the dishwasher. Rushing to the lounge, he picked up his phone from the arm of the sofa and answered the call from Grace.

'Hi, Matthew, you okay to chat?'

'Yeah. Hi, Grace, how are you?' He could hear seagulls squawking in the background.

'I'm good, ta. Thanks again for last night.'

'You're welcome. You're part of the family. So, about Melly. Like I said, I'm concerned. The last few weeks. I can tell, Grace. Something's not right.' He balanced on the edge of the sofa, placing his free hand on his forehead as his knees gently bounced. 'She's looking pale, tired, like thoughts are heavy on her mind and well…' He sighed.

'I know, you're right. Erm, there's someone she likes, a guy. I think it's just a bit complicated.'

Matthew straightened his back. 'Is it Brandon? Are they getting back together?'

'No, no, it's not him. I personally don't think it's going to go anywhere. It can't really. But you know Melody, she falls hard.'

He felt his temperature rising. 'Is he married?' He stood and began pacing his lounge.

'No, I just think perhaps she's more interested than him and, well, I think it will fizzle out soon and she'll be fine. Don't worry. I'll keep an eye on her.'

Don't worry. That was like saying, 'Don't breathe,' to Matthew.

He swallowed. 'Who is it?'

Grace was silent for a moment.

'Grace?'

'I'm still here, sorry. Erm, I think he works with her or something. Listen, Matthew, don't worry and if she appears to be struggling, I'll ring you, okay?'

Matthew puffed out air. He knew something was up. If some bastard hurts her… 'Alright, thanks, Grace. Please keep me updated. You're being a good friend, looking out for her.'

They said goodbye and Matthew tapped his mobile to his chin. This bloke better not upset his daughter. She was still stinging from her breakup with Brandon. Matthew was sure of that. His hands were restrained for now. He just had to monitor and, as Grace said, she would let him know of any concerns. She was a good friend and friendship includes looking out for one another, protecting one another. Matthew could rely on Grace, couldn't he?

Chapter 33: Melody

Despite a tense few days, Melody had enjoyed attending Fit for Life, doing a circuit class for beginners and using the cardio machines. During one visit, she had felt dizzy and wasn't sure if it was dehydration or a side effect of stopping her anti-depressants. She had yet to see Nate at the gym, but knew it was only a matter of time and she could find out his patterns if needed.

Just like she had discovered where he lived and had arranged a viewing of his house that Friday after work. Ringing the estate agent on Monday, Melody gave a false name and said she would view alone. When she hung up on the call, she had almost convinced herself of her fake persona and felt a cantering of excitement, holding her mobile phone to her chest.

It would be a shock for Nate, her turning up at his front door. A surprise that may make him apprehensive at first. But she would convince him to let her in, to talk, and then she would seduce him in his home — where he was in his own environment and not bound by the restraints of his therapist title. He could relax, the power of authority dissolved. Nate could follow his true feelings and give in to the lust. Smiling to herself, she felt positive for the rest of the day, knowing that week would be the week they progressed their relationship and ditched the therapist-client one.

On Tuesday night, Melody and Grace had gone to Matthew's for dinner. Grace loved Matthew and after coming to

London to study, leaving her own family in Nottingham, she enjoyed the cockney father figure he provided now and then. It wasn't the same for them after Felix died, and further strained when Zoe left, but the pair got on and Melody was pleased Grace was an extension to her family.

It was cosy at her dad's, with the fire blasting and after a meal of pizza, followed by warm chocolate brownies with ice cream, and lots of chat, it was time to go.

'That was lovely, thanks, Matthew,' Grace said as they got ready to leave.

'You're welcome, and well done on working so hard.'

She jolted, for a split-second wondering if that was a dig by her father given Melody hadn't studied further than GCSEs, which she didn't even obtain at school. Placing her hand on the bannister to steady herself, she put on her trainers, then gave her dad a hug and said goodbye.

The pair walked up the garden path and got into Melody's car, driving off as Matthew remained at the door, waving until out of sight. Grace turned up the radio. 'Sugar' by Maroon 5 came on and the pair began singing the words. And as Melody sang along, she felt it was a sign and she could have been singing those exact words about Nate.

It was Thursday, the day of Melody's last therapy appointment. She had hoped that he would provide more sessions, feeling she still needed them, or at least needed to see him — replacing her anti-depressants with the medication that was Nate Lundie. However, he had made it clear last week that today's session would be the last and instead, she would supposedly have a catalogue of worksheets and information for her toolkit to help keep her well and manage a crisis in the future. She made a pffft noise at the thought and then grinned; he wouldn't get away that easy.

Taking a day's annual leave from work, Melody had a little lie-in that was cut short by stomach cramps, another possible impact of her medication withdrawal, but she was also nervous about the prospect of the session with Nate. He had to see, realise they were each other's destiny. It was crucial it went to plan, and much of that was annoyingly out of her control.

That morning, she tried to relax at home. Grace gave her some emotional support along with the simple message that if it wasn't meant to be, some other lucky man would meet her and become her boyfriend — joking at the end that Nate Lundie wasn't all that. Melody didn't appreciate it and brushed off the comments, changing the subject. She knew it was complicated. That hers and Nate's relationship was not top of the list of conformity. But you couldn't help who you fell for, and Melody deserved happiness. She deserved happiness with him, and Grace would have to get used to it.

Grace left for work mid-morning, to Melody's relief. She made a cup of tea and began painting her nails a vibrant pink shade as she sang along to music. The aim for her look today was mature and attractive, rather than sultry. As her nails dried, she began to daydream about her future with Nate — her own happy-ever-after on reel in her mind. Smiling, she stared at his photo on her phone. Kissing her fingertips, she placed them on the image of his mouth. Sighing, she thought of all the places they would visit together, from restaurants to the theatre. To weekends away and holidays abroad.

Nate had an image of the Eiffel Tower in a frame on the wall of his office. Along with the many others, Melody had stared at them all during her sessions. The iconic tower in the picture, creating a magical, romantic scene. There was a slogan along the bottom about strength, love, and light. Tilting her head, she imagined the two, walking hand in hand along the River Seine, the magnificent structure in the background. One of the most romantic places on the planet. She hugged herself momentarily before scowling in case her nails were still damp. Pulling her hands back, she blew on her fingernails and placed her palms on her lap to daydream a little longer.

Melody's clothes had been chosen. A long-sleeved floral midi dress with calf-length brown boots that had a small heel. Luckily, it wasn't raining outside, so she would chance wearing her suede brown biker-style jacket. More autumnal than winter wear, but she had lust and excitement heating her. The dress, with its v-neckline, was perfect to show enough flesh to hopefully arouse his desire. With her hair and nails already done, she would have a late lunch, then spend an hour or so making sure she looked her best before travelling to King's Cross for her 3:30 pm appointment — hoping her best was enough, and knowing she could convince Nate, if needed.

Chapter 34: Nate

The viewing scheduled last night for Nate's house sale hadn't turned up. He was hacked off about it and narked at the time-waster who felt it was acceptable. He had another viewing to-morrow evening and one on Saturday morning. An earlier viewer had put in an offer £25,000 under the asking price, so that was a definite decline. Hopefully, the viewings over the next few days would prove fruitful.

However, he had more pressing matters occupying his mind, namely, the last therapy session with Melody that afternoon. Nate had never spent so much time preparing for a therapy session in all the years he had been practising. Determined to get the session right, for Melody's sake and his own, he wanted to ensure that she had ample information to take away, to prevent her from making further enquiries or contact. Or, God forbid, try to book more sessions, despite him saying he couldn't. Feel-ing a thick band of tension around his head, another thought came into his mind that she could threaten him — that if he didn't provide further sessions, she would report him to the BACP. He shuddered and felt a gust of sickly heat flush through him.

'Harm min,' he said aloud, looking at all the printouts and flyers on his desk that he would put in a folder and present to her at the end of the session. Like a car salesperson giving the MOT and log book details and wishing the new buyer a good-bye, praying they never returned with issues.

Nate knew it was for the best. She was bad news, despite having the allure of a *Baywatch* babe from his adolescence. He needed the door connecting them shut, locked, and bloody boarded up. The sooner the better. Even so, within him lay that dirty desire. The urge. The fantasies about undressing her, smelling her scent, tasting her skin. Devouring her. The need to have her. He sniffed up and tilted his head back, his neck resting on the top of his armchair. Closing his eyes momentarily, he inhaled deeply.

If Nate were to be honest with himself, he would acknowledge that, like his clients, he too had a problem. Likely many problems and issues that he had run away from. He had spent part of his career trying to fix others whilst walking with his own broken bones. Masking his thoughts, behaviours, emotions, and desires, instead focusing on the other messed-up people in the area. Advocating his services and therapy where in his mind, he perhaps thought he was too masculine, too trained, too professional to deal with his own shit and, perish the thought, ask for help.

There was a switch in Nate that he could turn off, disconnect from — and at times, he wasn't sure if it was a blessing or a curse. However, when it came to sex and women, that switch often got stuck and wouldn't turn off until it was forced. His shredded marriage proved that.

Clenching his jaw, he placed his interlocked hands on his head. Turning, he faced the window and puffed out air. 'Sixty fucking minutes. That's all you have to do. Just behave,' he said aloud, pushing his glasses to his head and rubbing his eyebrows. He would go for a walk in the park, on his alternative route to avoid any possible sightings of Melody, then come back, have lunch and distract himself with admin until she arrived.

There was a knock on his office door and Nate closed his eyes, taking in three deep breaths before heading to open it. Pushing down on the handle, he pulled the door back to reveal Melody in her hypnotic, dangerous appeal. He smiled, flickers of nerves consuming him, yet he couldn't help but move his eyes down over her body. She was wearing a multi-coloured dress. Pretty, understated, still sexy, with a plunging neckline that showed the softness of her inviting chest and her youthful décolletage.

'Melody, hi. Come on in,' he said in his best holiday-rep-happy voice.

She strolled through the door, a little clink from her heels touching the wood flooring as she moved towards the sofa. Nate tingled, inhaling her scent as she passed and wished he knew what her signature scent was, unsure whether he would always look to spray it or always aim to avoid it.

'Hi, Nate,' she replied, passing him.

Her long, dark, curled hair cascaded down her back. He remembered his fingers in it on the night at Survivor Bar. Grabbing it as he frantically consumed her, lips dancing and a sexual need he hadn't experienced in so long — despite bedding women from the dating app — that made him starving for her. He poured her a glass of water, realising his hand was shaking. Coughing, he cleared his throat and tried to clear his mind of his urges.

'There you go.' He handed her the glass of water. She took it, smiled, and placed it on the table next to the sofa.

Shaking her shoulders, she slid her brown jacket off. Nate wrestled with his eyes, wanting to look away, especially as her breasts bounced.

Putting his glasses on, he took a sip of his own water and

picked up his notepad, glancing at the folder of handouts and information he had prepared for her to take home at the end of the session. He inhaled, crossing his legs at his ankles.

'So, this is our last session, Melody and I suggest after this session you put into place all the things we've discussed. All the techniques you've learnt and the processes we've gone through. I have a load of information for you to take away,' he said cheerily, trying to put a plaster over the raw graze. Taking his eyes from Melody's, he looked at the folder, then back to her. Swallowing, Nate uncrossed his legs and leant forward slightly in his chair. 'This session will be summarising, reflecting, and looking at the next steps for you.'

She nodded, staying silent as her gaze remained on him. He pushed his glasses up his nose and continued talking, asking Melody questions around mental health management, avoiding anything about intimate relationships.

'What about your father? Do you feel there has been a shift in his behaviours towards your independence and recovery?'

She explained her father had been less intense and also started to have a level of social interaction outside of work again. As Melody talked about this and her father, Nate noticed her eyes lit a little and a genuine smile travelled across her mouth. A smile of fondness and pride that her father was doing well and their relationship was improving. It made him smile momentarily. That was what recovery was all about; not just the person, but the impact on the people around them and their relationships.

'That's brilliant, Melody.' He leant back in his seat and she nodded at him. He wanted to celebrate her progress with her: hug her, kiss her, screw her. They shared a moment, looking at one another in silence and Nate's heart rate increased.

'Thank you, Nate. For everything. You've helped more than I thought a non-doctor could.'

He let out a little laugh. 'You're welcome. I'm pleased you feel positive about your well-being.'

She nodded, glanced at her lap, and then back at him. 'I do feel positive on the whole. But...' Melody bit her lip and sat forward, reducing the distance between them.

He could see more of her breasts, almost begging to be caressed. Instinctively, he licked his lips.

Her eyes widened. 'I can't...' She took a sip of her water and turned her eyeline to the office window before returning her gaze. 'I can't stop thinking about you.'

Nate rubbed the back of his neck and took a deep breath. 'Melody, I...'

'I'll not be your client anymore. We can go on a date, see what it's like?' Her voice went higher at the end of the sentence. Perhaps trying to convince, perhaps trying to contain the emotion that threatened to leak out.

Taking his glasses off, Nate leant forward and looked into her doe eyes. He wanted her there, then. To take her clothes off and expel the screaming urges inside him. He inhaled deeply, nostrils flaring and then spoke, softly but firmly. 'Melody, we can't. You're beautiful, you really are. And I am attracted to you, but it can't happen. You have to understand.'

Tears formed in her eyes and Nate felt a vice squeezing him.

'Not beautiful enough.' She pressed her lips together and turned her gaze down to the floor.

He shook his head. 'No, it's not that. It's just not right. You need someone your own age. I'm old enough to be your father and, well, it's uneth...'

'Unethical. I fucking know.'

She stood up, and he rose with her. 'Melody, c'mon.'

Standing in front of him, her body was only a foot from his. 'Tell me you don't want me.' Melody leant in quickly and kissed his neck.

Nate groaned. Her mouth felt like maple syrup trickling down his throat. She turned him on so much. He did want her, and badly. However, he just wanted her for sex, nothing more. There was no long-term in Melody, and for that reason, she wasn't worth it. He *still* wanted her, just with none of the aftermath. Moving her mouth to his, she gently bit his lip. He jerked his head back.

'Stop! We can't.' He almost shouted, his eyes on her. She stood like a scolded child. 'Sorry, this isn't right. You need to go.' He tried to remain calm.

A shift changed in her face, and her jaw stiffened. She reached for his hand and he snatched it back, shaking his head. Melody leant over the sofa, grabbing her jacket and the folder from Nate. Then she picked up her almost empty glass of water and screamed as she threw it against the wall with force, making one of the framed photos fall and smash, along with the glass. His jaw dropped and he went to speak, but she opened his office door, rushed through and slammed it so hard it shuddered in its frame — leaving Nate standing speechless.

Chapter 35: Melody

Melody was shaking with anger as she barged through the double doors into the foyer of Nate's office block. The receptionist jumped slightly in her seat as she spoke on a phone, eyes following as she stormed out of the building, propelled by the fuel of frustration. *How could he reject her again? Their sessions had finished. Their client-therapist relationship was done. Why had the bastard done it again? She'd seen him perving on her, wanting her. Then he'd pulled away from her kiss. Rejected her, again!*

She wanted to scream for the whole of London to hear. Rage threatened to bleed out from every pore in her body as she marched to the Tube, not stopping for fear her shaking legs would seize up. She needed the realisation from Nate that she *was* the one for him. Dizzy with anger, she reached King's Cross St Pancras Station and leant against the wall of the entrance as people rushed by, feeling out of breath and like she was shrinking.

In her head, it was all meant to work out differently. He was meant to see, realise that they could now have a relationship. A non-professional, intimate relationship, based on the lust and love they had growing in them like an embryo. He had ruined the moment, destroyed her fantasy, and crushed her future. It left her with only one option, and that was to go ahead with the viewing of Nate's house arranged by the estate agent, under a pseudonym. She had no choice. He had left her with no choice and it was the last card up her sleeve, or at least the last card that didn't resort to playing very dirty indeed.

Melody arrived home, grateful that Grace was at work until late. She sobbed as her entire face pulsated with pressure. Getting her mobile phone out from her handbag, she screamed and dropped it to the floor, stamping the heel of her boot into it with rage. The screensaver photo of Nate's LinkedIn profile picture distorted under the cracked screen. Leaving the phone on the floor, she headed for the shower.

Remaining under the hot water for twenty minutes, she tried to wash away the rejection and gain some soothing for the fire that scalded her insides. Then she took a bottle of Grace's sauvignon blanc wine from the fridge and went to her bedroom, drinking the tart, acidic liquid, grimacing as she swallowed — until the whole bottle was gone and her eyelids were too heavy to keep open.

Waking up on Friday morning, she groaned, turning over in her bed and smelling the foul wine scent of the empty bottle that lay a few feet from her. Her immediate thought was Nate and she let out a yelp, needing someone to fix the broken mirror of her life. She looked at her watch. It was just after 8 am and she was due at work in an hour. There was no way she could face the arsehole brigade at Crawford's Insurance.

She had almost booted rat-face Selina again earlier that week after one tut too many. Someone would get her wrath if she went to work today, which would undoubtedly result in her P45 being handed to her by dog-wet-nose Glen in his sweat-stinking office of ego. No, she would have to call in sick. But first, she needed a gallon of water to drink and some paracetamol.

Sitting up in bed, she felt a wave of nausea. Managing to not succumb to projectile vomiting, she got up and walked to her bedroom door, clutching her head and moaning. The lounge was empty, Grace still in bed after a long shift at South of Here bar. Going through to their tiny kitchen, Melody let the cold tap run as she grabbed a glass from the cupboard. Seeing it reminded her of the fact that she threw a glass at Nate's office wall and she closed her eyes, trying to wipe away the image. Gulping a full glass of water, she refilled, yawning in between. Her stomach grumbled.

She drank the second glass of water, refilling it for the third time, and moved into the lounge, plonking herself on the sofa with a groan. Her cracked-screen mobile phone lay on the coffee table. Grace must have placed it there after she assaulted it and left it for dead in the hallway. Putting her head back, she grabbed the fleece blanket draped over the armrest and covered her face with it. She wanted to sob and scream, and she really wanted a hug from her mum. Popping two paracetamols, she hoped they would at least end the Mardi-Gras-level drumming going on in her head. Her stomach cramped, and she placed an arm across it and groaned again. Picking up her phone, she tapped the cracked screen and rang reception at Crawford's.

'Crawford's Insurance, Joanne speaking. How may I help?'

Melody didn't bother with a greeting. 'Joanne, it's Melody Dartford. I won't be in today; I've got the worst diarrhoea. I've been on the toilet all night.'

Joanne cleared her throat. 'Oh dear, sorry to hear that. Get well soon and have plenty of fluids. I'll let your team leader know.'

'Thanks. Bye.' Melody hung up quickly.

Saying you had the shits always worked. Either that or periods. People didn't want to get into the details of it as it embarrassed them, so using either was a good lie to tell that would avoid further probing. Dropping her phone onto the rug, she put her legs up on the sofa and lifted one of the fluffy cushions, leaning her head against it before she closed her eyes and waited for the paracetamol to kick in.

Melody was awoken two hours later by Grace coming into the lounge. 'Oh, not at work?' she asked as Melody stirred.

Stretching her arms over the side of the sofa, she shook her head. 'Phoned in sick.'

'What's up? You alright?' Grace perched on a tiny patch of sofa not occupied by Melody.

Nodding, she pulled herself up, creating space for Grace. Clutching the fleece close to her neck, she began to cry. Not expecting it, Grace leant over and tapped Melody's leg.

'Oh, Melody, c'mon. What's up?' she soothed, head tilted.

'He rejected me again, Grace. The bastard led me on and stamped on me again. He doesn't give a shit.' Melody buried her face in the fleece and sobbed.

Moving up the sofa, Grace put her arms around her friend and shhh'd her comfortingly. 'Oh, hun, I'm so sorry.' She stroked Melody's hair and the blanket dropped from her face.

'Why is he being such a bastard? I know he wants me and he had a chance yesterday. Our sessions have finished. He's a massive headfuck and a cruel tease.' She clenched her fists.

Brow furrowed as she nodded, Grace held her hand. 'I know. He's messed you around. I think he's wanted to be with you at first perhaps, but can't. Cos of his job and that. I know it hurts, but you can't have this.' She rubbed her friend's arm over the blanket. 'He doesn't deserve you and I don't think he'll change his mind.'

Melody bit back rising anger and upset. Grace wasn't helping by being so blunt and negative. Nate *did want her*. She just had to convince him it was safe to do so. He wouldn't get into trouble, as she was no longer his client. She felt rejected by him and the dismissal by her closest friend stung like a wasp attack.

Holding a hand to her chest, she spoke. 'He's just frightened. I know he feels it, Grace. I'm going to his tonight to talk to him away from his office.'

Grace straightened her back. 'How do you know where he lives?'

Melody rubbed her chin, then wiped her eyes on the fleece blanket. She giggled slightly. 'It sounds mad, but I followed him home one night. He lives in Stratford.' She picked a corner of the blanket, averting her gaze from Grace. 'I just had to know where he lived. And well, his house is on the market, so I've arranged...'

Shaking her head, Grace stood up. 'Melody, you can't do that. You shouldn't have followed him.'

Melody put a hand to her messy bun of hair. 'Calm down, it's not like I was stalking him or anything.' She puffed out air and ran her tongue over her top teeth.

'It's out of order, and he's made it clear he doesn't want a relationship. You can't follow someone and turn up at their home. Plus, he's likely gonna be angry.' She tutted. 'I know I would be!'

Melody felt rage taking off from the starting blocks, whizzing around the racetrack of her body. She clamped her jaw together and breathed through her nose as Grace stared at her, eyes wide and eyebrows raised. 'Grace, that's not fucking helping. You don't know him — what he's like with me. What *we've* got.'

Rubbing a hand over her mouth and chin, Grace perched back down on the sofa, still shaking her head. 'This is insane. You have to stop and just forget him.'

The furnace in Melody ignited. *Insane? Grace didn't know what the hell insane felt like.* 'It's none of your business and if you can't be supportive, then I'd rather you kept your nasty opinions to yourself,' she sneered before looking away from Grace.

'Nasty opinions? You're deluded, and this is no good for you. Your dad, he's worried.' She lifted her hand to move to Melody, in an attempt to reassure her.

Instead, Melody flipped, jumping off the sofa. 'How the hell do you know how my dad feels? Have you been talking about me behind my back?' she shouted, waving her hands in the air.

'No, no. He just asked if you're okay. He cares, Melody. I care.' Grace's eyes softened, but she stood up, giving distance between them.

'If you care, you'd let me be. I know what I'm doing. So just leave me the fuck alone!'

Melody stormed into her bedroom and slammed the door, seething with Grace and her dad and wishing she could just run into the arms of Nate.

After not speaking to Grace for the rest of the morning, Melody heard the flat door shut. Pleased her flatmate had left for work, she went to the kitchen. The viewing of Nate's house was at 5:30 pm and she would have to sort herself out before then. Looking like she had been auditioning for *The Walking Dead* certainly would not lure him into surrendering to his lust. Sitting down with some toast, five minutes later, she began going over her plan for the viewing again. Her outfit was sorted. She bit into the thick bread smothered in butter and kept her teeth still for a moment, using all her concentration to predict his response.

A beep from her mobile phone jump-started her out of her daydream. Chewing on her toast, she saw through the cracked screen it was a text message from her dad. Rolling her eyes, she couldn't be bothered with his crap, especially as she suspected her dad had been gossiping about her with Grace. She wanted to give him a piece of her mind, but now wasn't the time and it would only lead to a barrage of concern splattered on top of her. Instead, she replied to his message and said she would see him tomorrow. Switching her phone to silent, she placed it on the coffee table, Nate's cracked image face down.

It was soon almost 4:45 pm and time for her to leave for Nate's. She wanted to leave early, to account for the traffic and allow time to calm her nerves. Her legs felt like slinky toys as she slipped a foot into one of her new over-the-knee boots. She had bought them from some smutty website and they felt as cheap as they looked, but Melody knew they were a turn-on for any man. Damn, they were uncomfortable. She grimaced as she tried to line the boot up to where it landed above her knee, without it digging into the flesh of her leg. Getting sweaty, she swore to herself and took it off, deciding she couldn't drive the few miles to Nate's in them and would put them on in the car on her arrival.

Looking at herself in the full-length mirror on the back of her door, she turned to see herself from different angles. Even without the smutty boots, she looked the part. Her hair was full — big, brown waves cascading down her neck, over her shoulders and resting near her breasts. Her make-up, done to perfection given her hangover. Red lips glistening in the bedroom's light, full and inviting. Smokey eyes, cat-like, intense and alluring. Then her outfit, well, that spoke for itself. Melody giggled. *Who could resist this?* Certainly not Nate.

Popping her lipstick and perfume in her handbag, she slid some ballet pump shoes on and grabbed the ridiculously long high-heeled boots. Leaving the flat, she rushed to her car, feeling a flurry of excitement through her like a kaleidoscope of butterflies taking off.

Twenty-five minutes later, Melody pulled up close to Nate's house. She was a few doors down, on the opposite side of the road, cursing about the lack of parking spaces. It was just after five, meaning ample time to put her boots on, reapply her lipstick and perfume, and compose herself.

She reached into her bag and took out a miniature bottle of some peach schnapps drink. It had been gifted to Grace in a hamper last Christmas. Neither had been desperate enough to drink from the strange, brown-tinged bottle that shared product information in another language. Not desperate enough until now. Melody shrugged. Anyway, she'd already consumed Grace's wine yesterday, so why not? She opened the little bottle, the aluminium seal coming off with the finger-nail-sized red lid. Sniffing the contents, Melody nodded. It smelt good. She tilted her head back and necked the shot.

'Pahh,' she said aloud, grimacing. Flippin' heck, that was vile. Like syrup mixed with toilet cleaner. She shook her cheeks. It would do. Take the edge off her nerves until she got inside and Nate saw her; unable to resist. She sat, going over what she hoped would happen. It was 5:22 pm, according to her mobile phone. Sliding the cover to reveal the mirror on her car visor, she touched up her lipstick before spraying perfume.

It was dark outside, so Melody rationalised it was okay to stick a bare leg out of the car to make putting the plastic fetish boots on easier than doing Twister moves in her small Fiat 500. It proved a lot easier, as did the cold air in reducing the sweatiness of her feet and therefore them sticking to the synthetic material. Boots successfully on, she got out of the driver's seat and shut her car door, clicking the central locking into place. She smoothed herself down, glanced around, and began travelling to his house. Taking deep breaths, she walked slowly, shoulders back and said to herself repeatedly, 'He will be mine. He will be mine.'

A lamp post stood outside of Nate's house illuminating the *For Sale* sign. Walking up the path, his blinds were closed in what she assumed was the lounge and the light from what must have been a nearby lamp seeped out to the gaps where the blind met the window. A little conifer tree sat proudly in a slate pot by his wooden front door. She rang the bell to the left of the door quickly, fearing that not even glugging the peach flavour alcohol toilet cleaner would keep her from running away. Ten seconds later, she heard a latch turning and he opened the door. His jaw dropped immediately, but his words were not quite the romantic, passionate welcome Melody had hoped.

'Melody. What the hell are you doing here?' He crossed his arms, blocking the doorway, a scowl on his face, as she stood three feet away, smiling.

'Surprise! I'm your half-five viewing!'

Nate shook his head. 'You can't be serious?' He ran a hand through his hair as she watched.

'Yeah, I am. So, are you going to let me in?' She lifted a leg onto the front doorstep revealing more of her footwear and a flash of flesh peeping out of her black, belted raincoat. Nate's eyes moved down to her leg and back to her face.

He raised his eyebrows and pulled a hand over his mouth and chin. 'How did you even know where I live?' His tone was neither angry nor pleased.

She put a deep red painted nail to her mouth and seductively bit it before removing it and speaking. 'Women have ways of finding stuff out. So, are you going to let me in?' She twirled a long strand of hair and pushed her shoulders back, which lifted her chest slightly.

He sighed and tilted his head back. 'We've been through this, Melody, umpteen times. And quite frankly, after your explosion in my office yesterday, and still finding shards of glass this afternoon, I don't want you in my home.'

'Does that mean I have to walk back to my car like this, then?' She unbuckled the belt on her raincoat and pulled back the chest area, revealing a red lace bra underneath that matched the colour of her lipstick. She bit her lip as Nate's eyes widened and he swallowed. He shook his head again, puffed out air, and stepped back silently, allowing her to walk into his hallway.

Immediately, she felt a whip of jealousy being inside a house that Nate had shared with another woman. She viewed the geometric-pattern tiled vestibule and beautiful, varnished wooden bannister of intricate spindles, reaching the ground and meeting a grey carpet leading up the stairs. Thoughts of Nate and his ex sent an electric shock of frustration through her. Nate popped his head out of his front door and looked up and down the street, before coming back inside and shutting the heavy wooden door. He spun around, and as he did, Melody let her raincoat drop from her body, revealing just underwear on her curvy, feminine frame.

She heard his intake of breath and smiled. 'You like?'

Nate nodded silently as he looked her up and down. Dark red lace knickers matched her bra, displaying her womanly figure. The over-the-knee boots added a sordid streak that Melody knew would immediately arouse him. She was halfway along the hallway. Nate stood, his back to the now closed front door. She beckoned him with a curling of her finger and he licked his bottom lip, obeying and walking slowly towards her. She knew this plan would work. Of course he wanted her, he always had, she just had to give him the right opportunity.

Chapter 36: Matthew

Taking an earlier lunch break at work, Matthew sat in his car and called Grace. She had texted him that morning saying she was worried about Melody. It rang twice before she answered.

'Hi, Grace, how are you?'

'Good, thanks. You?'

'Yeah, good. Bit worried about Melly after your text. What happened?'

He sat, his feet bouncing on the small bit of space near the car pedals as Grace explained her conversation with Melody. Matthew felt his stomach drop, knowing he was right to be concerned.

'Well, I don't think she will talk to me and it sounds like she is lashing out at you. What about her therapy sessions?' He ran a hand over his brown hair. 'I could pay for some more. She seemed to really get something from them.'

Grace let out a pffft noise and Matthew's brow furrowed.

'No, that definitely wouldn't help,' Grace said, sarcasm in her tone.

He looked out of his car window at some colleagues leaving the office for their break. 'Grace, what's going on?' Then it clicked for Matthew — like a seatbelt into its safety slot. The boyfriend. Grace being evasive. But surely not? He was a professional. 'Grace, is she seeing her therapist romantically?' Matthew's mouth went dry and he felt a balloon of nausea float up inside him.

Grace didn't reply.

'Grace?' He knew he sounded more urgent as every nerve in his body became alert.

'Yeah. Well, not exactly.'

'What does that mean?' Matthew's voice was loud and angry. It wasn't Grace's fault, but he needed answers.

'Well, they've kissed, but it was on a drunken night out and…'

'They're drinking together?' Matthew interrupted, shaking his head, flabbergasted by what he was hearing. 'He's a bloody professional.' His palms were sweaty. He wiped his left hand on his trousers, then swapped ears with his mobile to wipe the other.

'Matthew, no. Erm, it's more complicated. So, her therapist, Nate, was involved in a sponsored spin at a gym, and Melody went along to watch. I went with her. Afterwards, we all went to Covent Garden for drinks, but I was working, so didn't stay long.'

Pushing his head back against the seat, he tried to take it in. His sister, Glynis, was a nurse. It was like her sleeping with a patient for crying out loud. She'd be struck off. Therapists have a governing body, a code, surely?

'Jesus. He's groomed her.' He let out a small yelp and rubbed his forehead. 'How far has it gone, Grace?'

Sensing the panic in his voice, Grace spoke slowly. 'No, Matthew. I think it's been Melody pursuing him as well, if not more from her side.'

Opening the car door, Matthew sucked in some fresh air. 'But she's not well,' he almost whispered, feeling sick that some pervert who the public trusted could manipulate his daughter.

'I don't think they've slept together.' She paused and

Matthew strained his ear to listen, desperate to protect his daughter. 'I don't think he's that interested. He's older, like your age.' She murmured the last few words, worried about offending him.

Matthew sighed, feeling helpless as he sat in his car wondering if his daughter was unravelling, spiralling into an episode of self-loathing and fear. He banged his hand against the steering wheel, annoyed with himself for paying for the so-called support sessions with some kind of pervy therapist that had made his daughter worse.

'And another thing, Matthew...' Grace paused and sighed. 'She's stopped taking her tablets.'

Matthew continued to chat with Grace for a further ten minutes, gathering more details about the therapist and trying to make sense of the situation and potential danger his daughter was in. As soon as they hung up, Matthew began a Google search for Nate Lundie on his mobile phone. His business, Lundie Therapy, came up and Matthew looked through his website, not gathering a lot of information but enough regarding premises address and contact details. Grace had said Melody was going to view the therapist's house that evening.

He sighed in disbelief at what the hell his daughter was doing. Unable to leave work early that day, as the company were getting audited, after work, he would drive straight to her and Grace's flat. Hopefully, he would make it there before his daughter went to this so-called 'professional' therapist's home. Matthew rubbed his mouth. He would drive there and gently get the truth out of Melody. For now, he would have to text her, being cautious not to make her spiral.

Reaching his daughter's flat at 5:10 pm, Matthew parked up. Glancing around, he couldn't spot her Fiat 500. Dashing to her door, he rang the bell twice, impatiently moving his feet on the spot. There was no answer. Matthew rang her mobile phone and got no answer. Knocking on the letterbox, he gave it one last shot before he would use his key. Thirty seconds later, he put his key into the door and opened it, before rushing inside the flat.

'Hello, Melly?' he shouted urgently as he walked in.

No reply. He looked around the flat, but she wasn't there. He had missed her. She had already left and Matthew didn't have a clue where she was going and what would happen when she arrived at her destination.

Chapter 37: Nate

After being stuck in extra heavy Friday traffic, Nate got home at 4:30 pm and completed a quick, last-minute tidy of his house. He had two viewings that weekend: one that evening and one tomorrow morning. Glad it was the end of the working week, he drank a cold bottle of beer as he tidied a little. It had been a draining few days, but he felt lighter for ending his therapy with Melody the day before and having since received two possible new referrals.

By 5 pm, the house was presentable and he jumped in the shower before drying and changing into black Calvin Klein jogging bottoms and a black T-shirt that clung to his biceps. Putting his feet into a pair of sliders, he opened another beer. Alexa played Teddy Swims on low and he began to relax, despite a stranger due in the next five minutes to neb around his house. On cue, the doorbell rang. Nate rose from his sofa, put his bottle out of sight, and walked to the front door, the music almost soundless in the background. Opening it, he looked twice. *What the fuck was Melody Dartford doing on his doorstep?*

'Melody. What the hell are you doing here?' He crossed his arms, blocking the doorway. She stood a few feet away, wearing long boots like what he had seen the exotic dancers wear in the strip club years ago and a black, knee-length coat. *Christ, she looked sexy.*

'Surprise! I'm your half-five viewing!' she said, opening her arms out like she had popped out of a giant birthday cake.

Nate shook his head, feeling an array of emotions but mainly wondering how the hell she had found out where he lived. 'You can't be serious?' He ran a hand through his hair as he tried to contemplate what to do. Pissing her off would be dangerous. He witnessed that yesterday. Leading her on would be even more dangerous. But, shit, she looked so inviting on that doorstep. He wanted to drag her in and have sex with her on the stairs.

She interrupted his thoughts. 'Yeah, I am. So, are you going to let me in?'

He watched her lift her left leg onto the front doorstep. He saw the heel and skin-tight fit of the cheap-looking, sexy boots that ran up to her thighs like a rainbow to a pot of gold. Looking at her leg, he felt a bullet of longing in him fire. Where the boot ended, a strip of flesh was visible. He wanted to touch it, taste her skin, and follow up the flesh of her leg with his tongue. He shook his head, trying to shake the filthy thoughts from his mind. *She's your fucking client and a dangerous one at that.*

After asking how she knew where he lived and receiving an evasive reply, Melody requested to come in. In his rational mind, Nate would have rather invited Vladimir Putin into his home at that moment than the sexy mind mess that was Melody Dartford — especially after her kick-off the day before. He glared at her, wondering if it would ever sink in that he couldn't have a relationship with her.

She raised an eyebrow. 'Does that mean I have to walk back to my car like this, then?' Opening the belt of her black raincoat, she pulled back the chest area slowly, keeping her vision on him. He glanced down, unable to stop his curious, greedy desire. A red lace bra was revealed from under the raincoat. No top, just a bra that matched the colour of her lipstick. She bit her lip and Nate's eyes widened as he swallowed. He shook his head again, knowing she would likely cause a scene outside, and stepped back, allowing her to walk into his hallway.

Sticking his head out of his front door, he looked left and right in case the nosey neighbours were curtain twitching. No one could be seen and he was grateful it was dark. Inside the hallway, Melody let her raincoat drop from her body, revealing just underwear on her feminine frame.

Back to the closed door, Nate gasped. A hunger desperate to be fed, his desire ramped up.

'You like?' she said nonchalantly, playing with her hair.

He nodded, looking her up and down, feeling like a teenage boy. He licked his lips as his pulse quickened. Matching dark red lace knickers and bra showed her sexy, curvy figure and the trashy over-the-knee boots added a sleazy vibe that just made him want frantic sex with her more than ever. By the smug look on her face, she knew this.

Standing halfway along the hallway, Nate remained on the spot. She beckoned him with a curling of her finger and he swallowed, obeying and walked slowly towards her, feeling himself getting increasingly aroused. Melody had planned this meticulously, and Nate knew he was wobbling on the tightrope, balancing between getting to the other side unscathed and a catastrophic fall.

Chapter 38: Melody

Her legs were shaking but Nate didn't notice — his eyes focused as he walked towards her. The hallway felt the longest in the world, but he tentatively got closer until he was standing inches away from her touch. Melody could see his chest rising and falling. Placing a hand on it, his pec muscles clenched underneath his tight, black T-shirt.

Moving her free hand down his arm, she took his hand and placed it on her left breast. Her brown eyes looked into his forget-me-not blue eyes. Their gaze intense, intentional, as if nothing and no one existed outside of that space in his hallway. A vortex of passion. He groaned quietly before she moved forward another step and placed her lips on his.

Frantically, they kissed. His lips were soft, moving in sexual sync with hers like a well-practiced waltz. She felt the lightest of grazes from where stubble was beginning to pierce his skin, peaking through his chin like the first glimpse of snowdrops after a long winter. She ran a hand through his hair as he moved a hand to grab her buttock, and his other cradled the side of her face, fingers reaching round to her neck.

Mouth dancing with his, she knew this chemistry was like no other. An energy, connectivity. Melody slid her hand down Nate's chest and stomach, pausing momentarily before moving it over his jogging bottoms and rubbing a hand over his crotch. He let out a moan that made her need him right there in the hallway. She eagerly pushed his hand from her breast to her underwear. Within a split second, Nate pulled away rapidly. He stepped back, mouth downturned as if she had dissolved into a pool of blood and guts.

'Shit!' he shouted, tilting his head back and moving his knees on the spot. Bending forward, he clutched his head in his hands.

Melody moved towards him. Putting a hand out, she touched his shoulder and he retracted as if she were contaminated.

'Jesus! How many fucking times?' He barked, shaking his head, before glaring at her. His eyes turning piercing ice blue as he wrung his hands together.

'I…' She moved a hand towards him again and he recoiled.

'Melody, I've told you, this can go nowhere. It's not on.' He pulled his hand over his mouth and chin. 'You turning up like this and seducing me. My fucking career is at risk being near you. Why can't you get that?' He sat on the bottom stair as she put her raincoat back on.

She slowly walked to where he sat on the grey-carpeted stairs and sheepishly looked at him. 'But I'm not your client anymore,' she whispered.

Nate shook his head, his gaze dropping to his hands on his knees. 'It doesn't matter, Melody. You are, were my client. All of this should never have happened. *It's never going to happen.*'

'I won't say anything until we can. I know you feel the same.' Her voice was pleading, childlike, as if asking for another hour playing out.

He sniggered and rose from the step. 'I don't feel the same, Melody.'

She glanced at the wood panelling travelling up the stairs, and looked back at Nate as if he would change his mind after a moment of realising his mistake.

'You do.' She went to touch his hand and he whipped it away sharply, sneering at her.

He moved closer, their faces almost touching, but this time it wasn't to kiss, and desire had been replaced in Nate with defiance.

'Melody, I fucking don't. Don't tell me of all people what I feel!' He grimaced as he gestured up and down her body with a hand. 'This, it's sly and slutty and I don't find it or you attractive. So please leave my house and leave me the fuck alone!' He clenched his fists and moved to the front door. Opening it, he turned to her with no hint of a mood change, and put a hand out in a 'there-you-go' action.

She sniffed and wiped her eyes with the sleeve of her raincoat as she shuffled towards him. Reaching the front door, she spoke again. 'Na…'

'No, Melody. No! This is the end,' he barked, before tensing his jaw, his eyes drilling into her, devoid of softness.

She quietly left, and Nate slammed the door. Shuddering as she walked up his path, Melody opened his gate and looked back at the house, willing him to change his mind. Instead, she was left out in the cold and as she walked to her car, sobbing, she felt familiar feelings of old. Feelings that had previously clawed and cut her mind and soul until she fought back with a sharper knife.

Chapter 39: Melody

Melody stirred as Grace plonked herself on the end of her bed. She was saying something, but Melody was too drunk to comprehend what it was. Four empty cans of Sprite and the remains of some vodka lay on the light grey carpet of her bedroom. Turning over, she ignored Grace and fell back to sleep. She woke again, as vomit catapulted through her insides, looking for its escape. The putrid-smelling, acidic burn overflowed from her mouth onto the carpet by her bed. Wincing, vomit-laced drool dripped from her mouth and she let out a groan. Almost immediately, Grace appeared at her bedroom door and rushed over.

'Urggh, gross,' she said, pinching her nose and looking at the carpet. Walking to the other side of the small room, Grace fished her hand through the gap in the cerise curtains and pushed the bedroom window open.

'It's okay, hun. Drink this.' Grace handed her a glass of water from her mirrored bedside cabinet.

Propping herself up, she gulped the water and made another groan. Grace left the room, returning a minute later, and began cleaning up Melody's vomit, gagging every few seconds.

'You owe me for this,' she muttered, as she mopped up the sick with kitchen roll and began spraying carpet cleaner on the offensive soiling. 'You cannot handle your drink.' She laughed, trying to bring light to the situation.

Melody began sobbing.

'Hey, hey. C'mon.' Grace sat on the bed next to her friend and stroked her hair. 'I take it things didn't go well?' Tilting her head, she watched for a reaction.

Melody shook her head as tears plopped onto her pillow, streaking across the bridge of her nose. She coughed. 'He doesn't want me, Grace. I think he did, perhaps, at some point. But now, he just doesn't want me.'

Grace continued to stroke her friend's hair. 'It's shit, but you'll get through it. You're made of harder stuff. And, well, he doesn't deserve you.' Tilting her head, she smiled empathetically at her friend.

'But I love him. Maybe in time…'

Grace shook her head lightly. 'You need to accept it, hun. It's no good for you.'

Melody closed her heavy eyes, not wanting to talk and acknowledge the truth.

'I'll make you some toast.' Grace rose from the bed and left.

Looking at her phone, Melody had a missed call and text message from her mum and four missed calls from her dad, along with a load of text messages and some WhatsApp messages. *Shit, he would be hysterical with worry,* she thought, as she texted him.

Dad, I'm fine. Just hungover. Sorry if you were worrying. Xxx
She saw he was replying.

Thank God. I've been so worried, Melly. Are you okay? Xxx

I'm fine, Dad. Just got a little drunk, but I will be okay. I'll come over tomorrow after lunch with Mum. Xxx

As long as you are alright. I'm always here for you. Xxx

Melody put her phone on her bedside cabinet and heard Grace in the kitchen. She closed her eyes, not quite able to face her friend and the 'told-you-so' vibes, again. A few hours later,

Grace said goodbye, heading out to work, and Melody promised she would text her later. Then she was left in the flat alone, only her thoughts harpooning around her mind.

After being asked to leave Nate's last night, Melody had worried she would crash her car — her eyes so blurry from the tears and smudged mascara. She got home and took her sexy lingerie off, ripped the smutty boots off and threw them all in the bin. It had been her last shot, her last attempt to get him to see that they could be together; were meant to be together. Instead, she had experienced the most intense, passionate kiss of her life before being kicked out of his house, like a rejected toy being discarded from the production line. It stung like no other pain she had experienced. Even losing Felix didn't feel like this: a stabbing rejection.

Nate told her he didn't feel the same and it was the end. Sobbing all the way home, she couldn't believe he could be so cruel. A therapist, so cold and hurtful, like a doctor who poisoned his patients. She spent the rest of the day cycling the emotions of heartbreak, denial, and rage. The last thing she remembered as she fell asleep was a familiar feeling marching in her stomach, the beat getting faster, louder. It was anger, a fuel that could propel her across the earth. Nate was beyond cruel, playing God with her feelings, and he would not get away with it.

After a broken sleep, Melody woke the next day feeling just as bad as the day before, minus the hangover. She wondered if she should take some of her anti-depressants. Would reintroducing them take the edge off? Probably, but it would take time to get into her system and, well, she needed mental clarity for her next steps — not to be frozen in a coating of false reality.

Dragging herself out of bed and to the bathroom, she felt submerged in darkness. Melody had arranged to see her mum for lunch, then visit her dad. She would have to share a massively muted version of the truth, while inside she would feel like she was clinging onto a rope, trying to swing between canyons.

'You can do it,' she said aloud, holding back tears whilst brushing her wet hair.

Walking into the kitchen, Grace was at the small dining table, eating cereal and reading from her Kindle.

'Hey, lovely. How are you? I'll make you a cuppa; the kettle has just boiled.' She jumped up, abandoning her cereal and switched the kettle back on.

'I don't know. Devastated, angry, heartbroken, hopeful.' She shrugged, bringing a finger to her mouth.

Grace threw a spoon into the sink and handed her a strong cup of coffee. They talked for a bit and Melody nodded at the things she thought Grace wanted her to, even though she didn't agree with most of it, and it didn't help. Groaning, she knew she would repeat some of this process with her parents that afternoon.

Arriving at her mum's apartment, Zoe was getting her shoes on and they left straight away, walking to the local pub for Sunday lunch. Zoe immediately sensed her daughter wasn't herself and as they strolled the five minutes' walk, they linked arms.

'What's up, Melly? And don't say nothing, you look exhausted.'

Zoe was the type to cut to the chase. Perhaps her legal training made her factual — never fluffing things up much, unless absolutely needed. She tilted her head to Melody and raised an eyebrow, her long chestnut-coloured hair swaying as they walked.

Melody shrugged. 'Boy trouble, as usual.' She sighed and Zoe rubbed her forearm.

'Brandon?'

'No, just some guy from the gym.' She sniffed up and wiped her eyes with her free hand. 'I really liked him and I think I've blown it.'

'Oh, darling. Love is bloody painful. I'm sorry, baby.' Zoe squeezed her. 'If it doesn't sort itself out, it's his loss, Melly.'

Melody was about to speak but they had reached the pub, the entrance doors flying open as a group exited, laughing. Holding the door open for them, the opportunity was gone — although she wasn't even sure what she would have said.

Arriving at Matthew's two hours later, as usual, he was standing next to the lounge window, giving her no time for any last-minute preparation. By the time she had grabbed her bag from the passenger seat and unclipped her seat belt, he had the UPVC front door open. Worry dug into the lines on his face as she approached and feigned a smile. His brown hair, usually tidy, looked dishevelled and in need of a haircut.

'Hi, Dad.' Walking into the house, she kicked off her trainers and Matthew embraced her.

'Oh, Melly, I've been so worried.' He held her out at arm's length, eyes like a bloodhound dog: heavy and sad.

'I know, Dad.' She swallowed and they moved from the hall-way into the lounge. Melody sat on the sage green sofa and began picking at the wool blanket draped over the arm.

Sitting in his armchair, he glared at her, and she felt one hundred times worse.

'What's happened, love?'

Melody bit back her desire to scream. 'Just boy trouble, Dad.

But I'll be okay.'

'Who is he?' Matthew asked quickly. 'I told your mum I was worried. Did she speak with you?'

Melody nodded. 'Yeah, we spoke. He's no one, just a guy from the gym I joined.' Technically, she wasn't lying.

Matthew lifted his chin up, his expression serious. 'And, it's over?'

Melody swallowed. 'Yeah. He doesn't want a relationship. So, it is what it is.' She shrugged and let out a sad laugh.

'Did you like him a lot?' He frowned.

Swallowing, she looked at her lap as her voice cracked. 'Yeah, I did. I do.'

She began crying, despite desperately not wanting to and knowing it would impact her dad and, therefore, herself. However, she just couldn't stop it and as Melody sat with her father, her tears fell like torrential rain.

Chapter 40: Nate

Nate's weekend had been like something out of a TV drama. Melody turning up at his house, in her underwear, then seducing him, before he made her leave. He had been shaking, his heart pounding, and after shutting the front door on her, he'd gone into the kitchen and grabbed a bottle of rum. Standing over the sink, for a moment he was unsure if he was going to be sick, scream, or neck the rum until he passed out. He went with the latter, attempting to silence his emotions with alcohol.

Nate had been harsh with Melody, but not as harsh as he'd wanted to. Granted, his desire to have sex with her had almost taken over. However, her pathological inability to listen to him and her calculated attempts at domineering him, deceiving him, and the danger he knew she was capable of — made him flip from wanting her to the rationality of knowing she had the power to knock him down to a pile of rubble. The whole performance at his house just made him realise even more that Melody was young, naïve, and trapped by teenage trauma that made her inexperienced and entitled.

And for that reason, he had to ensure that there was no way she could cause more harm. He wouldn't let another woman ruin his career, especially one that he had no emotional investment in.

If she reported him to the BACP, she had no proof. If they investigated, there were only a few emails that could be open to interpretation. But really, they indicated nothing of substance.

Checking over them, the emails mentioned he was drunk and that was about it from his end. However, it was out of work time and he was allowed to consume alcohol. God, he needed it at times, especially with bloody Melody as a client. She required a help he could never give her as a therapist and he just needed out, away from her *Venus fly trap* grasp. Hopefully, now he was.

On the positive, the viewing on Saturday morning went well, with the young, professional couple loving the house, the décor, and the convenient location. Nate was talkative, despite his hangover, and he received a call from the estate agent that afternoon, stating the couple would like to return for a second viewing early the following week. It took the sting out of the incident with Melody the night before.

Over the weekend, he had received several emails from her. Many were drunken nonsense repeating themselves with the message of loving him and knowing they could be happy together. Not responding, his anger increased as each one landed in his inbox. *What part of fuck off did she not understand?* He saw himself as a nice person. Decent, caring, and a good therapist. He'd made mistakes, but he was just like everyone else: human.

Yes, he liked women and flirting, no harm in that. But he wished he had never set eyes on Melody Dartford. As the emails landed and he answered none, Nate saved them into a separate folder, just in case something came back and he had to prove that it was, in fact, Melody who was harassing him. He knew the capabilities people could stoop to and someone like her, who was desperate and unwell, had a level lower than a snake's belly.

Knowing the new week would be difficult if she continued bombarding him and aware that she could turn up at his work or home, Nate felt edgy and suspicious. Despite it being under two weeks until Christmas, he had a diary full of clients and new referrals to pick up and was unsure whether an upcoming busy week at work was a blessing or if it would break him.

Monday came and went without incident until the late evening when he received messages on LinkedIn from an account with no profile photo. He knew it was Melody. It was full of mistakes, so he assumed she was intoxicated and as with the emails, he didn't respond. Instead, Nate had a restless night. Paranoid — and rightly so — that she might turn up at his house and cause a soap-opera-worthy scene that would no doubt, be the highlight of the year for the neighbours. He just had to focus on getting through the next several weeks and then, surely, she would begin to comprehend the meaning of no, get over him, and meet someone else.

In the meantime, he would go to the early morning spin classes, before work. If she saw him there and caused a scene, it would be embarrassing. And with Anita, in particular, he didn't want to acquire an image as a player, especially not with a younger woman. He'd already had that in his old circles and it set everything alight — leaving a stink of burnt reputations and relationships.

He rolled his shoulders as he sat on his sofa. The tension evident with the grinding of his cartilage and creaking as the pressure tried to escape with each rotation. The young couple who viewed his house on Saturday morning were returning tomorrow. Nate had a positive feeling about it and wanted more than ever, to move house and start afresh.

Scrolling on his laptop, he looked at properties on the market in East Hertfordshire. Beautiful countryside still with connection and the ability to commute at only thirty miles from the capital. Searching through the properties, there were a few that stood out. Not shy of DIY and a little renovating, Nate saved some that required modernisation. He spent the next hour short-listing properties to arrange viewings. It was inevitable, and Melody's antics had simply sped up the process.

After emailing estate agents, Nate went to make some dinner and picked his mobile phone up from where it had been charging in the kitchen. He saw there was a notification from his business Facebook page. He didn't have a personal profile. After he split with Sarah, people who weren't friends, and even those who were, had a lot to say about his marriage. Clearly, with no life of their own to occupy them, he had received snide comments or read them on Sarah's page. So, he had closed his account, receiving enough drama for his plate during his day job.

The alert from Facebook was a new review on his business page. He smiled, thinking about the clients who had been signed off from Lundie Therapy over the past few months, with new coping strategies, having digested and processed previous trauma to a manageable level. Then he felt a jab of panic. There was one very disgruntled client. Clicking on the comment that took him to his page, he saw the post. It was by someone called 'Song Bird' and he knew immediately that it was Melody.

I went to Lundie Therapy with high hopes that Nate Lundie would help me manage my emotional and psychological well-being. Instead, I was discharged after six sessions feeling worse. This man is not a therapist, he is a tormentor and women should stay away from him.

Nate gasped. What the hell? It had been posted almost an hour ago. His hands trembled with rage as he took a screenshot and promptly reported the comment and then deleted it, before blocking Song Bird. A firework of anger exploded through him.

How many people would have seen it? Christ, what a bitch. Nate had ignored her emails and her fake LinkedIn profile, spouting illegible, begging messages, so she had resorted to this. He leant against the kitchen bench and looked at the image of the comment from his mobile camera roll.

'Fucking tormentor!' he said aloud, hand on his forehead. Nate acknowledged he had likely led Melody on. She was vulnerable, psychologically unwell, and she was his client. But hell, he was entitled to change his mind and realise a quick fumble couldn't happen with someone like Melody, even if she wasn't accessing his service. She was the type of woman who would have his name tattooed on her body after date three, and whilst she would have been okay for some fun in different circumstances, she would never have been anything more to him.

He knew he had done wrong, but would not admit it if it came down to it. Nate had let his sexual urges control him again and he was in trouble, just like he had been with Annabelle Graham. But this time, he would not let anything more be destroyed. He wasn't prepared to watch his reputation and career swirl down the plughole with dirty water. Melody was harassing him because he wouldn't entertain her fantasy and let her manipulate him into bed. Nate wouldn't allow her unhinged mind to control his. He wouldn't let her win. She'd never get what she wanted, at least not while he had fight left in him.

Chapter 41: Melody

Posting the review comment about Lundie Therapy on Facebook gave Melody some needed release after a day that had stretched her patience to the extreme. She'd have been lucky if she managed four hours of sleep the night before. Haunted by Nate, she ruminated on his words — or lack of them. Melody felt abandoned and rejected. Painful feelings of Lily, Felix, Brandon, and her parents' separation resurfaced.

Without alcohol and her prescription medication, the result was a terrible night's sleep. In the minutes she drifted off, she would be awoken in a pulsating panic, reliving the rejection or dreaming of him with other women. Nate was torturing her and so was her mind.

During the work day, customers were their usual unpleasant selves and she hung the phone up on four. Screaming abuse at them being the alternative. On her break, she sat in the staff kitchen eating noodles from a plastic cup. Stirring them around, the sauce looked as murky as her life. Hearing someone coming in, Melody glanced up and sighed. Lizard-like Dave walked over and sat next to her at the small wooden kitchen table. Raising his eyebrows in a sleazy way, she grimaced, then looked at her phone.

'Fancy a date yet?' He asked, mouth full, breathing tuna and onions in her direction as he chomped on a soggy sandwich.

'No.' Melody didn't even bother to look up.

'Ah, come on, Mel, you've gotta be over that Brendon kid

by now? A real man will look after you, if you know what I mean?' He chuckled at himself as if his line had just won him the audition for the next smutty comedy blockbuster.

'I said no, Dave,' she sneered, pushing her cup of noodles to one side.

His tuna-infused lip curled. 'You think you're so bloody great, don't you?' A bit of tuna plopped onto his sandwich wrap. 'Better than everyone else as you come into work and look down your nose at people.'

She shook her head. 'Piss off. I think no such thing.'

'You do. Well, you are no better, Mel. You need to remember that. And I don't even fancy you, just feel friggin' sorry for you.' He tutted and looked the other way.

Melody rose from the hard wooden chair and picked up her still-hot noodles before flinging them at Dave. She left the kitchen, not looking back, only hearing the audio of his shouting. She stormed to her desk, took her coat off the back of the ancient chair that gave her backache during each shift, grabbed her handbag off the floor by her desk, and left the office, signing herself out at reception for the day.

The next morning, Melody prepared herself as she entered Crawford's, knowing she would likely be hauled into dog-wet nose Glen's office, either because of Dave-gate, storming off her shift early, or both. After logging on and making herself a cup of tea, Selina appeared, towering over her desk, like a scrawny, evil stepmother.

'Glen wants to see you in his office, now.' She smirked as she said the last word, her glasses sliding down her thin nose.

Melody shrugged and stood. She grabbed her bag, and with her coat yet to come off, walked to Glen's office, Selina in front, her spindly legs marching as she led. People looked, having heard about the incident yesterday. Melody didn't care, they were all pricks, and well, she had it far worse than this when she was at school.

Glen sacked her, lecturing that violence of any sort would not be tolerated at Crawford's and that walking out on her shift was also a sackable offence. Melody tried to deny throwing her noodles at Dave, but two witnesses had seen it happen and, well, what was the point anyway? Selina stood, lips pursed like a balloon knot, and an eyebrow raised over her glasses, as Glen lectured about her recent behaviour and a level of standard and acceptable conduct. It all sounded like an old cassette being chewed up in a ghetto blaster. She left the office, escorted by Selina, who didn't speak but held the look of disapproval on her gaunt face.

'Wait a minute, I've left my phone on my desk.'

Melody hadn't, but she had some unfinished business at Crawford's. Pretending to pick something up from her desk, colleagues stole glances as Selina stood near the lifts, watching. Passing Dave, who was on the phone to no doubt some accusing customer, Melody tapped him on the shoulder. She saw Selina beginning to move towards her. Dave spun around, his headset on and Melody punched him as hard as she could in the face.

Screaming, he grabbed his nose as blood rushed from it and over his mouth, drops falling in as he yelped out. People next to him gasped, dashing to help as she strolled away towards the lifts, leaving him screeching in pain.

'I would expect a visit from the police for that,' Selina said loudly, as Melody pushed past her and went down the stairs to reception and out of Crawford's for the last time.

Walking away from the shitshow that had been her job, she couldn't help but laugh in between the sensation of wanting to run away forever. She hated her job anyway and was sick of men taking advantage of her. Almost breathless with rage and exhilaration dancing together, she reached King's Cross Station and sat down on the seats outside, catching her breath and processing the last thirty minutes. Now she had no job, she would have no income. *Shit, how would she manage?*

Melody dropped her head to her hands and puffed out air. Her mum might increase her financial support for a few months and she could look for another job, omitting Crawford's from her CV. Biting her fingernail, she realised it was already hard enough getting a job with an arson conviction and now she would have to eradicate Crawford's from her lame CV. It was a week before Christmas and this was her bloody present. It was all Nate's fault and she hated him and loved him in equal measures.

Watching a couple walking past, holding hands, she wanted to cry. Melody needed a drink. Looking at her watch, it was 1:15 pm. She had started on late shift, meant to be in until 8 pm. *At least I will be home for Coronation Eastenders,* she thought, laughing at the irony. Deciding to go to South of Here bar, she hoped Grace would sub her a few drinks.

Sheepishly walking into the bar, Melody searched for Grace's friendly face. She couldn't see her and hoped she was just temporarily away. Ordering a vodka, she hung around the bar, waiting for Grace. Five minutes later, she spotted her coming from the back.

'What are you doing here?' she said, eyes wide.

'Nice to see you too,' Melody said sarcastically.

'You know what I mean.' Grace smiled and looked at her

friend's hand wrapped around her glass. 'What happened?'

Taking a swig of her drink, Melody put the glass back down on the bar and tilted her head back. 'I got sacked. Then I think I broke Dave's nose.'

Grace's hand shot to her mouth, and she stifled a laugh. 'Crikey! I mean, good on you, he's a creep. But, wow, he's going to be pissed off. And your job?'

Melody laughed. It was funny; Dave deserved it. However, she wasn't amused by the potential consequences and the fact that she had no job.

Grace leant over and rubbed her free hand. 'Seriously though, hun. He could call the police?'

Shrugging, she spoke. 'I don't give a shit.'

Grace straightened her shoulders, and her face turned stern. 'All this. It's not good, Melody. I'm worried about you and so is your dad.'

Melody's tongue ran over her top teeth. 'For God's sake, Grace. Stop with the bringing my dad into it, will you?' She looked down at her drink and shook her head.

'He's already in it. He's worried. Can you not see how he'd be concerned? You've been going on well…'

Her shoulders stiffened and her head shot up. 'Like a mad woman. That's what you were going to say, wasn't it?'

Grace's neck went red and she swallowed.

'Like a fucking mad woman. And here I was thinking you'd make me feel better. You're just another Lily. Another Nate.'

She downed her drink and left the bar, ignoring the pleas from Grace to come back.

Chapter 42: Nate

Placing his cup and plate on the draining board of his office kitchenette, Nate looked at the clock. It was 5:10 pm and he had the second viewing with the young couple at 7:00 pm. After drying his hands, he picked up his laptop and bag, turning off the lights before leaving his office. Walking to his usual car park, he felt the start of drizzle against his face.

He would have to do some work that evening, needing to leave his office early the next day for a cottage viewing in the rural village of Much Hadham, East Hertfordshire. Lost in his thoughts of a new property, he reached his car and jolted on hearing his name. Glancing around, he saw Melody sitting on the floor, leaning against the side of his white vehicle.

'Jesus, what the hell are you doing down there?' Nate put his hand to his chest.

'Waiting for you,' she slurred, looking like a pleading puppy.

He frowned, his eyes on her as she pulled herself up from the ground, moaning as she stood. She moved towards him, her arms out.

'Hey, hey. Stop, Melody.' Glancing at her mascara-smudged eyes, she looked like she'd been crying and fighting with a flock of pigeons. He smelt the unmistakable scent of alcohol around her. 'You're pissed.' Shaking his head, her eyes began filling up.

'I wanted to see you. I'm sorry. I love you, Nate.' Her hands moved into a praying grasp.

She hiccupped and Nate sighed. Glancing around, he hoped

no one would see the kerfuffle. 'Melody, I swear to God, I am not having this conversation again.'

'But…' She swayed and leant against his car.

'And that fucking comment on Facebook. Listen, you need to leave me alone. Otherwise, I will have to report you for harassment.'

She burst out laughing. 'Report me? I'll tell them you tried to fuck me,' she spat, pointing a finger at him and sneering.

Through gritted teeth, he inhaled. 'You need to leave me alone. This is your final warning.'

Melody glared at him, and in a silly, mocking voice, she repeated his words. 'This is your final warning.' She released a laugh, and then, as if flicking a switch, her face straightened.

'Yeah, well, it's your final warning as well. So, just stop all this bull and take me home.'

Nate felt he was going to explode with anger. He leant into her and sneered, spittle gathering in the corners of his mouth. 'I will go to the police if you come near me again. So just go away, Melody.'

A grin spread across her face. 'Let's see who gets there first.'

Nate pushed her away. Falling backwards, she wobbled against the rear end of his car, bouncing off it and towards the car next to his — her hands out to try and steady herself as her hair fell across her face. Clicking his central locking, he opened the driver's door, desperate to get away from the scene.

He heard a growl and flash as she came at him from the right, a fist landing on the side of his jaw. His top teeth moved to the left and came down on the flesh inside his mouth, biting through the warm sponge of his inner cheek. Pain seared through as the iron taste of blood coated his mouth. Shocked, he turned to look at Melody, watching her back off and scurry to the red car next to his. Despite her previous extreme behaviour, Nate was stunned.

Just wanting to get away from her, for both their safety, he got in the car, locked the doors and started the engine — unsure if she would even contemplate jumping on his bonnet. Looking in his side and rear-view mirrors, she was nowhere to be seen. Nate began to drive, shaking. Leaving the car park via the barrier exit, he drove home, heart beating quicker than the speed of his vehicle.

It was just after 6 pm when he pulled up outside his house. Cutting the engine, his foot bounced, still with the aftershock of what had occurred. Rushing inside his front door, he swigged some rum straight from the fridge to calm his nerves. *What the hell had just happened?* His jaw throbbed, the pulsating pain darting around his head like a motorcycle on a racetrack. He touched his face and winced. Taking a strip of painkillers from the drawer in his kitchen, he popped the blister pack and swallowed two tablets with another mouthful of rum.

He had to talk to someone. This had gone way too far, and now he felt at risk from Melody — like a loan shark wanting a debt paid. Or he was at risk of doing something that he would regret and that would end his career forever. The phone rang three times before she picked it up. Julie's voice was always chirpy. He swallowed and spoke.

'Julie, something's happened and it involves a client.'

After ten minutes, his sister was updated on all that had happened between Melody and him. Nate had been honest, sharing the full story. Julie always looked out for her brother, just like he had for her when they were growing up. They had an unbreakable bond and she was the only person Nate truly trusted in the world. Tension dissolved slightly from his shoulders when he had finished talking.

'So, you've kept everything?'

He sighed. 'Yeah, but, well, I don't know what she has. She may have recorded me or she could make things up.' Nate touched his sore jaw and glanced at the Karlsson clock in his lounge, conscious that the couple would arrive for their second viewing in just over fifteen minutes.

Julie made a humph noise. 'Nate, I think it's a really dangerous situation and she doesn't sound well in all honesty. She also seems desperate and that makes people do extreme and risky things. Why don't you come and stay with us for a few weeks, just until things cool off?'

Nate sighed as he rose from the sofa, straightening the cushions as he spoke. 'I'm not bloody running away, Julie. I'm not in the wrong.'

There was silence for a moment. 'Nate, I love you. You're my baby brother, but you do have some part to play in this. Even if she is batshit crazy, you have breached your conduct in some way and you have to take responsibility for that. She's the vulnerable one, not you.' He heard her sigh. 'Well, she was to begin with. I think you're pretty vulnerable now. And that's why I think you should come and stay here.'

Tilting his head back, he closed his eyes. 'This isn't another Annabelle…'

'I know,' Julie interrupted. 'Come and stay here for a bit.'

'Maybe. I'll call you tomorrow.'

After saying goodbye, Nate rushed around the house, hiding the mess before going back to the lounge to sit and wait for the doorbell to ring, praying it wouldn't be Melody.

Chapter 43: Melody

Melody watched Nate's car leave the multistorey car park and felt consumed with sadness and rage. She had been struggling to accept he didn't want her, focusing on their intimate moments and chemistry. Until then. His sneer and venom in his eyes gave her all she needed to know, despite having drank vodka for hours. Staggering out of the car park, she felt overwhelmed with despair and the sixteen-year-old who was abandoned and blamed all those years ago was crawling up inside of her like a serpent.

Standing on the pavement, light rain was falling and Melody tipped her face to the coolness of the drizzle, wondering where she could go. Home, to dwell and drink herself into oblivion felt too heartbreaking. She didn't want to go back to Grace's bar and her dad's house was a no-go, despite three missed calls and two text messages from him.

Instead, she began walking, heading back towards King's Cross Station and took the Northern Line train. After a short ride, she disembarked at London Bridge and began walking. Popping into an overpriced Tesco Express, she purchased four cans of vodka and lemonade. Cracking one open outside the shop, the hiss of the gas escaped. She lifted the can to her mouth and greedily gulped the room-temperature liquid.

After a mile on foot, Melody reached Shad Thames. Extortionately priced apartments were set back from the footpath alongside the River Thames. Restaurants and bars occupied the ground floor of the apartments, which attracted people who had more money to spend than there were grains of sand on Brighton Beach.

She snorted, thinking of all the money some people had in the sixth richest city in the world, yet how unhappy people can be. Wealth doesn't bring the dead back to life. It doesn't heal a broken heart or make someone genuinely love you. Not that Melody knew; she had never had a fat bank account or the richness of love in her heart.

Strolling along the footpath opposite the restaurants and bars, she observed people coming and going in couples and groups, laughing, full of Christmas festivities. And she was alone. Rejected by Nate, yet again. Walking a little further, the rain continued to fall. The earthy smell collided with the fumes of the city, the mossy odour of the river, and the scent of the worldwide cuisine eateries. She stumbled along, trying to clear her mind but feeling stuck in her own rain cloud as the partygoers petered out, taking shelter from the rain inside the restaurants.

Melody was tired and thirsty. She sat on the edge of the pavement, her legs under the railings, dangling onto the walls of the river. Her coat came to just above her knees so she wasn't sitting in the wet straight away. No doubt the damp ground would soak through her layers, but Melody didn't care. She cared about nothing at that moment.

Time passed as she remained seated on the ground, drinking alcohol. It was dark and people passing barely noticed her — everyone in a bubble of their own joy or sadness. Melody stared into the murky, black water, and an hour later, she remained sitting, staring.

'Hello, are you alright?' A voice said as an older woman

appeared by her side.

Melody glanced up quickly. Not speaking, she looked away, refocusing on the water. She could hear a noise from the woman but couldn't make any of it out and didn't want to acknowledge her. The voice persisted and Melody felt her insides were like a pan, boiling on the hob. Tentatively, a hand gently touched her shoulder and the voice kept going.

Not acknowledging the contact, Melody stared straight ahead at the river. She opened her mouth and screamed. Not stopping for air, her shrieking filled the now-quiet street with an eerie alarm. The woman dashed off as she kept screaming, focusing on the water as the sixteen-year-old Melody crawled out of her mouth.

Chapter 44: Matthew

It was after 9 pm and Matthew still hadn't had contact with his daughter. Following a concerned text message from Grace, telling him Melody had been sacked and apparently assaulted someone at work, then turned up at South of Here bar, he had soared into full-blown panic mode. Ringing her multiple times produced no response, nor did texting.

He had hounded Zoe in between court cases for any update, seething at her blasé response of, 'She's just being Melly.' Matthew had gone around to Melody's flat, waiting there in case she turned up. Sitting in her lounge, wringing his hands, his thoughts spiralled as he prayed for communication from her. He had paced her tiny living space so much, that he'd almost covered his daily step count just there. Frantic, he didn't know what else to do.

Then his mobile rang, flashing up unknown on his screen. Answering, a gentle voice advised him she was a ward sister from the local hospital. Melody had been taken to Guy's Hospital after a concerned member of the public had rung for emergency help.

'Is she okay?' Matthew blurted out, tasting bile in his throat.

'Yes, for now. She's safe but not engaging,' said the ward sister. 'I've looked at her records, Mr Dartford. This could be a psychiatric episode and we will determine if we can support Melody here or if she requires a possible specialist stay.'

Matthew put a hand to his forehead. He knew what a

possible specialist stay was. It meant sectioning Melody under the Mental Health Act, like his daughter had been when she was sixteen. After further information was shared on the phone, Matthew hung up. Hands trembling, he went into her bedroom to gather some bits and pieces for what would be a few nights stay. Finding a sports bag, he emptied the contents. Not sure where his daughter kept everything, he opened and shut drawers, trying to get essentials in his blind panic. Gathering some pyjamas, underwear, and socks, she would also need toiletries and a phone charger.

'What else?' he said aloud, smacking the palm of his hand against his head.

Opening her bedside cabinet drawer, he saw boxes of her anti-depressants. The ones she hadn't been taking, according to Grace. He popped them in the bag, along with a phone charger from the drawer. Taking some toiletries from the bathroom, he grabbed both electric toothbrushes, not knowing which was Melody's. Matthew stumbled out of the flat, anxious to go quicker than his body would let him. Getting into his Lexus, he made his way to the hospital.

Crippled with concern as he parked his car, he rushed into Guy's Hospital, desperate to protect his daughter. He knew exactly what had caused this — who had caused this. That bastard pervert therapist, Nate Lundie. And in that moment, Matthew Dartford vowed to get revenge against the man who should have helped his daughter and instead abused his position.

Four Months Later

Chapter 45: Nate

'Thanks for everything.' Nate handed the receptionist of his office building a colourful bunch of flowers and a bottle of wine.

'You're making me blush, you charmer. You'll be a big miss,' she said, putting the gifts on her desk and giving Nate a hug.

Nate exited the door to the building and glanced up one last time at his office. Those walls had heard so many stories. So much trauma and recovery. Now, it was time for new walls and new clients. A new start — away from the mania of King's Cross.

Walking to his car with the last box of items from his office, he sighed, thinking about how much had changed in the last four months. After that evening when Melody Dartford confronted him in the car park, the young professional couple had viewed his house again. They'd made an offer the next day and even though it was a little lower than his asking price, he had accepted it. It was his ticket out of there, and the sooner the better.

Following a few days of feeling he was being watched and jumping at the slightest noise, Nate had taken Julie up on her invite and went to stay with her and Brian. There had been a niggle in him that Melody was waiting. Silent, like an eagle watching a vole. But the silence frightened him for a long time after the incident with her.

The day after the couple had viewed his house, Nate had viewed a small cottage in East Hertfordshire, in a tiny lane in the village of Much Hadham. The two-bed house had a huge back garden that led onto fields. It ticked all the boxes and the garden space was large enough to build a therapy room, meaning he could give up the lease on the city centre office that cost a small fortune. Nate had fallen in love with the property — that was one of only a handful in the peaceful lane — on the first viewing, making an offer the next day. Harm minimisation had been at the top of his agenda, unsure of Melody's next tactic.

His offer had been accepted and tied in nicely with his house sale in mid-February, two months ago. The keys were handed in for his house, and Nate had collected the keys for his new cottage a few days later. He was sure it was a relief for Julie and Brian, who had been supportive but were likely sick of their houseguest's extended stay. He had gone to the house he had shared with Sarah one last time, before dropping the keys off at the estate agents.

Standing in the lounge, Nate had looked up at the stunning period cornicing and down to the original fireplace and floorboards. The room felt so big, so empty, but he could still remember swinging Sarah around in there as Paul Weller played on the iPad. The house of their dreams, only it had ended as more of a nightmare. He had sighed, hoping the new couple would have more luck in the home. Walking around, he had said goodbye to his home and the ghosts of his life that he hoped would remain in the structure. Shutting the heavy wooden front door, Nate had thrown the keys up in his hand and caught them before walking away from his past.

The sale of his home completed, Nate had moved into his new cottage and spent two months doing some bits of decorating and building a summer house for his therapy practice. It was now mid-April and almost four months since the car park incident. Thankfully, he hadn't heard from Melody.

Although still aware she could turn up or contact him, Nate had relaxed, not fearing a call from the police or from the BACP asking questions and investigating his conduct. After all, he hadn't pressed charges against her. So perhaps, she'd just swallowed down the potent cocktail of love she felt for him, which was mixed with a good few shots of anger, and a splash of fear of him going to the police. He could only hope.

His new home was a lot smaller, but weirdly, with more space. Instead of the terraced style, Nate had a patch of land surrounding his cottage on Lawson Lane in rural Much Hadham. Close to the amenities, around thirty miles from the capital, but rural enough to have the countryside vibes that felt like another world.

The summer house in the vast back garden had been an immediate project. It was hard work, but Nate had some help from Brian. He knew it meant he could give up the lease and commute to King's Cross and practice from home. The pros outweighed the cons, even with the mixing of his property. After all, in his several years of practice, the only problem with clients he had encountered had been with Melody Dartford. Being the extreme, he doubted anything like that would happen again. Plus, Nate wouldn't let it happen. He wouldn't look and touch, he wouldn't fantasise about bedding his clients and use his authority to blur the boundaries. He would take responsibility and be the good therapist that he was.

Chapter 46: Melody

It was Melody's first weekend living fully in the flat, having moved back there gradually since leaving hospital, after a three-month stay.

'Pizza for tea?' Grace said chirpily, helping her and Matthew with the rest of her bags, which included new bedding and some new clothes.

'And for me?' Matthew joked.

'You're always welcome, Dad Number Two!' Grace said, receiving a hug from Matthew.

'Thanks, but I'm playing darts tonight.' He did a little movement on the spot, impersonating throwing a dart.

'He's so *dad*, isn't he?' laughed Melody, nudging him and rolling her eyes to Grace.

Matthew raised his eyebrows and chuckled. 'Keep that app on your phone, mind.' He pointed at Melody as she dropped her bags in the hallway of the flat.

'It's been on for three months, Dad. I'm not taking it off and you keep it on yours as well.' She pointed back, smiling.

With her consent, Matthew had installed the Find My iPhone app on both their mobiles, saying it could just be temporary. It allowed him to see where Melody was if he ever couldn't get in touch with her and was part of her recovery plan. For her to not feel under the microscope too much, he had also activated it on his mobile when she was in hospital and she had grilled him about where he'd been in a jokey way each time he visited. It had become a bit of a game and Matthew would quiz his daughter as to which pub he had played darts that week, then ask her the price of a pint there, knowing she wouldn't have a clue.

He leant over and kissed her on the forehead. 'Right, I will. Me and your mum will see you on Sunday, Melly. Keep in touch.'

Melody nodded and hugged her dad goodbye. She smiled to herself. She had grown closer to her parents during the last four months. Now, Sunday lunch with her mum at a pub then rushing to her dad's, had changed to Sunday lunch as a family — well, as much as a family as they could be without Felix.

It was good to be home and even better to feel content. Grace ordered pizza before helping her unpack. Her room felt different with her new belongings in. Cleansed in some way from the negativity and suffering she experienced before she stayed in hospital. Zoe had cleaned it meticulously; her way of processing what had happened, no doubt.

After that night by the River Thames four months ago, Melody had at last got the help she needed. On reflection, she'd struggled since leaving Hopewood Psychiatric Hospital at seventeen. Although the therapy was good, she was still a child and didn't really learn how to navigate in an adult's world. She'd been walking on a ledge for over eight years, trapped emotionally as an adolescent as she waited for the right counselling and therapy. The constant risk of slipping but pulling her foot back, regaining her balance, until Nate Lundie pushed her off her ledge, almost for good.

She'd been taken to hospital that night at Shad Thames and admitted to a ward that was mainly for older people, with cognitive impairment. However, it was the only place there was a bed for her to be assessed. Melody couldn't remember any of it. A mixture of alcohol misuse, mental turmoil, and pain that she had covered in a concrete blanket. Sometimes, a snippet would plop into her mind, like a drop of rain, and she would sense something. A smell, or sight, a sound that would take her back to when her soul felt consumed with anger and despair. All of the unresolved and haunting issues of her childhood, Felix's suicide, her parents' break-up, Brandon, and Nate, had overflowed.

Melody had been emergency sectioned and after three nights in the ward, she was admitted to St Ann's Hospital, where she was assessed further, before it was decided she would follow a treatment plan with monthly reviews by her clinician. She had spent twelve weeks in the hospital and the following month living at her dad's, popping home for the odd night. Now, it was time to return to her flat.

She had also been arrested for assaulting Dave at work, but once it was known she was in the psych ward, Dave dropped the charges and the CPS didn't pursue it. There were never any allegations from Nate about what occurred in the car park, which Melody was relieved about. The incident would have likely been on camera. If Nate went to the police, she would have told them the whole story. So, perhaps he knew it was probable he'd come off bad, if not worse than her.

She had been admitted to St Ann's Hospital in a vacuum of desperation. Now, she felt she had worked through her feelings for Nate and been honest to her parents about everything. They had wanted to take it further, Zoe quoting laws and court processes. Matthew panicked, wanting Melody to move back to the family home, claiming she had been groomed, she was vulnerable, and that Nate Lundie needed punished.

Melody had insisted on leaving it, knowing she could come off just as bad, and have to relive it all. She was tired and wanted to rebuild her life. Clarity now made her see Nate for what he was. The professional who broke the boundaries. She was vulnerable and he'd taken advantage. Even though Melody wanted it, craved him, he should have known better.

She had made admirable progress to reach the point she was now at. For a long time in hospital, Melody obsessed over Nate, daydreaming about their future. In those three months, she had thought about contacting him many times. Conversations they had, things she wanted to say were like a stuck record in her mind. Torturing her at first as her broken heart felt like a wound that would never heal.

However, as she received help and had breathing space, the rational side of her knew contacting him would never yield the fruit she desired and would likely result in more trouble from authorities. Melody was tired, weary; her head submerged in a pond of slime and mud that she needed to lift to see clearly. Clarity could only happen if she flushed Nate down the toilet. The professional intervention and support helped, and the medication alongside it made her find her way out of the murky water.

His house in Stratford had sold — she'd checked when she left hospital. Not in a stalker way, just as part of her moving on. Almost like her checklist for recovery. His office address had also been removed from his website and Melody wondered if this was to dupe her, before suffocating the thought, like her psychiatrist had talked about. She would be lying if she said she never thought about him and what could have been. In the early days, it threatened to crush her. But now, she controlled her thoughts more than they controlled her.

Back on her medication and back home, Melody knew she had a long way to go and would always have to check herself. However, she was walking in the right direction. Not running, but neither crawling. And she had seen a slight shift in her father over the past month, becoming less panicked, startled, and more balanced.

Zoe helped, a calming influence — the exact opposite of Matthew. She gave more time, more emotion in the way that she could. It helped Melody heal but also helped her feel less responsible for her father's well-being. Life was okay and each day, Melody vowed to herself that she could get through everything and she would continue to thrive.

Chapter 47: Matthew

Melody was home, and Matthew would never let any harm come to her again. He lived with the guilt of failing his son; he wouldn't fail his daughter. They'd been given another chance and he wouldn't screw it up. She had been staying with him, spending the odd night in the flat, and Grace had even stayed a few nights at Matthew's. Now it was time for his daughter to return to the flat.

'Perhaps I'll go back to college, train in something completely different and new. Try to build an actual career,' she had said that Sunday over lunch with her parents, the sparkle returning to her eyes. Zoe nodded enthusiastically, stating it was a brilliant idea and she should have a look online.

Zoe had agreed to pay Melody's full rent for six months, giving her a chance to recover. Even if she wasn't ready for work, she was now receiving benefits that supported her outgoings. Both her parents wanted nothing to happen that could be detrimental to Melody, and that included going back to work too soon or getting another job she hated. They'd lost one child and almost lost another, and they would never take a risk again. And for Matthew, it was time to get revenge against the bastard who caused his precious daughter's relapse.

Now she was back in the flat, he would worry about her. He knew his daughter had to live and be independent, but his whole twenty-four hours a day revolved around her being okay. And whilst Nate Lundie was around, Matthew knew he could never rest well. There was always that chance and now that she was out of hospital, Nate could get to her. Predators don't change, so Matthew had to take control himself.

Four months ago — since that night Melody had been sectioned — Matthew started to put his plan into place. Four months was enough time to move on, forget, especially when not contacted. Matthew had taken it slowly, researching, not rushing into anything that could cause alarm or suspicion. Nate Lundie would think Melody had gone, gotten over it all, like a schoolgirl infatuation. He had no clue that she had been in the hospital, sectioned by mental health professionals for her own safety and the safety of others.

Felix had never received an intervention. A silent cry for help wasn't heard, acknowledged, answered — even by those closest to him, who were meant to protect him. Matthew understood the fragility of life and how brittle his daughter had been and could be again as she clung to an eroding cliff. Mental health professional was a term that Nate Lundie used with pride, yet he had caused the cracking of Matthew's vulnerable daughter. Caused her to break, to almost irreparable levels. Yes, four months was a long time for a predatory therapist with a penchant for young women to move on and to think he had gotten away with it.

Matthew had contacted Nate Lundie two months ago after purchasing a pay-as-you-go mobile phone. He had rung one lunchtime at work as he sat in his car. The predator had answered with a bouncy hello and Matthew — mouth dry and armpits sweaty — had begun his rehearsed lines.

'Hi, I'm looking to possibly see a therapist, so I'm just ringing around to find out about waiting lists and prices, and that.' He had released a friendly laugh at the end.

'Of course, that's the right thing to do. Shop about.'

Condescending prick, Matthew had thought as he said yes, agreeing through gritted teeth.

'Really, I want to see someone as soon as possible, and I drive. I noticed you are in the city centre.'

'Actually, I'm relocating soon. There'll be a few weeks gap from my current premises to my new one. I'm offering a discount for new clients for any location move and inconvenience.'

'Discount? One of my favourite words!' Matthew had chuckled, knowing that keeping the conversation light would help with rapport. 'So, what's your waiting list and process?'

'I would invite you in for a free chat about the service. Then, if you want to proceed, we will schedule six initial sessions and try to work through the issues that brought you to therapy.'

Matthew had heard pages being turned.

'I have capacity next week for the initial, then likely a week or two after that,' the therapist had said.

'That sounds great, thanks. Erm, I do have two more places to ring.' He had paused momentarily to add to his act. 'Ah, you know what? I think I've heard enough. I'd like to book in for that initial chat, please?'

Nate had suggested a day and time early the following week and Matthew had agreed, writing it down.

'So, can I take your name and is this the best number to contact you on?'

'Yes, this number and my name is Matt, Matt Nichols,' he'd said.

'Okay, good. I have put the appointment in the diary and look forward to meeting you next week, Matt.'

'Me too, bye.'

Matthew had hung up, exited his car, and walked back from his break thinking that he could hardly wait to meet the bastard. Matthew was a kind, caring man. But he'd had enough of losing the people he loved, and the guilt had aged his body and mind faster than the years ever could.

He had managed eight years of looking after his daughter as he witnessed her struggle in the shadow of her former self. Daily panics, paranoia, fear. Frantic in case she got poorly again and feeling helpless. Then everything imploded once Felix died and his life revolved around protecting Melody. The suddenness of Felix's death and the helplessness they had all felt made Matthew obsessed with keeping his daughter safe. And when Zoe left, she was all he had.

After the last six months, seeing her decline to almost catastrophic levels — just managing to stay afloat with the support of professionals who didn't take advantage of her — Matthew wanted revenge against the man who caused it all. The man who was a professional and was supposed to help. And although Melody was stable now, Nate Lundie had taken another chunk out of her. Even though she had healed somewhat, the scar would always be there and the predator could return for another assault.

Now, as Matthew sat on his sofa, sipping a beer, he recalled his and Nate Lundie's initial meeting, those weeks ago. For the first meeting, Matthew had taken a half day from work. His employer had been good with him, giving flexibility where they could, and he had done some longer shifts and weekends around Melody's needs. He'd caught the Tube to King's Cross, feeling apprehensive.

Walking out of the hectic King's Cross Station, Matthew had strolled to the office that Nate Lundie would soon move from.

That was okay; Matthew would travel. He'd travel across the world and back to protect his daughter. Having rehearsed the story he would feed Nate Lundie, Matthew had felt confident he could lie convincingly. His tale would be to say his wife, Suzanne, had died suddenly and he was stuck in grief.

As he walked, he had laughed sadly. It was true, the stuck in grief part anyway. Shaking his head, he'd inhaled, feeling shit for lying and thought of Zoe. But needs must and he needed to protect their child. Once he duped Nate Lundie into thinking he needed therapy, it would be easy. He'd make that bastard pay and his upcoming office move had helped to formulate Matthew's plan.

On reaching his destination, a pleasant woman behind a desk directed Matthew to the right office. He had walked up the stairs, taking deep breaths, pushing his shoulders back. Standing outside of Lundie Therapy, he had closed his eyes and swallowed, clenching and unclenching his fists. He knew he would have to use all his mental strength to not lunge at disgusting Nate Lundie and punch him — and as revenge got closer, Matthew had realised how mentally strong he was. He'd cleared his throat, straightened his collar, and knocked on the office door.

During the initial assessment, Matthew was twitchy and slow to answer, conscious of building his lie and not making things too complex — worried it could trip him up in future sessions. He kept losing his rehearsed act, as the need to make the bastard pay had blared in his mind. He had hoped Nate assumed it was nerves as he offered a soft voice and sympathetic glances. Matthew wanted to confront him, scream at him, assault him — using all his restraint to not knock the sleazy grin from the patronising prick's face.

That hour had been a torturous, necessary evil. Suffocating his instinct to protect his daughter, Matthew knew he had to play the long game, and he had sat on his hands, remaining as calm as he could whilst he'd talked a little about the death of his wife. At the end of the discussion, Matthew had rose from the comfortable yellow sofa and shook the hand of the man who had broken his daughter.

'Thanks. This has been really helpful,' he'd said, a fake smile he had perfected in the mirror flashing across his face.

'Excellent. I'm so pleased, Matt. And well done for opening up about Suzanne. Have a think and if you want to book some sessions, just get in touch,' Nate had replied.

Matthew stood looking at him, as he tried to keep his face from reacting to his thoughts of disgust and malice. He had rolled his shoulder and cleared his throat before walking towards the exit. Nate had followed, leant past Matthew and opened the door for him. Biting back the rage and desire to punch him in the face, Matthew had fake smiled as he got a whiff of his aftershave. It was going to mentally torture Matthew but this had to happen. It was the only way he would pay for what he had done to Melody, and no doubt, countless other women.

Turning to face Nate again, Matthew had reached into the inside pocket of his Harrington jacket. His fingers touched what they were searching for and he had trembled, uncertain he could pull it out. Nate had watched, likely wondering why his possible new client was taking so long to leave. His shaking fingers had pulled an envelope out of his inside pocket.

'Here you go. I've thought already; I'd like to book six sessions, please. I need to deal with what's going on in here.' He'd tapped the side of his head and flashed a smile. 'I've got the cash here. A bit old school, I know,' he had chuckled, 'but cash is king!'

The therapist's eyes had widened. 'Oh, great. Yeah, absolutely. Cash is fine. I can write you a receipt.' He'd moved back into the room, towards his desk and Matthew had interjected.

'No rush. I will get it next time.' He'd glanced at his watch and back to Nate then pushed the door open. 'I have to dash. Just let me know when you have an appointment. Texting is fine.' Matthew had walked through the doorway.

'Thanks. Will do. Enjoy the rest of your week, Matt.'

'Oh, I will. And you.'

Matthew had taken the stairs, left the building and walked onto the busy city centre street. His insides had felt like a helicopter spinning out of control. Leaning against the building wall, he'd gulped in air as his legs wobbled.

After that initial assessment, Matthew had returned home and remained awake until 3 am, a destructive storm of revenge building inside of him. He had immediately understood why Melody had fallen for the therapist. Nate Lundie had the silver-fox charm of a man who had known he was good-looking all of his life. A cockiness that would have made him arrogant and popular in his late teens and early twenties, but in his late forties made him punchable and predatory.

Matthew could almost visualise him looking at his daughter and other women. Using his intelligence, authority, and good looks as a way to manipulate women. The knight in shining armour routine of this handsome, knowledgeable professional who was going to solve all their problems. Only he wasn't professional. Nate Lundie was a predator. A perpetrator who targeted vulnerable women and Matthew was going to stop it. He had vowed then to end Nate Lundie's career and make him pay for putting his daughter on such a dangerous trajectory. However, he had to play the game; get him on side.

It had been easy to bend the truth and get the assessment. Matthew had given Zoe's maiden name as his surname and provided an address randomly picked. No proof of identity had been required. It wasn't like it was a free service, Matthew had handed over a wad of cash, paying top dollar for this pleasure. The pleasure of being part of and witnessing what would be the demise of Nate Lundie. He would never again be the puppet master of vulnerable women. Matthew would see to that.

Since that initial assessment, it had been more challenging than swimming the Channel for Matthew to not put his hands around Nate's throat and throttle him during the three and a half hours he had already spent with the so-called therapist.

That first initial assessment, he'd been shaking, even noticed by Nate, who had spoken reassuring words to him about recovery, support, and being brave. Matthew had smiled, biting back the inferno of anger in him.

Brave? The piece of shit knew nothing about bravery. His daughter had been through so much. She and all the other people trying to survive their mental illness were the brave ones. The thought of what happened to Felix possibly happening to Melody, was enough to almost stop his heart beating. Never again would he let his daughter be at risk.

Matthew had taken his time at the sessions with Nate Lundie, speaking and answering after thinking, anxious he would trip himself up. He'd shown emotion, kept his story simple, and talked about his love for his wife — which was still true. Lying about her death had been difficult, but the emotion for Felix cascaded from him. This wasn't the type of thing Matthew would have dreamt of doing, but desperation had led him to it and now he wouldn't, couldn't stop. Getting into character, he had shared the 'death' of his wife of thirty years, claiming Suzanne had died due to a heart attack, leaving him and their adult son destroyed.

He had talked about their marriage, much of it true, omitting any reference to Felix and Melody, but referring to an adult son. He had made the odd mistake, referring to her as still 'being around' but Nate hadn't seemed to have realised, or he had nodded in the way of acknowledging that love never dies, even if the person does.

Many of the emotions had been real and Matthew had felt a reservoir of tears building in the sessions. Then, he would be snapped out of it by Nate opening his mouth and making a comment. Using his manipulation and charisma that Matthew was sure he had used to seduce his daughter. And it fuelled Matthew, giving him an unstoppable energy to get revenge.

He had asked Nate a few questions each time before their subsequent two sessions had started, and again on the third one at the library after he moved office location. Nothing too obvious, too personal. Just small talk, showing an interest. Matthew knew it would make him feel like a person as well as a therapist. Important, and no doubt it would inflate his already cruise liner-sized ego.

Nate Lundie was nothing more than an exploiter of disadvantage. Like a pimp getting a sex worker addicted to drugs to keep her in the role, Nate kept people poorly for his own gains — well, at least that's what he had done to Melody. However, Matthew had gained his trust over those several weeks, and was one step closer in his plan for Nate Lundie to get what he deserved; a punishment that would keep him away from young, vulnerable women. It may be next week that he would get to go to Nate's home or the week after, but as soon as he was there, Matthew would get his chance for revenge.

Chapter 48: Nate

Nate had lived in his new home for over two months and he'd slept like a bear in hibernation. The lack of noise, the calmness of a quiet street with only a handful of houses and spaced-out cars. No busy roads making a hum twenty-four-seven nearby. And the calming bird sound, that was heavenly. Well, for him, anyway. There was the added release of the anonymity he now had from his past. Not just Melody, but his former neighbours who knew about his marriage crumbling, and no doubt had spied on him since. Like the air releasing from a blocked radiator, he had felt the burst of relief from his fresh start.

Having handed the keys in for his office in King's Cross last week, he had explained to his clients that he was on annual leave for a week, then he would be in touch regarding a place for the next sessions. The plan was to hire a room in the library for a week or two, whilst he finished decorating the summer house in his back garden. Nate deliberately managed his diary the two months before to ensure he didn't have a large temporary waiting list.

It meant he knew, and therefore felt comfortable with most of his clients, only two being relatively new. In the future, Nate would assess new clients in a hired room at the library, perhaps even conducting the first therapy session there, before the remaining being in his summer house. The garden office would save a massive amount of money in the long-run, but he still had to be cautious.

After a week off and four days working on the final touches to the summer house, Nate arrived at the library for three sessions, back-to-back. The library was a great community resource and the library manager, Clare, had been very accommodating, offering to put posters up advertising his services. Nate was going to enjoy the slower pace of life that living in the village would provide. He'd even looked at a local gym he was planning on joining. Life was feeling positive and with his past firmly in the past, Nate knew things could only get better.

Walking to the library was in contrast to the stop-start of rush hour Nate had experienced from inner-city working. The smog and horns blasting that were demoralising after a full day. With a bounce in his stride, he soon reached the library, grabbing a cappuccino and treating himself to a slice of carrot cake from their small café. Clare showed him to the room he had hired, providing a jug of water and glasses. Thanking her, he set up and waited for his first client of the day. Three hours passed and Nate had his final client due in fifteen minutes: Matt Nichols.

Having already met a few times, he was gathering more information on Matt. A serious, middle-aged man, Matt had lost his wife suddenly, to a heart attack. He had an adult son who lived in another part of the country, and he wanted help to manage his grief and fear of further loss. The sessions were going well, despite Nate feeling Matt was a little strange. During the therapy, Matt had zoned out a few times, his expression blank and his eyes fixed on Nate. Then it was as if a switch flicked and he would blink and return to the conversation.

Matt would swing from being very open to aloof, and would laugh at inappropriate times. Nate had witnessed similar before but Matt Nichols definitely gave off odd vibes. He chuckled to himself. Most people were strange, that was the nature of Nate's profession. It didn't really bother him. He'd had his fair share of oddballs as clients over the years, and instead, he just tried various tactics and approaches to get the best for the client. After all, everyone dealt with things differently.

Matt Nichols was from the same generation as Nate and many men their age found it hard to talk. It could explain how at times, Matt seemed to fluctuate between being robotic, intense, and jittery. Nate was used to breaking down barriers and he felt he was helping Matt to do just that. His case was something Nate saw frequently, along with relationship problems. He felt equipped to support him and as a guy close to fifty, Matt was opening up and considering advice from him positively.

'How have you been this week, Matt?' Nate asked as he poured him some water.

'Actually, good. My son is doing well and has decided to leave his thankless job in retail and go back to college.'

Nate nodded, pushing his glasses up his nose.

'It's all you want, you see, as a parent. For your child to be safe. Happy. To be free from pain and predators in society.' He smiled, glaring at Nate, then took a sip of his water.

'Yes,' Nate replied, thinking predators was a strange choice of words, but perhaps Matt was alluding to the systems of employment, societal expectations, and so forth.

He began referring to some worksheets they had discussed in the first week, including the Dual Process Model. Matt was attentive and nodded. The session soon ended and Matt requested the last appointment Nate had available the following Thursday, as he was working late. Nate didn't mind. Many of his clients were employed and although mostly he worked until 6 pm with clients, Matt's request for a 6:30 pm session didn't bother him. After all, he wouldn't have the commute home.

'As mentioned last time, I am hoping that next week, my summer house is ready, Matt. However, I'll reserve this room and email you the day before if there is a change in the venue. It's only five minutes' drive from here and there is plenty of parking in my street, so hopefully that's not a problem?'

Matt smiled. 'Not at all. Thanks. I will look forward to seeing your summer house. It sounds lovely, even without the summer weather!' Matt chuckled and Nate joined in as he saw him out of the small room.

It had been Nate's last appointment of the day and after saying goodnight to the library staff, he strolled home, breathing deeply, absorbing everything around him, and feeling grateful.

Chapter 49: Melody

There was something comforting about simple things. The bread toasted to the perfect golden shade, fresh linen, biscuits dunked in a cup of tea, and flowers received as a gift. Melody smiled at the sunshine-yellow roses in a vase. Standing proudly, they glowed against her light grey wall. They were a gift from Grace, with a card saying she would always be there for her and she was proud of her. Those supermarket roses had meant more to her than she could express and she had beamed as her friend handed her them.

Sitting on the IKEA Poang chair in her bedroom, she sipped tea and leant back, stretching her legs out in front. It was definitely the simple things that meant the most. After the last six months, Melody hadn't thought she would ever be grateful for such things. Couldn't imagine seeing the beauty and joy in the everyday. So consumed by Nate's rejection and ongoing mind-screwing he had projected onto her.

The rage in her had risen as the lucidity of thoughts declined. The crescendo was that night by the Thames. Thanks to the kind woman, she was now mending. Not healed, but healing. She was a work in progress, and that was okay. She had the tools to sculpt herself and, if a crack appeared, Melody knew how to repair it.

She still thought about Nate. The what ifs? The could-have-been. She wondered if he thought of her. If he had regrets. The difference now was that she wasn't going to act on anything. He'd not called the police and reported the assault. Perhaps he knew he had more to lose than her — his professional career.

Melody had already lost so much: Lily, Felix, her parents as a unit, Brandon, her job. And she had been losing her mind — it trickling into the gutter like heavy rainfall. But that was the past and now she'd been out of St Ann's Hospital for over a month and was back in her flat full-time. She yawned, content in her room, looking at the flowers huddled together in their vessel.

Matthew seemed to be doing okay. He'd loved having Melody stay. She would make sure she kept going to his through the week and was cherishing her Sunday lunches — the three of them. In the hospital, she had noticed his demeanour, leaving her guilt-ridden for ageing her grieving father and mother with an elephant's weight of worry. Other people's children were grown up, with careers and houses. Some married and with babies. It had made her realise, reflect, and vow to be more emotionally responsible and mature. She was lucky people cared but she had to begin to manage her own emotions, her own life, and let her parents heal and enjoy their lives.

The anxiety Melody had created in her father was like Sellotape around him that got stickier and thicker in its layers, restricting his movement, his breathing, his freedom through the paralysing worry he held for her. As the curtains on her world opened, she could see how heavy his were and how near they were to closing. She'd been selfish and she would learn from her mistakes and no longer lie to her parents about how she felt.

But Melody had made her dad also promise to be transparent and learn to trust her. They had to heal together, the three of them. Zoe could begin to show vulnerability, not having to be the strong, together one all of the time.

Things would be alright, Melody felt it. She had no job, but working at Crawford's had been a slow poison. She was receiving financial support via benefits to help her manage until she felt recovered. Now she was hoping to start college in the future, maybe studying social care. Yes, things would all be okay and as she put her cup down on the carpet beside her, she yawned again, feeling relaxed and the happiest she had felt in a long time.

Chapter 50: Matthew

That Wednesday, Matthew had taken Melody to a new bistro for dinner. She was chirpy and talked about an appointment earlier that week at the local college with Zoe.

'You know, all this, Dad, it's made me think about going to college in the future.' She pulled some spinach from the side salad next to her flatbread and ate it. 'The last eight years, maybe my whole life, where I've struggled. I want to help people like the *decent* people who've helped me.'

Matthew squeezed her hand across the table. He forked some of his creamy carbonara into his mouth.

'If I know my triggers and keep managing, maybe I can use the shitty things I've been through to help other people. When the time is right.' She cut into her crispy sundried tomato and mozzarella flatbread.

Wiping his mouth, Matthew tilted his head. 'Well, there's nothing better than that lived experience, Melly. But you have to be ready. It's too soon and your past might make getting work harder?' He spoke in a gentle voice.

Swallowing her food, she nodded. 'The course doesn't start again for eight months and the health and social care courses are two years at college, then possible further study, so, it wouldn't be rushed. I've done some research, there are places, mainly charities, that employ people with a criminal record.' She said the last few words quietly, glancing at her plate as she pressed her lips together. 'That personal experience can help with empathy and rapport.' She shrugged and paused for a few seconds. 'It might not be the right time next year, but perhaps it would be a focus and I can get a part-time job, maybe somewhere like here,' she said, looking around at the quaint décor and quirky mismatched seats.

'Sounds like a possible plan, love. I'm proud of you. Your mum is, too. And Felix…' he swallowed, 'he would be as well.' Matthew smiled weakly.

'I miss him so much, Dad. He was stuck, you know,' Melody tapped her neck, 'in here. An enormous lump in my throat that I carried and became other things: Brandon, you and Mum separating, worrying about you. Then everything with Nate.' She looked down at the table, and Matthew tasted the bitterness of guilt on his tongue.

'But the hospital, getting the *right* help. Well, it did help. And it made me appreciate you and Mum more. I'm sorry, Dad.' Tears formed in her eyes.

'Shhh, love, you've already said sorry a hundred times. There's nothing to be sorry for. I'm sorry for being overbearing sometimes. You're just so precious to me, Melly. And well, I nearly lost you.' His hands became fists as he thought of that bastard therapist. 'That predator, Lundie, he shouldn't get away with it.'

Melody shrugged. 'I know, Dad, he's a total pervert scumbag. I hate him. But what can I do? I assaulted him, remember?' She chuckled, but he saw the vulnerable, young sixteen-year-old beneath his adult daughter's façade.

'It still stings but I'm tired and want to just move on.' She shook her head slightly and swallowed.

'He's dangerous. He could do this again. It all…' Matthew sighed and scrunched his eyes shut for a moment.

'I'm here, Dad, and he'll get his karma.' She shrugged before popping some more flatbread in her mouth.

He nodded, determination heating his body. Swirling the spaghetti around his fork, his eyes watched his food dance. 'Yes, love, he will.'

Later that evening, Matthew sat on his sofa with a cup of tea, watching the news. It was the night before his next fake therapy session with Nate Lundie. He checked his cheap mobile phone and was pleased to see a text message from the bastard himself.

Hi Matt, I hope you're well. My new office is now completed, so if it works for you, can you please come to my address: 4 Lawson Lane, Much Hadham, East Hertfordshire. There's parking throughout the lane and my property has a red front door. Any problems, give me a call. Thanks.

Matthew clasped his hands together, a shiver of adrenalin rushing through him. This was his chance; his way to seek revenge on the pervert who had stripped another layer of confidence off his daughter that she had fought so hard to build. And in a way, it was for Felix and the failings Matthew carried each day like wearing an iron suit. Nate Lundie needed consequences for his actions. The things he couldn't do to have saved Felix, he would do to save Melody. He quickly replied.

Hi Nate, I am good, hope you are too. Great, thanks, I will see you then at 6:30 pm.

His hand was trembling and he took a deep breath. 'It has to happen. For Melody,' he said aloud. It was his duty. He turned the TV off and walked up the stairs, staring at the beige, worn carpet under his feet. Reaching the top stair, he glanced along the landing to the empty rooms that used to be full. Felix's shrine, Melody's old bedroom, and the master bedroom — now his room minus Zoe. He opened the door to his bedroom and like he did each time, Matthew hoped he would see Zoe in there, singing as she straightened the never-ending cushions they had crowding the bed. Every time, he was greeted with emptiness. He was doing this for the happiness they used to have. And because he knew, no matter how strong Zoe pretended she was, she was a broken jigsaw, with lost, damaged pieces.

Matthew bent down and opened the drawer under the king-sized divan bed. It glided out and revealed blankets and spare bedding, neatly folded and tucked into place. Matthew slid a hand in between the rows of uniform material and pulled out a pillowcase containing something. He unfolded the cream material — the smell of fabric conditioner being replaced by the scent of metal — and pulled out a gun.

Turning it over in his hands, he remarked at its authentic look. Then he sniggered to himself. He had never seen a real gun. However, after much research, he had ordered a Retay S22 9 mm blank firing pistol. It looked the real I am, and he'd paid good money for the handgun. Matthew wasn't in the business or knowledge of where to get real guns and, well, even though Nate Lundie had to pay, he didn't want anyone to die — unless it came down to self-defence. The gun definitely looked genuine as the metal glimmered in the bedroom light. Matthew turned it over in his hands a few times, his thoughts temporarily travelling elsewhere. Then he lifted it, holding it at arm's length and made a 'ptchooo' noise, as he pretended to shoot.

Chapter 51: Nate

The summer house was complete and it was the perfect therapy room. Nate had cladded the inside on one wall with wood panelling. Painting the other three white, he had hung black and white photos of London Landmarks. Buckingham Palace, Tower Bridge, the Houses of Parliament and Big Ben, and one of the famous skyline. His old office chair and yellow sofa sat in the room, with a new faux-fur rug and wooden table, carved and containing a river of gold resin, from a local craftsperson. New grey cushions and a grey throw decorated the sofa and dimmer LED lights and a standing lamp added brightness for the dark nights.

Looking around his new office, Nate sighed in satisfaction. He'd worked hard to create it, with Brian's help, and now the tranquil space was ready. For Nate, his new office indicated a fresh start in another element of his life. Despite rent costs, he had been happy enough in his city centre location. Although the commute was far from ideal, and that was just living a few miles away. After Melody had polluted it, there was always a stink in the room and an air that made him feel suffocated.

The summer house had cost a small fortune but would add value to the property. Plus, no city centre rent and commuting costs meant it was a clear investment for Nate. Many other therapists worked from home and it was successful for them, so why not? There were still some bits to do in the house: a new kitchen and bathroom at some point in the near future, and decorating. But it was liveable, homely, and Nate was in no rush to do everything. In fact, the project would be something he would enjoy as he settled into his new community.

Having found the local amenities, including the library, supermarket, shops, and pubs, Nate felt like Much Hadham was home within weeks. He would join the gym, looking forward to getting back into a routine. Still on the dating site, he'd not been as active, only going on a few dates over the last few months. In truth, he couldn't be arsed with the chase, much of which was for something he would never catch nor want to.

Perhaps he would meet someone local now that he was becoming part of the community. He'd taken some chocolates into the library for their hospitality and reduced room rates, joining as a library member whilst there. Tomorrow, Nate had his first two clients attending the summer house for their therapy sessions: his 2 pm and then Matt Nichols at 6:30 pm.

It was 6 pm the next evening and Nate was finishing his dinner of ribs and mashed potato. Wiping a slice of bread around the meat juice and buttery liquid, he enjoyed the silence. No TV on, no cars fighting for parking spaces, and no slamming of doors from neighbours as the cottage was detached. Just peace, calmness, and ease, in his often-silent street. Placing his plate and cutlery in the dishwasher, Nate washed his hands and tidied a little before sitting near his front window, the blinds half shut, to wait for Matt Nichols' arrival.

The summer house had easy access through the side gate in his front garden. He had taken his earlier client straight through the gate, preventing the person going through his home, which felt like a good way to separate the sites and have a more professional vibe. Nate was hoping people didn't ask to use his bathroom, but as appointments were only an hour, he predicted this would be seldom. He would just ensure not too much water was offered!

It was 6:28 pm when he saw Matt Nichols march down his garden path. Raising his eyebrows, he sniggered at odd Matt's wooden, abrupt manner as he approached his door. Notepad and Matt's file in hand, Nate opened the door a few seconds after the bell rang. The security lighting came on and he saw Matt step back, slightly blinded by the bright light.

'Hi, Matt, sorry about that light!' He chuckled. 'The street lighting isn't great here, so it's just for some added security.'

Matt nodded, looking around. 'Hi, erm yes, I understand.'

'The therapy room is just this way.' Nate stepped out of his front door and around the side of the cottage, followed by Matt.

Another security light came on as he reached the side gate and Matt followed. Nate didn't see his car.

'Where did you park?' He asked, looking over his shoulder as he slid out the bolt in the gate.

'Ah, just up the top of the lane. I saw a parking space and, well, I wasn't sure how far down your house was.'

Nate nodded. Matt seemed more tense than usual. Perhaps it was the new venue. 'Here we go,' Nate said as they approached the summer house, lights shining into the dark garden from inside. Opening the door, he held it for Matt to walk in.

'Very nice. Scandinavian style.' Matt glanced around. 'You must help a lot of troubled people to afford this.' He laughed a strange laugh and Nate just said yes, thinking Matt must feel awkward on his property.

'Take a seat, please,' Nate said as he pointed to the sofa and poured Matt some water.

Matt opened his black Harrington jacket but left it on as he took a seat. 'Hope you don't lure young women to your house,' he said as Nate put the jug back down.

Matt's face had no expression. There was no smile of a joke or wink in a bloke-like way. Nothing, just a glare at Nate. *What a weird thing to say,* thought Nate, shaking his head, more dismissing the comment, and took a seat opposite Matt. They talked for ten minutes, with Matt discussing his son starting a relationship with an older woman.

'Funny, isn't it? We shun an older woman for having a relationship with a young man. They get called all names like cradle snatcher, cougar, desperate. Yet, a man and a younger female, well, the man is always cheered for pulling a younger woman. Why do you think that is?' He took a sip of his water and focused his eyes on Nate, awaiting an answer.

Nate's views on age-gap relationships were a little off topic, but it was something that was going on in Matt's life that attributed to his emotional well-being. He uncrossed his legs, crossing them back on the other side and straightened his glasses.

'You're right. Society judges age-gap relationships, but it's always an older woman who gets the most stigma. Maybe it's the maternal element that people focus on. The could be his mother type of views, whereas the parental comments don't seem to be thrown around as much when an older man dates a younger woman.' Nate rubbed his mouth and took his glasses off, placing them on the side table.

Matt nodded, resting his clasped hands on his lap.

'I mean, look at Leonardo DiCaprio. Apparently, he's dated no woman over twenty-five. Then again, Matt, successful relationships are based on more than just the age of two people. It's the people, really. So, I hope it works out for your son.'

Nate smiled at Matt, picking up his pen again, hoping to move the conversation from his views back to his client's current emotional blockages and stresses. Instead, Matt adjusted his shoulders before asking another question, eyes fixed on the therapist.

'Would you date a younger woman then? How old are you? Mid-forties? Would you date a woman who was under twenty-five?'

Nate cleared his throat and moved slightly in his chair. 'Well, I'm not sure it's relevant, but yes, I would if we had a connection. I know you mentioned the importance of your son being happy and how much you worry about him. Hopefully, this new relationship will provide some assurance.' Nate wanted to steer the conversation away from his views on dating younger women.

'Do you mind if I use your toilet, please, Nate?' Matt stood up quickly.

Christ, the second appointment and already someone wanted to piss in his house! he thought as he rose from his seat as well. 'Of course.' He opened the door of the summer house. Pointing to the back door, he continued. 'The back door is open. It's through the kitchen and straight on your left-hand side. Just watch your head as it slopes under the stairs.' He smiled as Matt passed him and walked into the garden.

At least people pissing in his house could use the downstairs toilet and not his main bathroom. That was one thing. Perhaps he would need some room spray to leave in there. Crikey, if a client took a dump in there, it would make Nate cringe. Whilst Matt used his toilet, he quickly checked his phone, scrolling through the dating app. There were a few messages, two of which were replies to messages he had instigated. Smiling to himself, he looked at the profile of a woman who had sent a new message.

'Nice,' he said aloud, quickly replying.

What was bloody Matt doing? Ah, he better not be having a shit in there, Nate thought, looking at the clock on his wall. He would give it another few minutes and then go and check Matt was okay. Picking up his phone again, he scrolled the news app, seeing what political nonsense was going on. After spending a few minutes reading various local and national articles on his mobile, Nate looked at the time on his phone. Matt had been gone for over ten minutes. He was definitely having a dump in his downstairs toilet. Rolling his eyes, Nate placed his mobile phone on the side table, got up with a groan, and opened the door of the summer house.

The security lights beamed down and Nate walked to his house. Opening the door, he stepped inside his home. Weirdly, the hallway light was off. Nate was certain he had left the light on as he opened the front door when Matt arrived. Walking slowly through the kitchen, he stretched his neck out as he stepped gently on the cream porcelain tiles.

'Matt. Are you alright?'

The back door to his house swung shut, pulled slightly by a sudden light wind. He jumped and looked back, a shiver going through him. *Why did he feel on edge?*

'Matt? Is everything okay?' Something felt off. Maybe Matt Nichols had fallen. *But why were the lights out?* Nate walked into the hallway. He knocked on the door of the downstairs toilet that was directly on the left after the kitchen doorway.

'Hello? Matt?' He tapped again on the door

There was no light coming from the small bathroom and for a moment, Nate relaxed, believing Matt Nichols had left through the front door and gone home — turning the hallway light off on his way out to conserve energy before he buggered off. Opening his mouth, he was about to chuckle. He'd snuck out of a few women's homes in his days, but he'd never experienced this type of moonlight flit.

'I'm here,' said a low, steady voice.

Nate's body turned as the hallway light came on. Blinking, his eyes focused on Matt Nichols, who was standing in his hallway with a gun in his hand, pointing it directly at Nate.

Chapter 52: Matthew

Matthew had practiced holding the gun for the past week and it still felt weird, unnatural. Because it was weird and unnatural for quiet Matthew Dartford — who worked in accounts and played darts twice a week — to be aiming a gun at a therapist in his own home. It was almost laughable. But nothing about what had happened to his daughter because of this bastard was humorous. Even in the session there, the scumbag had talked about dating younger women.

He was nothing but a sexual predator. A pervert, preying on vulnerable women. Women like his daughter and look how that ended. Three months in a psychiatric hospital after the risk of jumping into the River Thames. Despair and desperation and God knows how many triggers that Melody was still trying to work through and manage.

He would never know the extent, because Melody would never tell him the full truth; still wanting to protect him and his own mental health. But Matthew could imagine, and even more so after meeting the therapist. Charming, sleazy, sleek Nate Lundie with his silver hair and piercing blue eyes. His square jawline and broad shoulders, and what looked like an all-year-round bronzed glow. He made Matthew sick, and it was time for revenge.

Standing, as he waited for the prick to come and find him — like they were playing a childhood game — he fished his free hand into his jeans pocket and pulled out his mobile phone to check it was on silent. Shit, there were missed calls from Zoe, his sister Glynis, and Melody, plus a text he didn't read. Placing the phone back, he returned both his shaking hands to holding the replica pistol. Hearing the therapist coming into the house, Nate called out, asking if he was okay. The stupid prick probably thought he had diarrhoea. He sure as hell would have hoped it was the explosive shits after finding the alternative less than a minute later.

Matthew stood, deadly silent, hidden out of view, to the side of the bottom of the stairs. The bastard had taken ages to come into the house, and Matthew had wondered if he could go ahead with it. Then he realised he had to, for her and all the other Melodys of the future.

'Matt? Is everything okay?' Nate had said as he approached the small bathroom and knocked on the door. Ten seconds later, he had tapped on the door once more.

'Hello? Matt?'

Matthew moved from the bottom of the staircase, just a metre or so into view. Holding the gun out with both hands to reduce the shake he felt, he stood in the hallway as Nate turned his body slightly, away from the bathroom door.

'I'm here,' Matthew said as he took a hand from the weapon and flicked on the hallway light. Eyes unblinking, he watched the bronze colour of health drain from Nate Lundie's face as he looked in his direction, standing on the spot, his mouth open.

'Matt, what the hell?' The panic was audible in his voice as the words wobbled and his pitch became higher.

Matthew was concentrating on his own breathing, trying to remain calm, in control, retaining the power.

'In there,' he said, pointing the gun at the lounge doorway.

Nate put his palms up and followed the instruction, his wide eyes on Matthew.

'Sit,' Matthew ordered, reaching to tilt the ajar blinds shut in the room that was already dark, only the light from the hallway seeping in through the open door.

Nate hovered over his black leather sofa as Matthew twisted slightly, pulling the cord of the blinds with one arm as he kept the therapist in his sight, gun pointed towards him.

'I said fucking sit!'

Nate quickly sat on his sofa as Matthew kept the gun pointed to him whilst switching on a small table lamp by the side of an armchair. Nate leant forward, eyes glued on his captor.

'Matt, listen. I do-don't know what this is about, but I can he-help. I can get you the ri-right help,' he stammered as Matthew took a seat in the armchair opposite Nate.

'Right help? You're the fucking problem, Nate. You're the problem and you've been a problem in my life for over a year. *You're* the one that needs help.' He shouted, anger coating his throat.

Nate looked utterly perplexed; a frown of terror on his face as he shook his head slowly whilst his knees bounced. 'I don't know what you mean, but we can talk. Find a solution?'

Standing up, Matthew flared his nostrils and leant into Nate's face. He jerked back, his body going as deep into the sofa as possible, whilst he held his palms up.

'Please, please. I'll do whatever you want.'

Matthew sneered, noticing he was pissing himself — liquid seeping into his blue trousers, turning them darker. He rolled his eyes, curling his lip at Nate soiling himself, and sat back down. 'You don't even know who I am, do you?'

Nate swallowed and shook his head frantically. 'I d-don't

understand.'

'Of course, you don't understand. Because you're so up your own arse, your breath smells of shit.' Matthew could feel his face getting hot with anger. Nate Lundie was so narcissistic he didn't even remember the trauma he caused.

Laughing, he shook his head. 'Ironic, isn't it that you are *meant* to help people? You are *meant* to assist people to move through hard times and be able to manage, thrive even. But instead, you make people poorly. Abuse your authority, your power.'

Leaning over from where he sat on the edge of the armchair, he smashed the replica pistol into an ornament by the side of a wood burner. It shattered and Nate flinched. His eyes, filled with terror, flashed on the broken ceramic, then returned to Matthew's face. Seeing Nate's legs trembling, the man who thought he was God's gift to women had turned into a wriggling worm. Spittle formed at the side of Matthew's mouth as his body moved closer to him, less than three metres separating them.

'*You*, Nate Lundie, are the man who put my daughter in hospital.'

The therapist put his hand to his head and began shaking it, nothing becoming clearer as Matthew spoke.

'I… I really do-don't…'

Matthew sneered, twisting his mouth as his eyes bore into Nate's, which resembled a child's watching a horror film. 'My name, you son of a bitch, is Matthew Dartford.'

Chapter 53: Nate

There was a deranged glint in his eyes as Matt Nichols ordered Nate into his lounge. With a gun gripped in his hand, he'd closed the blinds with a menacing grin and sat pointing the pistol at him from the armchair. His body took over, and Nate pissed himself. Feeling the warm spread of urine soak his trousers which then clung to his hot skin, he felt a rush of embarrassment similar to when he wet the bed as a kid — through fear of his father.

He thought he might faint and hoped odd Matt was going to burst out laughing and say it was all a joke. Albeit the most twisted joke he would have heard in a long time, he studied the madman's face, thinking in the next few seconds it would all be revealed as a sick prank. But his captor said no such thing and Nate realised that it wasn't a prank: it was real.

This unhinged bastard, in his home, with a fucking gun, ranting sentence after sentence of shit. If he got out of this holdup, he would make sure the mad prick went to prison for a long time. Day one of opening his home up as a therapy office and this is what he gets. He almost wanted to laugh at the ridiculousness of this wannabee-hard man in his lounge. But as a gun was pointed in his direction, he chose instead to listen to his insane captor and if need be, try to recall hostage negotiation skills that he had learnt all those years ago as a teacher.

Attempting to take deep breaths to keep his heart from bursting, he listened as Matt Nichols talked in riddles and accusations. He didn't bite back, unarmed and in the company of a psychopath, he didn't fancy his chances. After Nate's initial approach of offering help, the response soon made Nate realise this was more than an episode of instability. He didn't have to wait long to discover what it was all about.

Mentioning putting his daughter in hospital, Nate felt his brain was melting like the contents of a freezer during a power cut in August. *Daughter? Matt only mentioned he had a son. No daughter was ever discussed?* His facial expression and dropping his head to his hands must have displayed his perplexed thought process.

'I… I really do-don't…'

Matt sneered at him, his eyes looking sunken in the low-lit room and his mouth contorted into an almost unnatural position. 'My name, you son of a bitch, is Matthew Dartford.'

Nate felt acidic bile rise in his throat. He swallowed and winced, feeling certain this was his last night on earth. Melody's dad. The father who she had described as overbearing, overprotective, and who had sounded pretty fucking unwell himself. Yes, he was definitely fucking unwell and here he was, in his lounge, looking like he should be in Broadmoor, with a gun as an extension to his hand. Nate placed a shaking hand to his mouth to stop sick and a scream escaping. He needed to speak, but couldn't.

Mad Matthew Dartford began ranting again. 'Yes, my daughter is Melody. Beautiful messed-up Melody who you almost destroyed. And you know what's the funny part, you predator?'

Nate stared at him.

'Do you fucking know?' he screamed at Nate.

Nate shook his head frantically as he felt sweat dripping

down his back.

'I'll tell you. I will tell you what the funny thing is in all of this, Mr Lundie.' Matthew tipped back his head and laughed.

Jesus, he was like the bloody Joker.

'It's that I paid for those fucking sessions. Me! I paid for her to go into the monster's lair.' His jaw stiffened and he waved the gun from side to side in the direction of Nate's left and right shoulder.

Nate swallowed. His mouth was drier than sand and he wanted to shoot himself for putting his mobile phone on the side table in the summer house.

'Do you have any idea how that makes me feel?' He began tapping the gun into the palm of his other hand. Nate's eyes were wide, watching the gun, frantic it could go off.

'Since she was a teenager, and sectioned after the fire,' he inhaled, flaring his nostrils and moved his jaw from left to right, 'I've made it my life, my whole life, to protect her. My whole life, everything I've got to protect my baby.'

He stared off into space and Nate looked around quickly for something to use as a weapon. Matthew's eyes darted back to his prisoner and he leant forward, closer to him.

'My other baby, my precious son. We lost him, suddenly. Melody is all I have left.' He let out a manic laugh, stopping abruptly, and his eyes bore into Nate. 'And I paid for her to see a bastard like you.'

Matthew stood up out of the armchair and Nate put his palms up. 'Please… please Matt…'

'It's Matthew, you fucking pervert.'

Nate felt a crack in his cheek as the weight of metal chipped at the bone of his face. His neck jerked to one side and he let out a low groan.

'You! You have to pay for what you did to her,' he screamed in Nate's face, spittle gathering around his twisted mouth.

He held his hands up, a feeble attempt to cover himself as he felt a loose tooth plop onto his tongue. 'I didn't know!' he blurted. 'I didn't know she had gone to hospital. Our sessions, they'd finished.' Nate began crying, desperate to explain and to get out of this frenzied situation.

Matthew sat back down and laughed sarcastically. 'Oh, they'd finished alright. I know that and I also know that you tried to screw my daughter and for some reason that I absolutely fail to see myself...' He chuckled again, menacingly, as every fibre of Nate's being detested the day he met Melody Dartford. '...Melody was in love with you!' He hmphed.

Nate wiped his face on his jumper sleeve. 'She is a lovely woman,' he began as Matthew's maniac eyes glared at him. 'Very intelligent and strong. We were drunk and kissed and that was so wrong of me.'

Matthew raised an eyebrow before grasping the gun a little tighter. Nate felt dizzy, but he had to try to explain. It could be his only chance of getting out alive.

'Your daughter. I think she became a little infatuated with me.'

Diving up out of his seat, Matthew put the gun right in front of Nate's face. Screaming, he curled up on the sofa, his whole body shaking in terror.

'Please, please...'

'Don't you fucking dare blame her for this. You're some kind of doctor. You have a code of practice. You groomed her, my vulnerable daughter. I could have lost her like I lost Felix,' he screamed, emotion painting his face as he almost hopped on the spot, the gun moving with him.

If he doesn't shoot me, that gun will surely go off anyway, the way that disturbed prick is using it as a juggling ball, thought Nate as he slowly put a hand up. 'Please, let me explain.'

Matthew stepped onto the geometric rug and sat back in the armchair.

'She's very attractive, but you're right, I have a code of conduct. After that drunken kiss, I tried to tell Melody that it couldn't happen between us, even if she wasn't my client.' Nate licked his lips, his mouth so dry he was sure his tongue would crack open. His legs were bouncing like a rubber ball and he moved a hand onto each thigh, trying to steady them. The maniac's stare burnt into him. Unblinking, fuelled by hatred and revenge. 'I even offered to refer her to another therapist and return all the money.'

Matthew let out a pffftt noise.

'But she insisted that she wanted the last two sessions. That all would be fine. It wasn't and your daughter wanted a relationship. I tried to be considerate and not hurt her feelings but...'

Matthew got up again but paced the room rather than pointing the gun in Nate's face. 'She was vulnerable, you filthy old man.' He put a hand to his head as he walked back and forth, the table lamp creating an eerie shadow. 'She came to you for help and you abused your power.' Standing on the spot, he snarled at Nate like a rabid dog.

Nate nodded frantically. 'It went too far. I should have been firmer in telling her. I tried.' He frowned, his heart racing.

Matthew shook his head. 'I bet you do this all the time. London's own Leonardo DiCaprio.' He curled his lip. 'My baby, she ended up back in the psychiatric hospital. Eight years later. Eight years of waste, to go back to square one. Because of you!' he screamed and began sobbing.

Nate felt panic soak him. 'I'm sorry. I had no idea she…'

Then Matthew lunged at him, striking the gun against the side of Nate's head, and it all went dark.

Chapter 54: Melody

Looking at her mobile phone, Melody saw her auntie was calling.

'Hi, Auntie Glynis. You alright?' she said as she carried her plate through to the kitchen.

'Hi, Melly. I've been to your dad's to drop the cakes off for the darts competition tomorrow night. He wasn't in. Is he there?'

'No. Maybe he was in the shower?' She tucked her head into her neck to hold her mobile as she scraped some remnants of food into the bin.

She hmm'd. 'I don't think so, love. I rang twice and his car wasn't there.'

After chatting for another minute, their call ended with Melody saying she would let her auntie know once Matthew had been in touch. Checking her phone to read their text messages, her dad hadn't texted back after her lunchtime text. Usually, he would message after work, commenting what he was eating for tea and ask her what she was having. Melody scratched her head. Perhaps he had gone for a walk? But Auntie Glynis said his car wasn't there on the driveway. Maybe he went to practice for darts and forgot to tell his sister or he might have just popped to the shops. Melody shook her head at her spiralling thoughts as she tied her hair up into a messy bun and tucked her feet up on the sofa.

She called her dad and got no reply, before texting. At least she would see when he had read it. Within five minutes, two ticks appeared, showing he had. Waiting for the three dots to start, that indicated he was texting back, she watched the screen. A few minutes passed and there was no sign of her dad replying. She would give it ten minutes or so. Perhaps he was on the cusp of winning the darts round.

She tutted, thinking she was worrying about nothing and turning into her dad! Getting up from the sofa, Melody went to make a cup of tea. As the kettle boiled, she washed her dishes from dinner. Scooping the pasta bake out of the oven dish, she put it in a bowl for Grace, who was staying at the library late, her final exams approaching. A cuppa and an episode of her current box set later, Matthew still hadn't replied. Unlocking her phone, she texted him.

Dad, just me, again. Text, so I know you're okay, please xxx

Putting her phone down, she tapped her lip, unable to shake the feeling of unease. She rang her mum; it went to voicemail. No doubt Zoe was working late. Melody left a message saying she was trying to reach Matthew. A few minutes later, her phone beeped. Seeing his name, she felt a bubble of anxiety pop until she read the message.

I'm okay. Dealing with something that should have been dealt with a long time ago. Love you, Melly xxx

Melody frowned. 'What the hell does that mean?' she said aloud, re-reading the text message. *What could he be dealing with?* The unease whooshed back in like a snowstorm.

What do you mean, Dad? You're worrying me xxx

Tapping a fingernail against the side of her mobile phone, she waited for the two ticks against her text message. They didn't come and almost ten minutes later, they still weren't there. Biting her lip, she texted her mum asking her to call as soon as possible.

'Shit!' she said, as she got up from the sofa and began pacing the small lounge of the flat. What the heck was going on? What did her dad's message even mean? *Dealing with something that should have been dealt with a long time ago.* She squeezed the side of her head with her hands.

'Agghhh,' she screamed quietly. What was it? Something to do with Felix? Melody hadn't seen her dad as much the last few weeks after moving back to the flat. Even so, she'd been around and he had seemed okay, good, in fact. Her phone rang — it was Zoe.

'Hi, darling, I'm just at the directors' meeting. What's up?'

She heard the sound of office life in the background. 'It's Dad, I can't get in touch with him, Mum. I'm worried. He isn't answering his calls and Auntie Glynis went round and he didn't answer.' She rushed out the sentence, feeling panicky.

'Maybe he's just out with friends, at darts, darling? Or he's gone for a drive. I'm sure he will reply.'

Melody was silent, biting her fingernail. Something didn't feel right.

'Melly, I'm certain he's fine but I will drive by after the directors' meeting and check to see if he's home, okay?'

'Thanks, Mum.'

'I have to go, darling. Speak in an hour.'

She felt helpless, despite a little comfort from her mum. She could drive to her family home herself and got up from the sofa. Then she realised, the Find My iPhone app. They both had it on their mobiles. Breathing quickly, she opened the app to locate where her dad's phone was and, therefore, his location. The little dot appeared on the screen and she zoomed out, trying to see where it was. She scratched her head. What was he doing in East Hertfordshire at 7 pm on a Thursday night, dealing with something that should have been dealt with a long time ago?

A heavy sensation occurred in Melody's stomach — like a bowling ball clattering through skittles. Sitting down to steady her wobbling legs, she tapped her phone to LinkedIn. As she searched, her fingers trembled against the screen. There it was: Lundie Therapy. Scrolling through the profile, she saw it under his service description: East Hertfordshire.

Her throat was closing up. She gasped for air, scrolling through his page for any posts, any information. Heart pounding, she read four posts before seeing the confirmation she needed but certainly didn't want.

'Fuck!' she screamed, grabbing her scalp as her knees bounced.

Delighted to announce Lundie Therapy has located to East Hertfordshire. Thank you to all that have used the service over the years in my King's Cross base. I hope current (and new) clients will love the new premises as much as I do.

And now Melody knew exactly what her father's text message meant.

Chapter 55: Matthew

Matthew glared at Nate as he sat on his black sofa, the top half of his body slumped to the left. The hard metal of the gun had hit his head at the right point with a furious force from Matthew, leading to Nate being knocked out. Lying there, as if sleeping, with his face looking distorted and swollen, Matthew stared at him and felt enough rage to fuel a power station.

Placing the gun on the floor next to where he sat, he checked his mobile phone and turned it to sound on. More texts had arrived over the hour he had held the therapist captive. All from Melody and one missed call from Zoe. He read the first text message.

Hi Dad, Auntie G went to yours with cakes and you weren't in. Let me know all is okay xxx

Twenty minutes later, there was another.

Dad, just me, again. Text, so I know you're okay, please xxx

Matthew dropped his head to his knees and sighed. All he wanted to do was protect her. He squeezed his hand a few times, clenching his fist to try and make it feel normal after grasping the gun. Beginning to type, he stopped, deleted it, and started again.

I'm okay. Dealing with something that should have been dealt with a long time ago. Love you, Melly xxx

The ticks to show she had read the text message appeared almost immediately, followed by the three dots indicating she was replying.

What do you mean, Dad? You're worrying me xxx

Matthew rubbed his mouth and slid his mobile phone back into his pocket. Looking at Nate Lundie passed out on the sofa, he knew he had to think about the next steps. He hadn't planned to kill him. He didn't have a real weapon — unless he used a knife from Nate's kitchen. Matthew didn't want to go to prison for murder. He didn't want to go to prison at all and had hoped that his strategy would be executed in a way that prevented that. But watching films and making a plan, for someone who hadn't even stolen a chocolate bar in his life, meant Matthew was never going to accomplish being a criminal genius. Instead, he now thought perhaps he would have to kill Nate Lundie and hope to get away with it.

The bastard hadn't taken any level of responsibility for grooming and manipulating his daughter. No remorse for making her poorly again. Just excuses and blame towards Melody. He was a narcissistic prick, no doubt about that. Murder and possibly getting away with it? Well, that was unlikely but Matthew wanted to ruin his career and it could be worth a prison sentence.

Feeling like his head was in a vice, he needed a drink of water. Matthew looked at his victim, flat out, and rushed to the kitchen. Putting the gun between his legs, he cupped water in his hands and gulped it down before promptly returning to the lounge. Walking in, the sofa was in immediate view, but Nate wasn't there. A vase struck Matthew's head, and he tumbled back a little against the wood door.

It wasn't enough to knock him out and he was blocking the doorway for Nate to escape. Instead, Matthew reacted by pointing the gun in his face, about thirty centimetres from the end of his nose. The therapist's mouth dropped open and Matthew smelt the potent scent of sweat coming from him; the smell of fear.

'Sit on that fucking sofa and if you dare to move again, I swear to God, I will put a bullet in your head,' Matthew said through gritted teeth, as his free hand touched his head where the vase had struck him.

Nate tried to make himself as small as possible and returned to the sofa. Whimpers came from his mouth as Matthew watched him, thinking what a disgusting man he was. Touching his head, Matthew pulled his fingers away. There was no blood, but it stung.

'Perfectly nice vase you've ruined there. But nothing is sacred to you, is it? Like my daughter's heart, you smashed that as well as her mental health.'

'I'm sorry,' he wept.

'But are you? Are you really sorry, you bastard?'

Matthew was back in his face, pointing the gun. His phone began ringing in his pocket and Nate's eyes widened as if it were someone coming to rescue him. Matthew ignored it and stepped back.

'Where is there some paper?'

Nate looked at his captor blankly. Matthew leant in and saw no colour on one side of his victim's face and red and purple hues on the other where he had assaulted him.

'Bloody paper? Made from trees?' He rolled his eyes at him like he was stupid.

Nodding frantically, Nate pointed to a wicker box by the side of the fireplace. Matthew opened it and pulled out an A4 notepad and a pen. He handed them to Nate, who took them with trembling hands.

'You, Mr Lundie, are going to write a letter to your medical board, or whatever it is. What's it called?'

'B-BA-C-C-P,' Nate stammered.

'Who?' Matthew asked abruptly.

'BACP,' Nate blurted out.

'Yes, those people. You're going to write and tell them that you're a pervert, grooming and manipulating patients for your own sexual needs.' Matthew waved the gun around as if he were showing a baby to a room full of guests. 'You're going to write what I tell you to.'

Nate nodded, but his hand was so shaky, Matthew wasn't sure he would manage.

'Concentrate, because this will take all night if you don't do it right. Now, write as I speak.' He ran the gun over the mantlepiece like it was a duster, before returning to the armchair, opposite Nate. 'Put your registration number at the top. Do you know it?'

He nodded and began to write slowly.

'And this address and your mobile number.'

Nate followed his captor's instructions.

'Dear Sir/Madam, I am writing to inform you that I have breached the BACP code of practice.' Matthew paused and leant forward, making sure Nate was writing. He was, slowly, but it looked like a five-year-old had written it due to his shaking hands.

'That's a mess, you daft bastard. I'll do it and you can sign it.'

Snatching the notepad and pen from his trembling hands, Matthew moved back into the armchair and rested the paper on his knee, placing the gun on it to prevent the pad from moving.

He wrote for a few minutes. Glancing up at Nate every ten seconds or so, he couldn't help but feel smug at his constant rabbit-in-the-headlights expression. Taking the pen away from the paper, he read over the letter, then nodded to himself before reading it aloud.

Dear Sir/Madam, I am writing to inform you that I have breached the BACP's code of practice. This occurred multiple times over a period of around four months where I practiced in an unethical way.

This included several instances of sexual misconduct, aimed at a vulnerable patient. I abused my authority and put the young woman in question at further mental harm for my own sexual gratification. The woman subsequently spent a period of time in a psychiatric unit after being sectioned.

I am unable to lie about this any longer and feel I need to be punished for my predatory behaviour. I understand this is a breach of the code of conduct and an abuse of my power. I will therefore be resigning from practice as a therapist and understand there may be an investigation into my behaviour.

Yours faithfully,

Nathaniel Lundie

Pushing the notepad under Nate's nose, he spoke, 'Sign it, you pervert.'

Nate swallowing, taking the paper and pen and signed his name. Matthew ripped the letter from the notepad, folded it neatly, and put it in the back pocket of his jeans. As he did so, his phone rang again. Holding the gun with one hand he fished the mobile from his pocket with the other. It was Melody calling. She would be worried, he knew that, but he would sort this, one way or another. It was his duty.

Chapter 56: Melody

Matthew wasn't answering his phone and as Melody travelled nearer to the location identified by his Find My iPhone app, she became cripplingly anxious about what she might discover. Struggling to regulate her breathing as she drove, she felt like tarantulas were walking across her scalp. Nate was much stronger than her father. He could have hurt him in a confrontation. Matthew wasn't answering his phone and that text message had intent. She had left another voicemail for Zoe, saying she was worried that her father had travelled to East Hertfordshire to Nate Lundie's.

Rubbing her cheek as she surpassed the speed limit on the country roads out of London, Melody prayed no animals were strolling around. Glancing at her phone, the signal kept going and returning, but the app identified the rough location and she had to keep driving, knowing that every minute could be critical.

Passing a church and some shops, she continued to follow directions to where her dad was. A few minutes later, Melody hit the dark lanes again. Slowing down in the unfamiliar area, the signal on her phone fluctuated in strength. Lights shone a little distance ahead and the location app was as detailed as it would get in a small geographical area.

Slamming her hands against the steering wheel, Melody screamed. *Where the hell was she?* And more importantly, *where was her bloody dad? And why was her mother unavailable, yet again?* Driving closer to the lights, she followed the road around, then turning left, spotted a car at the top of a lane. Still with limited street lighting, driving closer, she recognised her dad's blue Lexus. There was space behind his car to park on a small stretch of pavement. Pulling up and looking around, a street followed down from where Matthew's car was and there was another street at the end of a grassed area to the left.

'Shit,' she said aloud, not knowing where he would be. Melody could see a few lights and roofs of houses down the lane and more in the nearby street, but it was relatively dark. Her phone rang; it was her mum.

'Melly, I'm coming up. Where are you?' she said calmly but firmly.

'No, Mum, it's okay. I'm here now. I'm sure all is okay, but I will let you know if we need you.'

'Don't be stupid, darling. You can't just go up there and knock on doors. Give me the street name.'

Melody felt her patience depleting and Zoe was wasting time. 'Mum, let me deal with this. It's my mess and unless I need you to be involved, you're really best kept out of it.'

'Now listen here, Mel…'

Melody hung up on her mother. She didn't need her taking control right now and well, in many ways, she was trying to protect her career, if nothing else. Digging her fingernails into her head, she knew time could be critical and rang her father again.

'No street lighting but good mobile reception, eh,' she said to herself. The phone rang several times before going to voicemail. Hanging up, Melody made a grrrr sound. Fingers trembling, she texted him.

Dad, I'm right by your car. I know you're at Nate's. Answer the phone or I'm calling the police xxx

Her phone rang less than two minutes later.

'Dad, are you okay? Are you hurt?' Melody rushed the words out.

'Yeah, love. How did you…?'

'Are you hurt?' she screamed.

'No, no. How did you know where I was?'

'The Find My iPhone app. What the hell is going on, Dad?'

Melody was met with silence. 'Dad, for fuck's sake. Where are you? Talk, or I'm ringing the police.'

'No, no, Melly. You can't do that.' He said quickly.

'Then tell me where you are and what's going on? Mum knows,' she cried.

She heard her dad sigh. 'I'm at number four Lawson Lane. But don't come through the front, the light will come on and the neighbours might see,' he said calmly, quietly.

Her heart raced and her mouth felt dry. 'What's happened?' she said breathlessly as she began walking down the lane. 'Dad. You're scaring me. You haven't hurt him, have you?' She began sobbing, frightened by what she was about to discover. Silence followed. 'Dad? What's happened?'

'Melody, just do as I say. Come around the back of the houses. It's fields and there's no lighting until you're in the garden. This bastard's house is the second one down and you'll see a summer house with lights on. There's a small surrounding fence. Keep to the edge of the garden in the dark so the security light doesn't come on. See you soon.'

The phone went dead and Melody walked back the few steps she had taken, heart racing, nausea rushing through her. *Why was she having to creep about? What had her dad done?* Shivering, she realised she could walk into a crime scene, and she let out a quiet yelp. Going back to the car, she opened her boot and pulled out a box of rubber gloves that Matthew had got for her during COVID-19. Her hands were shaking like a child holding a snow globe as she put each hand into a glove — knowing she had to protect herself from any fingerprints that would match hers on record after the fire.

She walked past the lane to some green space. Travelling over it, her foot squelched in something she couldn't see but hoped was sodden mud from the rain earlier that day. After walking thirty or so metres, grass turned into a narrow footpath with trees on each side. She wiped the mud off her shoes against the firm surface and felt nauseous.

There was a noise in the trees and Melody jumped before something with wings took flight. She came to the first house that was in darkness from the back and could see the outline of the roof of a house a little further down, which she assumed was Nate's. Continuing down the footpath, she saw a light, which must be Nate's summer house. A fence separated the footpath and his garden. She reached the side nearest a ten-foot hedge — a barrier between his vast garden and the neighbour's land.

Her heart sat in her throat and her legs felt like elastic bands about to snap as she climbed over the fence, wobbling. Sneaking down through the large garden, she glanced at the summer house, lit up. She bit her lip, thinking how it could have been her and him in there, enjoying watching the stars over a glass of wine. Then she clicked out of her daydream, replaced with the reality that he had almost destroyed her and now, something serious and potentially dangerous was going on in his house between Nate and her dad.

Reaching his back door, there was a closed blind at the

window to the side of the door. Melody pushed the UPVC handle down. It opened and she walked into a large kitchen.

'Dad? Dad?' she said, her voice shaking.

'In here,' came a voice from the hallway.

Melody was both desperate to see, and dreading to see her father as she walked tentatively through the unfamiliar kitchen and hallway. There was a door ajar on her right. It creaked slightly as she pushed it open. Her jaw dropped and she clasped her hands over her mouth. In the room, stood her dad, his complexion grey as he held a gun. To the left was Nate, sitting on a sofa, swellings all over his face, wet trousers, and a look in his eyes she had never seen before.

Chapter 57: Nate

Nate was losing faith that he would make it through the night alive. Matthew Dartford was like Frank Spencer from "Some Mothers Do 'Ave 'Em" in one breath and like Charles Bronson in another. Worse still, he was driven by the most dangerous fuels: love and revenge. Face pulsating with the throbbing pain from his assaults, he sat, silently listening to his frenzied ranting, wanting to punch him until he stopped breathing. Mad Matthew's phone rang and his captor answered.

'No, no, Melly. You can't do that.'

And Nate didn't know what it meant, and he didn't know if he felt relief or more concern. A minute later, Matthew ended the call.

'My daughter is coming. You can apologise to her in person before we make sure you never practice therapy ever again.'

Nate swallowed the boulders in his throat. He was desperate for some water and felt like his head was filling up with blood, drowning his brain. Matthew was peeking out of the smallest of gaps in the blinds, but keeping an eye on Nate, who now wished he had moved to somewhere with more houses and better street lighting. This would never have happened in his old street with the houses all joined, everyone coming and going, and curtain twitching being a team sport. A minute later, he heard a click. His back door opened and Melody's voice quietly called out.

'Dad? Dad?' She sounded like a child and he winced.

'In here,' Matthew said, his eyes remaining fixed on his prisoner.

Melody walked into the lamp-lit lounge and her face dropped. She switched on the main light and Nate saw a fear in her eyes as they darted back and forth between him and her dad.

'Dad. What the fuck? Why have you got a fucking gun?' she screamed.

'Shhh, Melly. Just sit down.'

She shook her head. 'This, this… can't happen. What have you done, Dad?' she said, shaking her head frantically.

'Not enough to match what this bastard deserves, Melody.' Matthew's eyes filled with tears and she moved towards him.

'Put the gun down, Dad.' Concern was etched across her face, as she held her hands towards her father.

Matthew shook his head. 'He has to pay, love. He has to. I can't let him get away with what he did.' He pulled the table lamp that had been lighting the room from its socket and smashed it against the wall above Nate's head.

Nate screamed and glared at her with pleading eyes. He began to speak, to ask for her help.

'Mel…'

She looked at him and Nate saw a switch in her. The worry in her eyes dissolved as a grin flashed across her face. A knock at the front door made them all stop.

'Help!' Nate screamed as loud as he could before Melody pounced on him and put a gloved hand over his mouth. He grabbed her hand, twisting her arm, and screamed again as he pulled her palm half off his mouth. She scowled and slapped his cheek, baring her teeth like a wolf.

'Shut up, you prick!' she snarled quietly.

Matthew leant towards him, jaw clenched, and put the gun in between his eyes. Feeling the cold metal on his head, Nate became more still than he had ever been in his life. Only his chest moved as his heart threatened to explode out of it.

There was another knock at the door and a female voice spoke, 'Hello, are you okay in there, Nate?'

Matthew released the safety button on the pistol and placed a finger to his mouth in a shushing motion. His unblinking watery eyes looked like a dark, dangerous lake.

Nate stared at Melody with pleading eyes. She smirked then glanced away from his eyeline towards her dad, her brow furrowing at him. They remained silent for a further minute until Matthew removed the gun from his head but kept it pointing at him, taunting him — a scheduled execution on Death Row.

'Dad, we need to go,' she whispered, as she touched her father's upper arm. 'They might call the police. Please, Dad.' Glancing at Nate, her mouth sneered and she shook her head. 'This piece of shit, he's not worth going to prison for.' She was negotiating with her father, despite the hatred in her eyes for Nate.

He watched father and daughter look at one another and despite the risk of death, the madness, the fear and torture that he'd had been subjected to and was still in — even then, he saw love in Matthew's eyes for his daughter. He inhaled deeply. Or perhaps it was just two mad bastards in sync.

Matthew stared at the therapist. Shorter in height but towering above him as Nate sat on his sofa prison and Matthew loomed over with his gun as God.

'I could kill you right now. You know that, don't you, you filthy fucker?' Spit formed around the corners of his mouth and the whites of his eyes looked red in the lounge's low lighting.

Nate wondered, after all the years of practising therapy, if there was no limit to these screwed up maniacs.

He nodded, quickly, attempting to keep the power with his captor — whilst desperately trying to remain alive and hoping Terry, his kind neighbour who knocked, had heard the shouts for help.

'Dad,' Melody implored, tapping his free hand that didn't have a killing machine in it.

Matthew lips were pressed so tightly together they looked like a thin line drawn where a mouth should have been. His face was turning red as he stared at Nate.

'You say *nothing* about this to the police or I guarantee, it'll be you going to jail as well. And I've got your letter, so if you don't resign from practising within a month, I will send them it. Whether the authorities believe it or not, they'll investigate and I bet my daughter isn't the only young woman you've groomed.' Matthew sneered, his face contorted with anger. Moving forward, he put the gun against Nate's head, who began to plead and cry.

'Please, God, please. I won't say a word. I fucking promise.'

Melody pulled Matthew's arm and the gun gently away from Nate's head as two tears trickled down his cheeks. She took her father's hand, before slowly removing the pistol from it and holding it herself in a gloved hand, as she nodded reassuringly to Matthew. She looked at Nate, then at the gun, then back at him, and giggled. Like a child laughing at a puppet show.

As Matthew stood back a little, Melody grinned at Nate. Gripping the gun, she moved closer towards him. He was so squashed into the corner of the black sofa, his body had almost melted into the fabric. Feeling breathless, his heart rate accelerated. Her mouth came towards the side of his head, unnervingly slow and Nate smelt that fruity scent she always wore. Vomit rose in his throat and he gritted his teeth, swallowing it down.

Her hair tickled his cheek as she leant in and Nate's blood chilled inside of him, as if it were being poured into his body from a bottle out of the fridge. He shuddered. Melody noticed and chuckled an evil laugh before her mouth touched his ear. Her hot breath circled his ear lobe — which would have been a comfort, a turn-on, in any other situation. But not with a scorned unhinged woman who had a deranged father as a side-kick. Whose love he didn't return, and who was currently pinning him down with a gun. His chest hurt from his heart beating at an exponential rate and he could hardly breathe, feeling faint as she began speaking, menacingly whispering in his ear.

Melody jerked her head up, her eyes in line with his. Confidently, with chilling calmness, she stared at him. Her irises almost looked black, blending in with her pupils — cold, dark, unnerving as they burnt into his. Nate's throat stung with bile as he nodded his response to what she had said. His jaw still with fear, fighting not to scream, sob, and stay conscious. She grinned and raised her eyebrows before kissing him on the lips, biting his bottom lip as she pulled hers away.

Glaring at him again, Nate saw a flash in her eyes. A softness, the way she looked at him in the sessions. Then her gaze narrowed, her jaw clenching. She nodded slowly, winked at him, and smirked. Melody rose from the bending position, grabbed her dad with her gloved hand and dragged him out of the room. Matthew Dartford turned back and made a shooting noise. Five seconds later, he heard the back door slam, then it was deadly silent.

Alone at last, Nate sat sobbing and screaming, gasping for air. Unable to move for what seemed like hours but was only around ten minutes, he sat frozen in distress until the sound of sirens filled the air on Lawson Lane. Blue lights flashed through the tiny gaps in the lounge blinds as Nate tried to get up from the sofa. But he couldn't, his legs couldn't take his weight. The heaviness of fear he'd had around him the past few hours, too restricting.

The doorbell rang and a thumping came. 'Police! Police! Open the door.'

Nate shivered, sobbing, but washed with relief as he crawled to the front door — dragging himself along the hallway on his hands and knees, mucus dripping from his nose as he sobbed. Pulling himself up with all his energy, he flipped the lever on his Yale lock that was meant to keep him safe and secure in his home. He pulled the door ajar slightly before the police pushed it open and Nate fell back, sobbing like a child.

Six Months Later

Chapter 58: Melody

Melody and her father had talked about the incident at Nate Lundie's that night and vowed to never speak of it again. Going straight to Matthew's house, Zoe had been waiting frantically. Getting their story straight in case of any comeback, they had made a pact to play the night down, as they scurried away from Nate Lundie's cottage to their cars. The pair had agreed that if the police became involved, they would say there was a fight and both assaulted one another.

Arriving home, they had given Zoe the PG-rated version of what happened — stating there had been a confrontation at the therapist's old office and Matthew had followed him one evening, seeing where he lived. He had gone to have it out with him that night and it turned into a scuffle, with both assaulting one another. Zoe had been understandably angry and concerned but had advised as a solicitor, as well as bollocking them as a mother and estranged wife.

'This has to end, Matthew. We've suffered enough,' she had said sternly before breaking down in tears.

Melody had hugged her mum as Zoe sobbed uncontrollably. Years of held-back emotion, eventually seeped out the sides into a flood of distress. Holding onto her mother, Melody had almost choked on her guilt, lying to her and seeing a fragility in her mum that she hadn't ever seen.

'This has to end, Melly. It has to stop — both of you.' Zoe had looked at her ex-husband and daughter through mascara-smudged eyes, her complexion pale. They'd nodded, both hoping it would be the end but knowing that night's events would haunt them, along with the fear of police involvement.

The three had drank cup after cup of tea until Zoe left, stating she would be back the following evening, leaving Melody and Matthew in their family home. Matthew had shut the front door after watching Zoe drive off and turned to face Melody in the hallway. His hands had reached for his face as he dropped to his knees on the olive-green rug. Rushing to her dad, she had embraced him for a minute before they'd sat in silence — only the sound of Matthew's low sobbing as their audio. Wiping his eyes on his sleeve, he had looked at his daughter, eyes pleading.

'I had to do it, Melly. I had to make him suffer for what he did to you, to us. Someone had to pay for all these years. For everything we've lost.' He'd yelped and she'd grabbed his shaking hand. 'I couldn't lose another child, lose you, Melly.' His words had choked in his throat and he'd coughed before scrunching his eyes shut.

Squeezing her father's hand, Melody had told him it was okay. And as aghast as she had been, something about what he had done made her feel the ultimate protection and validation that she was the innocent one. That Nate Lundie was wrong. He, the big bad wolf who should've known better. However, Melody felt heartbroken that her dad had been battling tumultuous seas in his mind alone. To go to the extreme of duping Nate Lundie and becoming a client, well, although she admired his creativity, it was insane and Melody could see that, with the clarity of her hospital stay and medication.

She now had the tools to manage. Her dad needed to heal, from everything. And it started with her helping him and being strong. Melody had taken the fake gun from Matthew's that night and thrown it in the River Thames, at the murky blue spot that she once thought about throwing herself into. Her dad had always been her protector, her strength. That evening, she had vowed to help him recover from years of anxiety that had gnawed at him like a parasite. He'd be okay, and so would she. They would be okay.

And as they slowly got back to some level of routine, the family unit became stronger, despite its new shape. Matthew began to lose the layers of desperate feelings. The pain of loss, fear of loss, guilt, and need for revenge that he carried, had transformed him into a muted version of the dad she remembered when she was a young teenager and Felix was alive. Slowly, glimpses of the former Matthew began to show, as if using a telescope on a sky that got clearer each night.

Melody tried and managed most days. She was human, not a robot. She knew that she would have spiralling thoughts at times that would need working through, using her tools. She was a work in progress and that was okay. But despite her progress, something remained unfinished in Melody. A shadow. A blemish that wouldn't heal. That she picked at in her mind and simply couldn't let scab over.

The reoccurring thought she had frequently about Nate Lundie, even though it had been six months since that night in Much Hadham. Despite her therapy, medication, and recovery, the thought lingered. A dark cloud that simply would not dissipate and the fact remained — that Nate didn't say sorry that night at his house.

Chapter 59: Nate

Pulling his lunchbox from the fridge, Nate rushed to the hall-way, put his trainers on, and grabbed his sports bag. Shutting the composite door to his flat, he dashed up the path and into his Audi. He sighed as he started the engine. A satisfied sigh of gratitude to be in a place he would never have dreamt of eighteen months ago, and felt lucky to be at after the incident and the last six months being completely unpredicted. Driving the five minutes to his new job at Goals Gym, he reflected on the last year and a half.

He still had the odd nightmare — Melody haunting his dreams. As a former therapist, he knew why. He had PTSD, and he had to use tools he had advocated to others for so many years to manage it. Despite all that happened, Nate still felt lucky he survived that night with Matthew and Melody Dartford. His neighbour on Lawson Lane, Terry, had likely saved his life. Well, Terry and her greyhound, Flynn. He had barked continuously at the window of her home, so she had taken him for another walk that evening and heard a smash and shouting in the otherwise almost silent country lane. Terry had heard the screams for help when she knocked at his cottage. Knowing something wasn't right, and with Flynn echoing her thoughts, she had rung the police.

'Better safe than sorry,' she had said to the call handler.

The police had asked questions, of course they had. The other two neighbours in the lane hadn't heard a thing. Elderly and used to the quiet street, no one had cameras — they didn't need them in a street like Lawson Lane. There was no risk, there never had been, until Nate moved in. A car had been parked at the top of the lane, a blue one, or maybe black. It was dark and Terry hadn't really focused on it as she walked Flynn earlier that evening. It could have been people visiting someone in the next lane. She'd not returned that way on the second walk, taking a shorter route, past number 4, Nate Lundie's house.

He had told the police the vaguest story he could. That the man was average height and build. Young with a voice he didn't recognise and that he thought it was a burglary gone wrong or mistaken identity. Perhaps he was after the former resident. Nate said he took some cash, smashed a few ornaments, and hit him.

There was little else to tell. No one pushed it, believing an honest, professional man. Of course, they'd found no one as Melody and Matthew took off over the back of his property and had driven away before the police and ambulance approached Lawson Lane. The police had limited resources and with crimes to investigate elsewhere, the case was closed.

After that night with Melody's father, Nate knew his career would be over. It had to be. Matthew Dartford had a letter as blackmail, and he didn't know what he would do with it or when. A ticking timebomb. The Dartfords had taken enough from him, Nate would control the termination of his career. Resigning, he folded the business, and cancelled his registration. How could he ever trust another client again?

The horror he had been subjected to that evening by deranged Matthew Dartford had broken his trust of people. After what his unstable daughter had done to Nate, he knew they should both pay. True, he wasn't all innocent in it, but her response to his rejection was more Hollywood thriller than it wasn't meant to be. He'd wanted to expose everything. Go back to the police and tell the whole truth from when he met Melody so the Dartfords would go to prison. However, Nate was scared. The Dartfords had created a fear in him that could match any horror story. An unease that felt insidiously evil and limitless, and it chilled him to the bone.

Nate feared Melody Dartford. There was something in her. He wasn't sure if it was obsession, anger, strength even, or just a little sprinkling of evil. But she unnerved him, haunted him, and he couldn't forget the look in her eyes and the words she whispered in his ear after she pulled her dad's gun-clasped hand away from his head. Uncurling her father's fingers and taking the weapon, before rushing off in the darkness as if a super-hero's antagonist. He shuddered at the thought.

It wasn't worth it and in those few days and weeks after the incident, it was like a nightmare or someone else's life in one of those trashy women's magazines. But it was a story that would never fully be told, kept only between the few that were in-volved as Nate resigned from BACP membership and vowed never to practice again. Ironic, given the investment he had just made creating his office in the summer house. Nate didn't want to tell his story — only to Julie, who listened without judge-ment. He'd lived in a hamster wheel of his own trauma and it had almost killed him. Now it was done, over. Well, he hoped.

He had stood in the summer house that had been used once. One genuine session before a psychotic charlatan changed his world, and tarnished the safety of his new home. He sold up, luckily making a profit with thanks to the summer house. Just six months after moving into his dream cottage, he was out, renting a flat in Brentwood, where he would buy a property when the time was right. When he felt safe. If he ever fully did. Each time Nate felt his guard drop, he thought of the words Melody whispered in his ear and it would make him shiver, look over his shoulder, in a cold-sweat panic.

Getting ready to leave work for the day, Nate said goodbye to colleagues and walked out of Goals Gym for the drive home. Hungry after a day of teaching spinning and several PT sessions with new clients as part of his qualification — including a rather attractive woman — he was looking forward to getting home to his rented two-bedroomed home for his leftover roast chicken, sweet potato, and brown rice. Then he may even have some ice cream. Everything in moderation, after all. He glanced around the car park, part of a retail park, and looked over at the Company Coffee café and takeaway a few shops away. *Bugger it,* he thought. He deserved an iced latte after a day of burning lots of calories.

Walking over to Company Coffee, he thought about his new client. She had worn tight leggings that showed the perfect curve of her backside. A strip of tanned torso separated the beige leggings and sports cropped top, revealing the shape of small but pert breasts. And that neck — beautiful, flawless like Annabelle's. She was giggly with him, twirling a necklace on her slender, smooth neck. He'd leant in, admiring it and inhaling her summery scent and told her she shouldn't work out with jewellery on. That despite it being a lovely necklace, it could get tangled or caught on equipment. He'd wanted to touch it, touch her, but he didn't and she had smiled, bit her lip and thanked him for his health and safety advice.

Nate shook his head to himself and then grinned. He could just ask about any possible boyfriend. He was in better shape than ever since starting his job and beginning a PT instructor course, thanks to the gym. Maybe he would just find out — ask her a few casual questions.

Strolling into Company Coffee, Nate stood in the short queue. After ordering his iced latte with extra caramel, he waited to the side whilst his drink was prepared. Looking at his phone for a minute, he texted back a friend from work and then texted Julie. The server called his name and as he glanced up, someone caught the corner of his eye.

His head jerked left and he got a glimpse of someone who, for a split second, stared at him, grinning, unmistakable blood-red lipstick shimmering on her full lips. Then she returned her gaze to look ahead and walked through the exit of the cafe. His heart raced and he felt faint as he saw the back of the woman. Tall with dark brown long hair, thick and wavy as it cascaded over her shoulders. *Was it her?*

His shaking hand quickly took his drink and he gently pushed through the small crowd of people waiting for drinks to take away, his heart pounding in his throat. Rushing to the exit of the café, Nate didn't even know what he would do if it was her. If she was standing there, waiting for him. Reaching the exit about twenty seconds after seeing her, he frantically looked around, sweat gathering in the arch of his back and the hairs on his neck standing in uniform.

He couldn't see her. Spinning around, Nate scanned all directions. Pulling his hand down over his mouth and chin, he felt nausea creeping up his throat. His eyes flashed to the car park, trying to spot her Fiat 500. But it was no use. There were hundreds of cars there and in his panic, they were all blurring into one in his vision. Gulping in air, the ice in his latte made the slightest of sounds as his hand shook it into percussion. *Why would she be in Brentwood? Twenty-odd miles away from her home? Was she following him? Coming for revenge?*

Just when he had almost stopped having nightmares about Melody Dartford, he'd seen her and, worst of all, she'd seen him. A shiver of fear coated his body as Nate continued to look around, eyes wide, legs trembling as he remembered the chilling words she had whispered and wondered if the score from the Dartfords would ever be settled.

Acknowledgments

Writing a book is a team effort, and I'm forever thankful for the support around me that enables me to write and create books. Thank you, reader, for choosing this book. Readers are our fuel to keep going, and I'm eternally grateful to each person who reads my work. A special thank you to the readers who diligently support every endeavour I embark on, cheering me on from the sidelines. I value each of you and cherish your friendship.

The biggest thanks to Paul, my partner in love and life, who encourages me, supports me, and carries me when I feel weak. Thank you to my parents and whole family, who always ask and support. And a huge thanks to Jarmila and Kathryn for your expertise.

If you enjoyed the book, please do leave a review and tell people about it — this is the ultimate thank you to an author. For more information and updates on my other publications and releases, please follow my website/socials and those of Write on the Tyne (CIC).

www.writeonthetyne.com
www.helenaitchisonwrites.com
Instagram: @helen.aitchison_writes
Twitter / X: @aitchisonwrites
Facebook: @Helen Aitchison Writes
Instagram: @writeonethetyne
Facebook: @Write on the Tyne

The Dinner Club

Five people. Five secrets. Each needing healing, support and acceptance. Derek's life has changed suddenly. His wife of the past few decades has left him, unable to live with his secret anymore. Inspired by a TV show, he decides to start a dinner club to make new friends, the kind that might accept him if he can be brave enough to tell them the truth.

Eddie is grieving, a widower, struggling as a single parent. The void in his life slowly destroying him and his relationship with his young daughter.

Florence, supported by her carer Jessie, craves one more adventure to round off the last 80 odd years.

Violet needs a focus, a new identity, until she has the confidence to escape her grim reality with abusive husband, Ben.

Cara is lost, with nowhere to call home and no one to go home to, now she's aged out of the care system.

Will this mishmash group fill each other's souls as well as their plates?

The Life and Love (Attempts) of Kitty Cook

Kitty Cook may be a great school teacher, but learning the lessons of online dating is a harder subject than she first thought.

Finding herself alone again in her thirties, she decides to take her friend Sophie's advice and sign up for an online dating site. After recently leaving a failed five-year relationship, Kitty is hesitant to get her hopes up.

All she wants to do is graduate from the school of love, but will she ever find someone who will make the grade?

The Life and Love (Attempts) of Kitty Cook is an emotional yet heart-warming read that takes you on an unforgettable journey through the highs and lows of online dating and looking for love in your thirties.

The 31 Days of May

In the wake of a devastating family loss, 24-year-old May finds herself adrift, her belief in love and happiness shattered. Struggling to navigate her new reality, May grapples with the persistent sensation of being a misfit in a world where she never quite belongs. But just as she begins to resign herself to this feeling of isolation, tragedy strikes once more, propelling May into action.

Determined to shield herself from further heartache, she concocts a radical scheme to safeguard against future abandonment. That is until May meets Mr. Parsley, a charming retiree who becomes May's unexpected neighbour. As May meticulously executes her plan, the presence of Mr. Parsley and his grown-up son, Sam, threatens to disrupt her carefully laid out path.

Will May stick to her meticulously crafted schedule, or will the warmth and kindness of the Parsley family lead her down an unforeseen, life-altering path? Join May on her poignant journey of resilience, love, and the transformative power of human connection in the face of life's most profound challenges.

Somebody's Nobody

A murderer is targeting the vulnerable in rural Northumberland.

Local day centre, Homeless Helping Hands, provides sustenance, support, and safety to people in the area. Until antagonism, anger, and an atmosphere that threatens stability surround the service. A body is discovered, followed by another, and the place of sanctuary is no longer safe.

The Homeless Helping Hands staff team, each with their own backstory, struggle to protect themselves and the people using the service. As rumours and resentment rises, danger drops its disguise, and the cracks of composure by a calculated killer threaten to expose the truth.

Detective Sergeant Ronnie Ericson leads the homicide investigation, supported by Detective Constable Polly McCardle. Holding a reputation for outcomes, Ericson welcomes the case - a much-needed distraction from his lonely, personal life. Alongside his team, Ericson vows to reveal who holds the fatal control, and bring the killer to justice.

With strained relationships, buried secrets, and a sinister obsession, no one is safe and everyone is a suspect.

A Home for Every Cat

Eric lives in a nice house with his parents, Helen and Paul. But his life wasn't always as safe and cosy. Eric was homeless as a kitten, walking the streets in search of food, friendship, and a loving home.

Thanks to some kind people, Eric found his forever home and the love he always wanted. After all, there is a home for every cat.

Non-fiction includes:

In the Footsteps of Walker Women

Recovery Voices

Veterans' Voices

Ramblings

Changing Futures – South Tees